KILLER DADDY

A Bad Boy Inc Story

EVE LANGLAIS

CHAPTER ONE

"GOING SOMEWHERE?"

Stowing her luggage in the back of her minivan, Audrey held in a sigh at her nosy neighbor's question.

No, I'm lugging around a suitcase for the hell of it. Pasting a false smile on her lips, Audrey slammed the trunk shut and turned to the suburban snoop. "Business trip."

"Another one already?"

As if Audrey's trips were any of this woman's business. The last one had been over a month ago and only lasted a few days. "Part of the job."

"Perhaps you should find a new job."

"This job pays my bills." She couldn't help the sharp retort.

Disapproval pinched the neighbor's features. "But the baby—"

"Is fine." Audrey cut her off before she could begin. Having been subjected to the preaching once before, she wasn't in any mood to hear it again. "I've hired a nanny with impeccable references." The agency she used only hired the best.

"A child belongs with its parents. You shouldn't be so greedy. Share her with her father."

Mrs. Crummb loved to give her unwarranted—and unwanted—opinion. Audrey knew of a place she could shove that opinion. She gritted her teeth. "As I've told you before, her father is *not* a part of her life." Nor was Audrey's life any of the woman's business. "If you'll excuse me, I do believe that is my nanny arriving."

Even if it weren't, she needed to get away from Mrs. Crummb before she did something she'd regret.

Without giving the neighbor any chance to reply, Audrey strode towards the car that slid to a stop at the curb. A four-door hatchback, red and generic. It lacked any kind of sign on the roof or decal on the door; however, in these days of Uber and Lyft, most taxi services went around anonymously.

"Gnah." The baby monitor clipped to Audrey's waist crackled with a small wail of complaint. Harper was finally waking. The 3:00 a.m. screaming fit—a result of a stubborn tooth struggling to penetrate tough gums—had tuckered her out, and she'd slept past her usual wake-up time. However, Audrey didn't have the luxury of sleeping in late like the baby. She had to get ready and leave shortly, or she'd miss her flight.

Since the baby would be fine in her crib for a minute, Audrey strode down the driveway to meet the nanny. If indeed it were a nanny because the woman getting out of the car looked nothing at all like the one she'd hired.

A frown wrinkled Audrey's brow. "Can I help you?"

The portly woman, her gray hair pinned in a tidy bun,

possessed rounded features and crow's feet at the corners of her eyes. Deep lines bracketed a mouth that didn't smile.

"You are Mrs. Marlowe, yes?" A strong eastern-European accent clipped the words.

"I am she, but you're not Mrs. Green." Mrs. Green was a willowy woman in her late forties who'd been her assigned nanny on two previous trips. For Audrey's day-to-day job, she used a local daycare.

"Mrs. Green is sick. I replace her." Spoken in an almost commanding bark.

It didn't help the pounding pain behind Audrey's eyes. "The agency didn't notify me of any changes."

"I get the call early this morning, and I go where they tell me." The words were clipped and heavily accented. The woman hefted her suitcase, already deposited on the curb by the driver—a slim man with pockmarked skin and short, greasy hair. The car drove off, leaving Audrey with a stranger who, so far, wasn't instilling much confidence.

"What's your name?" she asked. Because despite what the woman claimed, Audrey wasn't about to just leave without doing some checking with the agency first.

"I am Mrs. Nowicki."

"Where are you from?

"Poland. Here on work visa."

"I'll have to see some identification if you don't mind."

"Of course." The woman reached into her large purse and pulled out a battered wallet. Opening it, Audrey spotted several cards, including a Polish driver's license apparent through the plastic window. The woman handed her a work visa.

Audrey perused it and spotted nothing out of the ordinary. The full name on the document was Marja Nowicki. The date of birth matched the apparent age of the woman, as did the picture. The date of entry and expiry also seemed in order.

She handed it back. "Looks okay, but I still want to call the agency to verify your credentials." Because this last-minute change did not sit well with her at all.

Mrs. Nowicki nodded. "Call. They verify."

Entering the house, Audrey was conscious of the woman lumbering behind her. It made the spot between her shoulder blades itch. The entrance was tight with stairs going immediately up to the second floor, while to her right was the living room. The two-story home was barely larger than a townhouse, but the price had been right when she bought it.

The hallway led straight ahead to the kitchen. It fit the entire width of her place with enough room for a table for four with three actual seats and a high chair. The large island with the granite top had more room to sit, the three stools tucked under only rarely used. Audrey didn't entertain often.

Okay, she didn't entertain at all.

On the counter, she noted her phone, the screen lit up. She snared it and read the notifications. One missed call from the nanny agency, followed by a text message from them.

It essentially repeated what Mrs. Nowicki had said. A sudden illness had taken Mrs. Green, which meant a replacement. Still, she called the agency while the nanny looked on patiently. It was while she was talking to their switchboard operator that the monitor at her waist blared to life again. Harper finally decided that she was awake and let out a full-throated holler.

Before Audrey could move, Mrs. Nowicki trundled off, exclaiming, "I get the baby."

Unpinning the monitor from her waistband, Audrey listened as the woman entered the baby's room, crooning, "There's the sweet *misiu*. No crying. *Ciocia* Marja is here." Mrs. Nowicki then switched to Polish, her tone gentle.

Harper cooed in reply. Audrey's daughter loved being the center of attention. The fact that she took right away to the nanny soothed some of Audrey's nerves, as did the woman she spoke to at the agency. Marja came with glowing reviews, but Audrey still asked for them to send the woman's file over to her phone. She wanted to check it out in more detail.

Her wristwatch beeped, the alarm on it warning that she needed to be on the road else she would get snared in traffic.

Shoot. I am not ready to go yet. Having expected Mrs. Green, she'd not built in much time to show a new nanny around.

Mrs. Nowicki descended from the second floor, Harper balanced on her hip. "You have beautiful daughter," she declared, still not smiling.

"She is a cutie pie. Aren't you, baby girl?"

Hearing her mother's voice, Harper reached for Audrey. She grabbed her daughter and snuggled her close, breathing in the scent of warm baby. Mrs. Nowicki had done a quick diaper change before bringing her down, which raised her a notch in Audrey's esteem.

Her wristwatch beeped at her again.

"You go," the woman stated.

Audrey chewed at her lower lip. "I can't leave. I haven't shown you around."

"No need for showing. Baby stuff easy to find. I call if need help."

The nanny had a point. There wasn't much to show, and if she tarried any longer, she'd miss her flight. "The baby formula is on the counter, and there are freshly made pureed foods in the fridge. I've left instructions on her sleeping schedule, feeding schedule, as well as the play-groups she's involved in on the activity board." Pinned with a magnet that said *Number One Mommy*, which she'd bought for herself to give encouragement on the days when life overwhelmed.

"I care for many babies," boasted the nanny. "We be fine."

Once again, Audrey's watch beeped. Last call if she wanted to speed her way to the airport. Still, she hesitated. "If you need anything, just give me a call. My flight is only three hours."

"No worry. Me and the *misiu* will be just fine." The matron finally managed a smile.

Audrey's stomach tightened. She hated leaving Harper, especially with someone she'd just barely met. But the agency had reassured her that Mrs. Nowicki was a long-standing employee of theirs with rave reviews from parents. It was just mommy nerves, which was funny, considering this wasn't the first time she'd left on a trip. Although this would be the longest. Her previous ones were never more than a few nights. This one could last up to a week. She blamed the panic on the amount of time she'd be gone mixed with guilt about leaving her daughter.

But she didn't have a choice. Without her job, she and

Harper wouldn't have this house, this life…anything. *I have to do this.* She was going to be late for her flight if she didn't hustle.

Audrey kissed her daughter one last time before handing her over, then grabbed her phone and purse, before heading out the door. The nanny followed with Harper and stood on the front step.

The minivan pulled out on to the street, and Audrey did a quick sideways peek. The nanny waved, the baby on her hip.

The knot in her stomach didn't ease.

Audrey pressed her lips tight. *Harper will be fine.* Audrey would do her job and be back in a few days.

She made it to the corner when her phone beeped. Incoming email from the nanny agency with the file she'd requested. She ignored it. She'd read it once she got to the airport.

Except she got caught at a stupidly long light on the way out of her neighborhood and thought, why not? She thumbed open the .pdf attachment. Stared at the picture inside.

Checked the name above it.

Then cursed.

Audrey whipped the car around in a very illegal U-turn not giving a damn who honked at her. Speeding much faster than the posted limits, she raced back to her house, only to slow rather than barrel into the driveway. It wouldn't do to startle or give warning. She parked in the neighbor's driveway, knowing the tall hedges would hide the van from any glances out from her place.

But she'd better move fast. It would not take long for her nosy neighbor to notice and come knocking.

The middle console arm popped up, and she was treated to a packet of tissues, gum, and a stuffed bear, all tossed aside. Underneath, she pulled out the tray, the false bottom sticking only a little before giving. She grabbed the weapon she kept stashed inside.

As she exited the van, she glanced up and down the street. She would feel stupid if she overreacted. It was possible the agency had attached the wrong picture to the file. Possible, but not likely.

Gun in hand—and not easily explained if anyone saw her now—she eased up the steps and noticed the front door slightly ajar. Because of the damp spring, the wood had warped enough that it took a good yank to get it to shut. It being open meant she could quietly slip inside.

Immediately, Audrey heard Mrs. Nowicki talking to someone in her heavily accented English. "It is safe for Klaus to return. She left. I have the child."

Like hell you do. No doubt anymore. This woman wasn't here by accident.

Slipping out of her shoes, Audrey eschewed the hallway and padded in stocking feet into the living room with its sound-muffling carpet. The baby was in here—safe. For a brief moment, she debated grabbing Harper and running. But what if she overreacted. Perhaps this was a misunderstanding. She couldn't let paranoia control her.

She passed by the playpen with her daughter sitting inside. Harper cooed and clapped her hands. Adorable, but she didn't have time to play peek-a-boo. Audrey kept going, hugging the wall of the dining room, doing her best to sneak up behind the possibly fake nanny. Before she reached her, Mrs. Nowicki turned around and saw her. Her eyes widened in surprise.

The imposter nanny played innocent. "Did you forget something?"

"Who was that on the phone?" Audrey asked, the gun tucked behind her.

"Just agency. I call to let them know I am here with the baby."

"Stop the lying. Who are you? What's your real name?"

"I show you visa."

"No, you showed me fake identification. The agency sent me the real Mrs. Nowicki's file. So I'm going to ask you again. Who. Are. You?" For emphasis, the gun came into play, her aim steady.

The gaze in front of her narrowed. "You no want to shoot me."

"Who sent you?" Audrey was no longer worried about missing her flight. Screw her trip. The situation unfolding in her kitchen was more important.

The fake nanny's gaze went to a place behind Audrey, and she barked something in Polish.

Shit. They weren't alone.

Whirling, Audrey brought her gun to bear on an empty room. A ploy!

Before she could whirl back, the portly woman slammed into her, her hand chopping down on Audrey's wrist, causing her to lose her grip on the gun.

It hit the floor with a clatter, and the heavier woman tried to wrap her thick arms around Audrey. Since that would probably be much like a hug from a bear—with rib-crushing consequences—Audrey dropped to the floor and spun her leg around, meaning to trip Nowicki. Only the woman danced out of reach, lighter on her feet than expected.

Since she was already low, Audrey dove for the gun. She almost wrapped her fingers around it when Nowicki kicked it away.

With the weapon out of reach, Audrey flipped her hair out of her face only to freeze as she heard a click. Nowicki had pulled her own gun.

Stupid. How stupid. Audrey had never even thought to frisk the woman. Then again, who would think to frisk a nanny?

I should have. A few months ago, she would have. This suburban life had made her complacent.

"Put your hands over your head." The accent had disappeared.

Audrey did as she was told. "Who are you? What do you want?"

"I am here for the baby."

Words that made Audrey's blood run cold. She didn't have to fake the fear in her trembling voice. "Please, don't hurt her."

"The child won't come to harm, and neither will you so long as you cooperate."

Cooperate? Yeah, that wasn't going to happen, but she faked compliance. "I'll do anything you ask." Audrey ducked her head and nodded, appearing the epitome of meek submission.

Nowicki fell for it. "Hands behind your head. Stand up."

She laced her fingers behind her neck and pretended to struggle to stand, head still bowed.

"Weak." Fake Nowicki snorted. "I don't know why they were so concerned."

"Who is *they*?" Audrey asked.

"As if you don't know."

Audrey could guess, and it didn't bode well. Except for one thing. Her enemy wouldn't want her dead. Not by someone else's hand, which might keep her safe for a bit.

The barrel of Nowicki's gun drooped as she dug out her phone and used one hand to dial.

Audrey bided her time. Listening as a male voice answered, the buzz low in timbre, too low to make out words. All she had was the matron's one-sided conversation.

"The baby is fine. But the mother returned."

The voice barked something.

The woman sneered. "Dangerous? All I see is a sniveling coward." The hand holding the gun waved. "Tell the boss that I will expect extra for bringing them both in."

Oh, she'd get extra all right. An extra helping of trouble.

With the woman having relaxed her aim and her guard, Audrey made her move. She lunged, charging into Nowicki, wrapping her fingers around the gun. She shoved the weapon hand, straining against the other woman's bulky strength. A stomp on her instep made Nowicki falter, and the muzzle pointed at the ceiling. The gun went off, a loud retort that sprayed chunks of plaster and set Harper to crying.

"You made my daughter cry," Audrey growled.

"I will make your daughter an orphan," snapped the fake nanny.

"Like hell, you will." Bad enough that Harper only had one parent. Audrey wasn't about to let her lose another. "Don't worry, baby," Audrey shouted. "Momma's got this."

She wrestled with the heavier woman, their bodies twisting and turning in a grunting dance. Her hip hit the edge of the kitchen island, the granite hard and uncompromising. The bigger woman leaned Audrey back, causing the stone to dig into Audrey's spine, the fake nanny's lips pulling into a sneer of triumph.

A knee between the legs, while not as effective as on a man, still hurt plenty. The fake nanny gasped, and her hold loosened enough that Audrey regained some measure of control and let go of the gun hand.

Her fists shot out, fast and furious, hitting the woman in the face. *Whack. Whack.* She kept pummeling, feeling cartilage crack and the hot spurt of blood on her hands.

The matron reeled away from Audrey, her face a bloody mess, the gun loosely held in one hand. Audrey pressed her advantage, not relenting in her jabs, but now also aiming for other body parts: the diaphragm to shorten her breath, the tit because—as many women could attest —a tit punch hurt.

The fake nanny stumbled around the island, one hand cupping her broken face, an eye already swelling shut. But given whom she worked for, Audrey knew—because of a lesson hard-learned—there could be no mercy.

She reached overhead for a pot hanging from the rack, wrapping her fingers around the handle, and swung it like an expert ball player. It connected with a resounding twang, and the false Mrs. Nowicki went down.

But that didn't mean Audrey could pause. She quickly stripped the other woman of the gun, then searched her. The phone she'd pocketed, the switchblade in her bulky left sock, too. Then Audrey grabbed some twine from the drawer—because a good suburban housewife, even a single mother, always bound her papers in a neat stack. It also did a good job of tying up would-be kidnappers.

Job accomplished, but conscious of the ticking clock— someone would notice when Nowicki didn't check in—she took a moment and rinsed her hands at the sink, washing the blood from her scraped knuckles, cursing herself for being stupid.

This is my fault.

She should have known something was amiss the moment the woman stepped out of the cab. Should have listened to her gut.

"Waaah." Poor Harper still cried, her hysterics making her hoarse. First, though, Audrey peeked into the yard to see if she spotted anyone. Fake Nowicki obviously wasn't working alone. She checked the bar on the door. Drew the shades when she saw nothing.

Back entrance secured, she hit the front door next and locked it. Only then did Audrey head to her hiccupping daughter. She grabbed Harper's chubby body and cradled her close. "Shhh, baby girl. Momma's here." Momma had returned in the nick of time. But Harper was upset. And probably hungry. As she prepped the bottle she grabbed from the fridge, she hummed to her daughter. A soothing lullaby that never failed to work, the only thing she had left of her own mother. The words to *The Mockingbird* made up as she sang. Because the words themselves didn't matter, just the repetitive singing. It calmed Harper even before the bottle hit her lips. If only Audrey's problems were as easily solved.

Someone had tried to take Harper.

This place was no longer safe, and Audrey had to figure out what to do next. She couldn't call for help. Especially from the police. How would she explain the fake nanny she'd knocked out? Her safety depended on her not drawing any attention at all.

"What are we going to do?" Especially since she expected a knock at the door any minute. It wasn't even far-fetched to imagine someone busting in the windows and shooting.

Paranoia wanted to make her its bitch. She couldn't let it. She needed a clear mind to figure out her next step.

Something in her pocket buzzed. Not her phone.

She set Harper down on the floor and pulled out Nowicki's cell. Glanced at the screen. Unknown caller.

What a surprise.

Audrey answered but said nothing.

Neither did the caller.

For a moment, it was just dead air. Then a low chuckle.

Click. The call disconnected, and Audrey's blood turned to ice.

"We need to leave." Quickly, she grabbed the always-packed bag for her daughter that held clothes, diapers, and a small container of formula with a bottle. None of which would last long. She should grab the full can on the counter. She entered the kitchen, ignoring the prone body on the floor.

A *rat-tat-tat* turned her head, and she saw the woman's heels drumming on the tile as white foam oozed from her mouth. It lasted only a minute, and then the body went still.

Dead. Bloody poisoned. Some things never changed.

Just as ruthless as ever. And the fake nanny probably never even knew about the deadly bomb she carried inside her.

Explain that to authorities. *Yeah, so someone sent her after me to kidnap my baby, and when she failed, they set off a poison pill failsafe.* She'd end up in a psych ward for delusions.

Good thing she didn't plan to stick around.

Audrey turned to her stove and flicked on the gas burners, all of them, but didn't light it. She did, however, light a candle on the dining room table. The sweet vanilla scent not yet overcome by the gas.

Audrey headed for the front door, snaring the diaper bag on her way, along with the chest sling. Harper cooed as she tugged at the buttons on Audrey's shirt, unaware that their life was about to change.

Exiting outside, Audrey—with the baby in one arm, the diaper bag over her shoulder, gun still in hand—kept darting her gaze, wondering if someone watched. Would they come after her while she was vulnerable with Harper? She hated the seconds wasted strapping the baby into her car seat, expecting a bullet in the back at any moment.

Instead, she got a shrill, "What are you doing parked in my driveway?"

"Leaving," Audrey announced as she slammed the minivan door shut.

"I thought I heard gunshots. Coming from your place." The neighbor looked eager, her beady eyes and pinched face hungry for scandal.

"Probably just someone's television." Audrey sidled sideways, willing the woman to leave.

"What happened to your nanny?" said with a sneer. "Going to—"

Audrey snapped. "It is none of your damned business." She raised her gun. "And if you don't mind, I'm kind of in a rush. So move your nosy ass." Threatening the biddy probably wasn't her brightest move, but Audrey didn't have time to deal with her. She had to go.

Especially now since the woman ran back into her house, probably to call the cops.

"Hold on, sweet pea, because Momma's about to make this minivan fly." She threw herself into the driver seat before peeling down the driveway and spilling onto the street, not sure where she was going but knowing she had to put some distance between them and the house.

Quickly.

She went a few blocks before she slowed to a stop, hopping out only long enough to flip her plates. Literally. A simple clip allowed her to turn them over and give her an entirely new identity, and a bit of breathing room. Because—

Boom!

The detonation rocked the neighborhood as her house exploded.

—the police would be looking for her. They just wouldn't find Audrey Marlowe.

She jumped back into the van, throwing it in drive to soothe Harper's startled crying. "It's all right, baby girl. Momma's going to keep us safe."

Somehow.

Where to? Her identity was compromised, which meant she couldn't get on that flight. No flight meant ditching her mission. Yes, mission. Because her regular job as an interior designer didn't require her to go out of town. But her secret employer did.

A simple phone call would have her job reassigned, and get the work started on a new life and identity. But Audrey didn't want to admit defeat, and she hated asking for help. Her employer had done so much for her already.

However, how was she supposed to work with a baby in tow? She glanced in the rearview mirror at Harper, who'd discovered that she could grab her toes and eat them.

Who could she trust to watch Harper?

Later that night, after spending a few hours on her laptop, she found the answer.

CHAPTER TWO

THE KNOCK ON THE APARTMENT DOOR SET OFF HIS proximity alarm. Good thing something was paying attention because Declan slept like the dead.

The single knock wasn't repeated, so he slapped at his tablet flashing red by his nightstand. Probably just someone coming in from a late night and banging into the walls. He'd done that a time or two. Even tried to enter the wrong apartment before.

"Waaa. Waaa."

Did someone sob?

He lifted himself onto an elbow and looked around his loft apartment. The noise appeared muffled. Was the knocker still outside his door?

Please don't let it be some drunk chick. He didn't do well with snotty noses and running mascara.

He grabbed his tablet and tapped it to bring up the surveillance camera he'd installed in the hall, only to frown. It showed nothing but darkness. Someone had blocked the lens.

The intentional act put him into mercenary mode. He swung his legs over the edge of the bed and heard it again. A little crying engine that kept going. "Waa-waa. Waa. Waa-waa."

It came from outside his door.

He grabbed the gun from his nightstand and trod quietly in his bare feet to the portal, keeping to the side to avoid a shotgun blast. Although, it would take some pretty heavy-duty firepower. He'd had a steel-plated door put in when he remodeled the loft. The walls were thick cinderblock. He thought of it as his bunker against the world.

What he didn't understand was why he could hear someone in the hallway.

He paused by the door, arguing with himself against opening it, but that seemed cowardly. His buddy Calvin certainly wouldn't hesitate. Most of the guys he worked with at Bad Boy Inc. would fling that door open and confront whatever lay outside.

Probably just a sloshed partyer passed out in the wrong spot.

The tumblers in the many locks clicked as he turned them, and bolts slid out of their secure housings. His fingers gripped the gun tightly as he swung open the door and confronted a...

Baby?

Big brown eyes peered at him, a rosebud mouth pursed, and a note pinned to the blanket covering her said: *Congratulations, Daddy*.

Declan did the mature thing, the only thing a man in his position could do.

He slammed the door shut.

He then leaned against it for good measure.

Wrong address. Had to be. While a bit of a ladies' man, Declan was very strict when it came to protection. Always wear a rubber.

Always.

But, sometimes, condoms failed.

The nagging thought taunted and wouldn't depart, especially given that the wails got louder. He couldn't exactly leave the baby outside.

He couldn't exactly bring it in either.

As a mercenary, he'd trained for many things. Hand-to-hand combat. Weapons. Surveillance. Even bombs—both the creation and dismantling of. But a baby?

He needed help.

Speaking aloud, he commanded his house computer. "Hey, Uma"—because he just loved her in *Kill Bill*—"call Harry." Uma being his virtual personal assistant when at home. Harry being his boss, mentor, and the only guy he knew with baby experience.

A moment later, his boss barked, "Do you know what time it is?"

Time to panic? "I have a problem."

Instantly, Harry changed his tone. "What's happened?"

"There's a baby at my door."

"Did you call me because one of your lady friends is crying for seconds again?"

"Not exactly," Declan hedged. And he'd only done that once. Served him right for not checking her purse to see if she was on any meds.

"I'm going to hang up." Harry didn't hide his impatience. As owner of Bad Boy Inc., he knew how to take charge and not waste time.

"There's a real baby. At my door. Wrapped in a blanket with a note. Says I'm the daddy."

Harry coughed. "What the fuck did you say? Repeat that, because I'm pretty sure I misunderstood."

"I said, there is a baby in the hallway outside my place with a fucking note pinned to its pink blanket that basically says hello, Daddy."

A snicker emerged from the speakers. "Looks like your luck ran out. What's the kid's name? Who does it look like? Hopefully, not you. Who's the mommy?"

"How the fuck would I know?" Declan yelled, letting some of his panic loose. "Someone just dropped the kid outside my door. What am I supposed to do?"

"Um, Declan, please tell me you didn't leave the baby in the hall." When there was no reply, Harry barked, "Declan, bring that baby inside right this instant!"

"But—"

"No buts. Whether it's yours or not, you can't leave a child out there."

"But it's crying."

"Declan." The warning note in his boss's voice had him sighing.

"Fine. I'm getting it." Opening the door rose the muffled crying to decibels at wincing levels. Reaching down, he grabbed the edges of the contraption the baby was strapped in, shot a look up and down the hall—with only one door: his—and brought it in. As he turned, he noted a bulging bag tucked to the side of the door. He used his foot to drag it in, too.

He then slammed the door shut and carried his package to the table where he deposited it. "I got the baby.

You happy now?" he said, having to speak loud enough to be heard over the wailing.

"No, I am not happy. Pick the baby up and soothe it."

"Are you insane?" Him, hold a baby? He'd rather handle a live grenade.

"Now, Declan," Harry snapped.

Except now wasn't that easy. Declan held out his arms and gripped the squishy baby over the blanket. It stopped crying and blinked wet lashes at him. It didn't last because, though he tugged, the baby didn't leave the strange, rocking seat and began hollering again.

"It's stuck!"

"What's stuck?"

"The baby!"

Harry sighed. "Did you undo the buckles?"

"No one said there would be buckles," Declan muttered as he removed the blanket and spotted the harness holding it in place. *Click.* He quickly folded back the straps and then gingerly lifted the baby, holding it out at arm's length.

The crying subsided again, and he breathed a sigh of relief.

"Hold the baby closer," demanded Harry.

"How did you know...?" He shook his head. Harry always did have a sixth sense. Declan reeled the baby in until he cradled it against his chest. It smelled kind of nice.

"Was that so hard?" Harry asked as the baby tucked its head against Declan's shoulder and began to suck on a fist.

Yes. "Now what?"

"Is it a boy or a girl?"

"How can I tell? It's only got a wee bit of hair."

"The outfit will usually give it away. What color is it?"

"Pink." The duh moment hit him hard. "It's a girl!"

"Congratulations."

"No, wait. It's not mine."

"She is for the moment. Daddy." Harry snickered. "Tell me more about the note. Does it say anything else?"

"Dunno."

"Shouldn't you find out?"

Could he blame his lack of brainpower in the moment on shock? Balancing the baby against his chest, Declan retrieved the blanket, tore the card from it, and flipped it over. "I'll be damned. It's got more to it."

It read:

Sorry for the abrupt announcement. I didn't know where else to go. I've got something I've got to deal with, and I can't have the baby with me. This is Harper, your daughter. She's eleven months old. Everything you need is in the diaper bag. I'll be by to pick her up as soon as my business is done. Signed, ***your one-night stand.***

Harry was outright laughing by the time Declan finished reading it. "Well, I'll be, if the tomcat didn't finally get collared."

"This isn't funny," Declan grumbled. It was downright ludicrous. "How do I even know this baby is mine?"

Sobering for a moment, Harry replied, "DNA tests will clear that up easily enough. Swab her, and we'll have the lab run it against your profile."

"How long will that take?"

"At least a day, maybe two. They're pretty swamped right now."

"I can't wait that long!" Declan wanted to know now, this instant, whether this was a cruel joke.

"You can't rush science. And no matter the answer, you're still in charge. The mother left her with you."

"But I don't know how to care for a baby. Can't you and Sherry take her?" Sherry being Harry's wife and a mom already.

"I wouldn't want to deny you the chance to bond with your daughter."

"She's not my daughter." His claim might have held a thread of panic.

"Are you one hundred percent sure of that?"

Declan wanted to yell yes, he was fucking sure. But... what if there'd been a hole in a condom? What if this child was the fruit of his loins? Could he abandon her?

He knew how it felt to be alone. Declan had no family. Parents long gone. No siblings. Just him. It suited his mercenary lifestyle.

Speaking of which...

"I can't spend a week babysitting. I have shit to do. Or have you forgotten my new client?"

"I have not forgotten, and there's a simple solution. Hire a nanny to watch her while you work."

"I don't want a stranger in my loft. Isn't there a place where you can drop them off?"

"You mean daycare?" Harry snorted. "You want good daycare, you're going on a long waitlist."

"Does it have to be good?"

"Declan!" Harry barked his name. "This is your kid. You can't just leave her anywhere."

"I guess." Still, though. "I don't want to hire a nanny."

"Then I guess you'd better invest in a stroller since you'll be bringing her along with you everywhere you go."

"Why would I do that?"

"You do know a baby can't be left alone."

No, he didn't precisely know that, but he surely would have figured it out. Eventually. "The mother had no problem dumping her on my step," he grumbled. Just like his parents never had a problem making him a latchkey kid.

"Can you blame the woman for dumping and disappearing? Had you gotten wind of your kid, you'd have had that place empty and up for sale with no forwarding address."

"Are you implying I'd run from my responsibilities?" His reply emerged a touch indignantly.

"Yeah, I am. Let me ask, how long were you planning to leave the baby in the hall before you called me?"

Could a man squirm on the inside? "It took me by surprise."

"Welcome to parenthood. It's always a big surprise. You'll learn to adapt."

"But—"

"When I give you a mission, do you always know what to expect? Or what to do?"

"No, but—"

"There is no but." Harry didn't give him a chance to speak. "This baby, right now, needs you. She is your mission. And I expect you to do a good job."

"Even if she's not my kid?"

"Doesn't matter whose kid it is. She's your responsibility. So suck it up, buttercup."

There was no chance for a rebuttal because Harry hung

up, leaving Declan with a sleeping baby on his shoulder. The little girl had fallen asleep, half her fist shoved into her mouth, a warm, limp bundle that he didn't know what to do with.

Harry said to treat her like a mission. A mission usually involved things like stalking people and then either spying, kidnapping, or killing them. Easy shit. Stuff he understood and knew how to do. The only thing he knew about babies was that they cried and supposedly shat a lot.

In his world, the only ass he wiped was his own. As for crying, he never could abide it.

Yet Harry had made it clear. Declan had to deal with this.

I don't even think she's mine. But Harry did have a point. If he didn't care for her, who would? Child Services?

He'd had run-ins with them as a kid, and had friends who didn't have anything good to say about the agency either. Could he really subject the baby snuggled against his shoulder to their impersonal bureaucracy?

Sigh. No, he couldn't. But neither could he do this alone.

Beep.

His tablet signaled that he had a message, and he could have breathed a sigh of relief when he saw that it was from Harry.

It didn't say much, just contained a link for a nanny agency. He quickly fired off a request through their online form. Next thing he knew, he was logged in and searching their database for prospects. By lunch, he'd narrowed it down to a dozen that might work.

Being a man of caution, he did rapid background checks. One arrested in her late teens for theft. Off the list. Another with an ex-boyfriend in jail for drugs. He believed in second chances, but hello, this was his kid.

Maybe.

Anyhow, off the list, too.

By the end, he was left with five possibilities. He set up interviews for that afternoon.

The first one arrived just in time.

Declan flung open the door, surprised he'd even heard the knocking because the wailing of the baby had surely shattered his eardrums. "Thank fuck you're here. Help!"

CHAPTER THREE

Edith took one look at the frazzled man and had to bite her lip lest she burst out laughing. The guy framed in the doorway was the epitome of every cartoon in existence: hair standing on end, covered in wet spots and grubby hand marks. He looked an absolute mess. Less funny was the poor hollering baby.

"Mr. Hood?"

"Yes. That's me, I think. Please tell me you're the nanny." His voice held a thread of panic, the type that indicated he was about to completely unravel.

"I am. Edith Jameson. The agency sent me."

"Thank fuck," he muttered. "Come in." He swept a hand, and she stepped inside to see an open floor plan loft with super high ceilings, unfinished and showing off the thick metal girders and aluminum piping. Brick walls all around, and windows made up of many small panes grouped together to create a large one. The floors were scuffed hardwood, and the décor—in direct contrast to the age of the building—all chrome and leather. She didn't have to look hard to see underneath the yuppie décor to the warehouse it used to be.

It also wasn't hard to see that under the frazzled exterior existed a handsome man. Taller than her five foot eight, Mr. Hood was probably around six feet, broad of shoulder, his jawline softened by a beard. Not exactly her preference, but facial hair seemed to be the fad of the day. He looked comfortable in worn jeans and a steel gray Henley shirt showing signs of baby spit up and powder. White powder that'd better be milk and not drugs.

"I brought my resume." She held out the sheaf of papers bound together by a staple. Not exactly necessary. The agency had all her information online, but a starting point in case he'd forgotten anything.

He gave it a brief glance and shook his head. "Screw that fancy feast of words on paper. Education and courses don't mean shit if you can't apply them. Let's start the interview with you showing me what you'd do with a crying baby." He pointed behind him. "That's my, um, daughter, Harper."

The baby sat on the floor, surrounded by pillows, fists clenched, face red, mouth open wide in a wail.

"Oh dear." Edith hurried to her side and dropped to her knees with a soothing, "It's all right. Calm down, sweet pea." She began to hum. "Hush now baby, don't say a word..." The familiar words spilled out of her and penetrated the child's hysterics.

The screams turned into hiccupping sobs as the baby peered at her through drenched lashes. Edith held out her arms, and the baby mimicked her, pudgy arms flailing. She allowed herself to be plucked from the soft nest. Holding her close, Edith bounced the baby, cooing the lyrics to the song, hand cradling her head while the other hugged the sturdy body close. The baby calmed and snuggled in.

She pivoted to see the man staring at her, relief plain to see on his face.

"Thank fuck."

"Language," Edith said with a frown."

"Don't tell me you're a prude."

"No. But there's a child present."

"I don't think the baby understands me yet."

"No, but she will eventually. Do you really want her first words to be profanity?"

A line appeared between his brows. "Hadn't really thought about that. Kind of new at this whole daddy thing."

"Oh?" she said with an inquiring note. "Are you and your wife divorced?"

He looked startled. "Not married. Hell, not even in a committed relationship. I just found out recently, this morning as a matter of fact, that I might be Harper's daddy."

"Might be?"

"First I heard of Harper was this morning when I found her on my doorstep with a note. The mother didn't stick around to chat."

"How awful," Edith exclaimed.

"Tell me about it. Dumping a baby on me with no warning and shit."

She shot a glare at the man. "I meant for Harper. And watch your language. While you're upset about the inconvenience, the poor mite was left by her mother, the only person she's ever really known." The now calm baby sighed against her shoulder, her body relaxing as she began to drift off.

"Don't be giving me sh—erm, heck. I wasn't the one who did it. I'm the one who's trying to handle it, hence why you're here. I need someone to take care of her while we figure things out."

"I can start work immediately. You obviously need it." She couldn't help a disparaging tone.

He bristled. "I never said you were hired. I have other people to interview."

"Or you could cancel them. I assure you, I am more than fully qualified to handle your child. If you check my references, you'll see I've been a nanny for quite some time now."

"Yet you're available now on short notice? Why?" He eyed her suspiciously. "What happened to your last job?"

"They grew up. When children reach a certain age, parents find themselves needing a housekeeper more than a childcare worker."

"How old are you?"

"Twenty-eight."

"Marital status?"

"Why does my love life matter?"

"If you're gonna watch my kid, then I want to know if I have to worry about any boyfriends trying to come over or a husband forbidding you from working. I keep odd hours."

She rolled her eyes. "Single. And staying that way."

"Where do you live?"

"Right now, I'm just renting a room until I'm settled with a new family."

"You're a live-in nanny?"

"For people with hectic schedules, it's best to have a nanny full-time so that there are no issues if a parent suddenly has to go out, especially at night."

"What if I prefer you just come during the day? I like my privacy."

Her lips flattened. "Then I should mention that rather than a flat rate, it will be hourly, and should you call me with little notice for an evening stint, that hourly rate triples."

He waved a hand. "Money's not an issue. I don't know if I want someone underfoot all the time. Especially a young lady."

"Afraid you'll be inappropriate?" She arched a brow.

He snorted. "As if. More because there's not a lot of privacy and I don't have a guest bedroom as you can clearly see. And I'm not about to see my bathroom taken over by girly shit."

"Language."

He glared. "She's sleeping."

"She can still hear you."

"Are you always this bossy?"

"When it comes to taking care of my charges, yes. But in return, I can promise you exceptional childcare."

"What if I want something that isn't going to impede my lifestyle?"

"Then you're obviously not ready to be a father."

By this point, they were standing almost nose-to-nose, the baby tucked between them.

"I already explained this wasn't my idea. I don't even know if the baby is mine."

"Whether she is or not isn't the issue. Until you know for sure, you're responsible for her."

"I didn't ask to be. And, quite honestly, I'm still debating if I should call Child Protective Services."

Her eyes widened. "You wouldn't!"

"Why not? All I have is a baby dumped on my doorstep and a note saying I'm the daddy. What if they got the wrong address? What if the mother is never coming back?"

"What if the mother just has some issues she needs to deal with and thought, hey, maybe the father should help out for a bit while she gets her affairs in order?" Edith found herself in the odd position of defending Harper's mystery mother.

"We all have issues. Doesn't mean she's got the right to dump a kid on me without warning. And then what? I turn my life upside down for the kid and then I'm supposed to just let her waltz in and kidnap my daughter when she no longer needs me?"

"I thought you said she wasn't your daughter."

"I don't fucking know if she is or not," he snapped. "Not yet. But I plan to find out, and if she is, then I probably should be a part of her life."

"Probably?" She couldn't help niggling at his choice of words.

"Why is this any of your business? All I want is a nanny, not a lecture on how I should live my life."

"Maybe you need a lecture because your attitude sucks."

"And your interview skills leave much to be desired. I

find it hard to believe anyone would hire you with your holier-than-thou attitude."

"There's nothing wrong with me advocating what's best for a child."

"It is when it's none of your goddamned business," he snarled.

The verbal scuffle woke the baby, who let her displeasure be known with a wail.

"Now you've done it." Edith glared at him as she bounced the baby, trying to soothe her.

"I've done it?" His brow arched. "You're the stranger arguing with me about my life."

"But that's just it. It's not just your life." Edith turned from him and looked around for a diaper bag. She spotted it sitting on a table and ignored him to rummage through it, pulling out a fresh diaper—the last one, she noted—sleeper, and wipes. The talcum, sitting in a puddle of white silt, was already on the table. As were three open jars of baby food, a can of formula, and several bottles of milk, none of them the same in appearance, the texture in one thick and clotted.

I don't think he followed the instructions. No wonder the baby was unhappy, but she kept that observation to herself lest he start yelling again. But she did feel a need to mention, "You need diapers."

And food, and a crib, along with a whole bunch of other things. She set the baby down on the floor, using the rug to protect the mite from the cold concrete.

"I need more than diapers," he grumbled.

"If you mean furniture, then I'd suggest since the situation is possibly transitional that you invest in a playpen. The baby can sleep in it as well as play."

"Play with what?"

"Pretty much anything so long as it's not sharp, small enough to swallow, or easily breakable."

"You just ruled out everything in this place."

"Not quite. You just have to use your imagination." She finished dressing the child and then propped her amidst the pillows before asking, "Do you have any plastic bowls and spoons?"

"Yeah. Why? You gonna make me cookies to bribe me with?"

"You wish," she snorted. "It's to give Harper something to play with."

"Oh." He fetched the items then stood back, watching with a surprised expression as Harper snatched the spoon and began babbling as she whacked the bowl making a drumming sound.

"That's loud," he observed.

"Most kids' toys are. You'll discover children don't need fancy gadgets or the hottest trends in toys to keep them happy. Simple things—like kitchen stuff, a box, even a blanket to play peek-a-boo—will do the trick if you're stuck. As for baby-proofing..." She glanced around and shook her head. "Outlet covers are a must."

"I didn't have those growing up, and I survived just fine."

"And how many times did you stick your fingers in them?"

His lips crooked. "It was my tongue. And once was enough to cure me of that."

She almost smiled. "Your coffee table has to go."

He glanced at the plate glass set on a carved wooden bear. Modern rustic the sales guy called it. "But I like it."

"Have you seen the corners on it? Not to mention, do you want to be constantly cleaning baby prints off it?"

"How about I just get rid of all my shit," he drawled.

"It would be safer."

He frowned.

"Don't give me that look. You asked for help. I'm giving it."

"What about food? I tried feeding her the stuff in the bag, but she spit it at me."

"Because babies aren't always crazy about new flavors and textures."

"She didn't want the milk either."

Grabbing the one with lumps floating on the top, she shook it. "Can you blame her? You actually have to follow the directions, not just dump some in and hope for the best. She might also prefer it heated."

"This whole baby thing sounds complicated."

She laughed. "Complicated at first only because it's new. But you'll soon get the hang of it."

"Maybe." He grimaced.

Knock. Knock.

Having dropped to her haunches, Edith raised her head as Mr. Hood announced, "That must be the next nanny."

"Tell her the position is filled."

"But it's not."

"I told you I could do it."

"And I never said I was hiring you," Mr. Hood drawled. "As a matter of fact, I don't think you and I will mesh well at all. We've known each other, what, fifteen minutes? And already managed to fight."

"I wouldn't call it a fight, more an expression of opinion."

"Sorry, but I don't think it will work." He went to the door. "Thanks for coming."

Edith glared but couldn't change his mind. Not yet.

But he would call her back.

And soon.

CHAPTER FOUR

No way am I calling Edith back.

For one, she was bossy and had a way of making him feel guilty when he had nothing to feel guilty about. He wasn't the one who created the situation. How dare she rag on him when he was trying to do his best with the shitty hand dealt to him.

Second, he wasn't about to curb his language for anyone. His father used to swear around him all the time as a kid. A wallop on the ass by his drunken dad, and a mouth-washing of soap by his mom had curbed him of ever cussing around them. Although, once his mom died, he didn't really give a shit what his dad thought. Especially once Declan got bigger than him, and Dad couldn't threaten with his fists anymore. When Declan moved out on his own, he stopped restricting his language. In his opinion, fuck was a perfectly fine noun, verb, and adjective. While shit came a close second.

Take that, Miss Didn't-Like-His-Potty-Mouth.

But the best and final reason he wasn't hiring Edith?

The woman was too damned hot. As in 'wet fantasy with a trim figure in snug blue jeans and a demure blouse begging for stripping' hot. While screwing the nanny worked out in the adult movies he sometimes watched, in real life, banging the help was a recipe for disaster.

So, he told her she wasn't getting the job and ushered her out as he let in the next nanny interviewee, an older woman with a wide waist, round cheeks, and no sense of humor.

Mrs. Partridge, also a nanny of experience, arrived with a list of rules. No working before 8 a.m. No working after 6 p.m. She insisted on Sundays off for church. The list went on and on.

Declan sent her off just in time for the next, a lovely Filipino woman who spoke barely any English. He couldn't understand a word she said, but at the same time, given his business, he wouldn't have to worry as much about her overhearing anything. Plus, she didn't make his man parts tingle. He put her on the *maybe* list.

By the end of the afternoon, he had two firm nos, three maybes, and a baby who sat staring at him.

"So, diva"—because with lungs like hers, surely she'd end up being a singer on the stage—"which one did you like?"

"Gaaa." The baby clapped her hands.

"Yeah, that doesn't help me much." The resumes were layered in front of him on the coffee table. His gaze kept straying to the corners of the glass top. One of the many injuries waiting to happen that Edith had pointed out. She was the only one with the balls to declare that he should change his bachelor pad around to suit the baby.

Edith was also on his *no* list. He shoved her resume to the side.

He also shoved Mrs. Partridge away. He needed someone more flexible.

That left three.

Which one to choose?

Should he resort to darts?

Give them to Harper and see which one she drooled on?

Or how about being smart about it and actually doing a deep background check on them.

Duh. He was a killer for hire. A mercenary with access to databases beyond just the police ones. Before he allowed anyone into his life and near his kid, he should make sure they weren't a child abuser.

Rosa, his favorite nanny of the cut, wasn't here legally as it turned out. Which was a shame. He'd rather liked her. And might have hired her anyway if he'd not discovered a previous drug mule charge.

Her resume went into the *no* pile.

Theresa, the quiet woman who wouldn't meet his gaze. No convictions. Lived at home with her parents. Belonged to a cult.

He blinked. There was no mistaking it, though, and the only reason he found out was because the FBI currently had an open file on its leader, including his many wives. They worshipped the devil, which didn't bother him, but the fact that there were signs they made animal sacrifices did. He slid her resume to the side, as well.

Which left one resume. The Norwegian woman, blonde, good-looking, here on a work visa, whose nanny job fell through when the husband ran away with the chauffeur.

No flags were raised when he did a search. While attractive, he was pretty sure he could handle himself. The baby didn't seem to mind her, and she offered a flexible schedule.

He gave her a call.

She answered on the second ring.

"Hey, Petra, it's Mr. Hood. I interviewed you this afternoon. The job is yours."

"Not interested."

He frowned. "What do you mean, not interested? You seemed plenty interested this afternoon during the interview."

"I was hired elsewhere." *Click.* The phone hung up, leaving him staring at it perplexed.

He spoke aloud. "What the fuck?"

"Fuuu." The baby babbled, and he snapped his mouth shut. Surely, it was a coincidence.

His gaze roved to the resumes. Mrs. Partridge and Edith Jameson. Not his first choices.

He ran the old woman's name first. Clean as a whistle. But did he really want that humorless biddy around? And... what about the times he needed to go out at night? He couldn't exactly curtail all his evening activities.

It's only for a week.

But what if there were an emergency? He needed someone who could come in at a moment's notice. However, did he want that someone to be bossy Edith?

She's advocating for Harper. Is that such a bad thing? No. But her advocacy meant he was being put on the spot. She expected him to change.

If the kid is mine, shouldn't I be willing to change a little? Because there was no denying, in some respects, she was right. His home wasn't set up to handle a baby. Especially not one who could crawl. Kind of. What the heck was that weird hump and bump thing Harper did on her ass? It seemed a strange method of locomotion, but it worked. And she was fast.

He'd had to chase after her a few times when she went scooting across the floor, determined to explore: his cd tower, his kitchen cupboards, the basket of ammo shells—which he should note were spent and acted as a decorative thing in a basket some ex-girlfriend had given him.

The socket where she extended her finger, ET-like, was a close call. He'd put a chair in front of it, but was only too aware of just how many others remained at her height.

It pained him to admit that maybe he did need someone like Edith. If she was as good as she said.

Running Edith's information showed a clean record. Not even a single parking ticket. Everything about her seemed perfect, yet he hesitated because calling her meant sucking it up and admitting that she was right. She'd probably lord it over him. Did he really want to hire her bossy ass?

That oh so sexy, hot ass.

The fact that he could so clearly picture it reminded him of the real reason she was wrong for the job.

The doorbell rang, and he jumped from the couch. "That better be Harry and Sherry," he said to Harper, who was currently penned in by the chairs he'd laid on their sides to form a temporary pen. She still managed to grab them and haul herself to her feet, offering a toothy grin of victory.

"Don't you escape, little diva."

"Va!" she exclaimed as he went to answer the door.

It was Harry, without Sherry. Declan peeked out into the hall. "Where's your better half?" The kind of half that would take one look at the cuteness drooling all over his wood floors and insist on taking her home to help Declan out.

"Sherry is home with a cold. She didn't want to infect the baby. But she did send me with supplies." Harry held up a package of diapers and rattled something metal and vinyl. "Playpen," he said at Declan's drawn brows.

"Awesome. Edith said I should get one."

"Edith your new nanny?"

"Nope." He shook his head. "None of the ones I interviewed will do. I'll have to find some new ones to check out tomorrow."

"Seriously? I thought the agency sent you like five to check out."

"And none of them were any good."

"No good? How picky are you?"

Apparently, pickier than expected.

As Harry showed him how to set up the portable crib thing, he explained.

At the end, Harry was grinning and shaking his head "Look at you, being an overprotective daddy already."

The word daddy made Declan wince. "I'm just being smart."

"Then hire the girl who recommended the playpen. The bossy one. What did you say her name was?"

"Edith. And I don't think it's a good idea."

"Why? Because she pointed out that your place is a

death trap? She is right. I'll bet you keep your cleaning supplies in the cupboard under your sink."

"Where else would I keep them?"

"Locked cabinet or a high one out of reach of the baby. Wouldn't want her to poison herself."

"I can barely get her to eat. I highly doubt she's going to start chugging chemicals."

"Said hundreds of parents every year before they rushed their kid to the hospital."

Declan glared. "Fine. I'll move the damned stuff."

"Hire the girl and let her baby-proof."

"If that were all she wanted, I'd be okay with it, but she has also declared I shouldn't cuss around the baby."

"She's right. You shouldn't."

Declan gaped at his boss. "You telling me you don't curse around your kids? I call bullshit. I've heard you in the office. You use fuck as a noun and an adjective."

"In the office, I talk how I like, how it's expected. At home, around my kids and Sherry, you're tootin' straight I watch my mouth."

"Did you just seriously say tootin'?" Declan ogled him.

"Yeah, I did. Your kid is right there." Harry pointed.

"She doesn't talk yet."

"And? Part of being a good example is showing my kids I can control myself. So I watch my language, temper, and behavior around them to prove a point."

"Which is?"

"You act how the situation demands. You wouldn't go see a client and swear like a trucker."

"Depends on the client."

Harry growled. "Don't be deliberately obtuse. Take this new client of yours. Mr. Suarez, with his fifteen-million-dollar penthouse condo for sale. You going to drop f-bombs around him?"

"Hell, no. The commission on that sucker is going to pay for that vacation condo I've been eyeing in the Bahamas."

"Think of the baby as a high-end client. Not to mention, she's a girl. Do you really want your daughter to grow up sounding like a hillbilly trucker?"

Declan looked over at his daughter who'd taken the sweater he'd given her and played her own version of peek-a-boo. She grinned—and drooled—each time she saw him.

One day, she'd be a young woman.

And boys would look at her.

Declan was well-aware of what boys thought about girls. Especially girls with dirty mouths.

He frowned. "I don't like you."

Harry laughed. "Truth hurts, eh? Don't worry. You'll get used to it. If you still need to swear, just change it to something like fudge, or niblets."

"Niblets?" Declan arched a brow. "There are names for men who use the term niblets."

"Yeah. Happily married with kids, the oldest of whom just got into university on a full scholarship because of her grades. Which reminds me, Sherry said to let her know if you need a list of preschools for Harper."

"What the fu—heck do I need the names of schools for? She's a baby who doesn't even talk yet."

"Never too early to apply. The prestigious ones have waitlists."

"I doubt she'll be around for that long."

"What makes you say that?"

Declan snorted. "Come on, you don't seriously think she's mine."

"She could be. She does have your smile."

"Does not." Did she? Cocking his head, Declan tried to see it past the gums, few stray teeth, and the slobber. "Is it normal for her to drool so much?"

"She's teething."

Another term that didn't mean a thing to him. "You didn't happen to bring an instruction manual, did you?"

"You could try asking Google. Although, be careful with that. Else you'll be convinced there's something majorly wrong with her if you get the wrong site."

"How did you learn all this parenting stuff?" Declan asked.

"From Sherry. Who learned from her mother. But I will admit, we both sucked at the whole parenting thing at first."

"Not exactly reassuring."

"If it's any consolation, you kind of got a raw deal what with the baby being dumped on you. Which is why you need to hire some help. Sooner rather than later."

Scrubbing a hand through his hair, Declan sighed. "I know. Guess I'd better let the agency know I need more choices."

"Or just hire the bossy one. After all, if it's only for a few days, how bad could it be?"

That depended. Could a man die of blue balls?

He had to stop thinking like that. He was a grown-ass man with control. Just because she was hot and made his man parts swell wasn't a reason to dismiss her out of hand. She was the most qualified.

A pro.

Just like he was a pro.

He could do this.

Of course, wouldn't you know, she didn't answer when he called, meaning he got sent to voicemail. It beeped, and he hemmed and hawed as he left his message.

"Changed my mind. You're hired. Can you start first thing in the morning?" Because he needed tonight to nanny-proof his place.

Wouldn't do for her to find his collection of guns. Or grenades. Oh, and he'd better do something about the knife he kept strapped under the bathroom sink. Sharp enough to shave with.

CHAPTER FIVE

WITH THE BABY SITUATION SETTLED, AUDREY CLOSED the lid of her laptop and slid it into her messenger bag. About time he finally hired the nanny she'd chosen. She'd had a close call when he tried to hire the Norwegian one. Audrey had maneuvered certain information to ensure that he would call the person she'd selected. Except he was stubborn. Ignoring common sense.

Then to add insult, the DMV records hadn't cooperated when she'd tried to change them to make it seem like the Norwegian had a few DUIs under her belt.

But a dick pic sent to Petra arriving from his phone number with a note saying, *Work bonus*, just before he called took care of that situation. Good thing, because it would have been a shame to put her in the hospital. Accidents were so easy to stage.

And, yes, Audrey had meddled. Dropping her baby off for a temporary stay didn't mean she'd washed her hands of her child. She knew Declan wouldn't be able to handle a kid, but he had the means to hire help that could.

Now that she'd ensured the proper type of nanny for Harper, she could move on to other things. Even if she were a touch nervous about the fact that he'd opted to not have the nanny show up until morning. Surely, he could handle Harper for one night.

Just in case, she'd be back later and peek in on them. After she'd untangled his security again. For a real estate agent, he believed in keeping himself well protected. Had he been a victim in the past? She'd not found anything in her research to indicate why he felt the need for so many bells and whistles. She also didn't care. The fact that he kept his place locked tight was yet another reason Harper would be safe with him. Especially since no one knew about Declan but Audrey.

Exiting the coffee shop, she walked a few blocks to the car she'd bought on the drive out here. Bought with cash, of course—after she ditched the minivan and set it on fire to erase prints and any trace evidence. Anything to ensure that she and Harper disappeared.

Again.

Nestled in suburbia, she'd thought herself safe. It had been over a year—before Harper's birth—since their last attempt to get her. Somehow, somewhere, she'd been sloppy.

She couldn't let it happen again.

Her life and the life of her child depended on it.

I should have killed him when I had a chance. But at the time, she'd thought she had things under control. Thought she knew better. Wrong. All along, he'd been using her.

In the past. All of it was in the past, and this was the here and now.

She drove uptown, never having been to this city

before but finding her way via the GPS. Today wasn't about breaking in and finding the item her boss had requested. Today was about reconnoitering. Poking around the neighborhood. Walking casually past the front of the condo complex, the camera on the brim of her hat capturing images, heat signatures, electronic signals. Later, in the motel room she'd rented with cash, she'd peruse the data and look for weaknesses in the building's security and plan her point of entry.

When Audrey had done a full circuit, she left the area before anyone spotted her or wondered at the lone woman wandering around without apparent aim. She returned to her motel room and logged on via satellite to the main system.

Username. The box waited for her reply. That part wasn't encrypted.

She typed: *Frenemy Mom.*

Her code name.

Password. She quickly typed a stream of symbols, characters, and numbers.

A moment later, she was logged in. The KM logo lined the top of the screen. The company, which had offices around the world, was known for its interior design service for the elite. The fun part about her job was knowing how clients kept trying to guess what KM stood for. Killer Mansions, Knitted Memories. In reality, it stood for Killer Moms. An underground agency that only hired women— mothers, to be precise. Those who had nowhere left to go, whose lives were in jeopardy, and who would do anything —even kill—to keep their kids safe.

As to what KM did with those they recruited? Just

about anything they wanted. Which made it sound worse than it was.

KM offered second chances. For teen moms with no prospects to get that education they needed, and if that education also included pressure points to immobilize a body or how to load and unload a gun in the dark, then so be it.

It provided a hand up, not a handout, with only one thing expected of them. One mission a year. Just one. With no notice. And you could say no. But if you did... expect to be cut off.

Some moms, like Audrey, volunteered to be more active. She'd led an active life before she had to disappear. She wasn't content with being just a designer helping pick out patterns and paint. She needed adrenaline, and KM provided it.

Since no mission ever left a paper trail, she had to log in to the KM network see the case file. It was a slim one. Basically, just an address that was the last known location of an object. The object being a vase that had been smuggled out of Europe. It took some searching to narrow down the possibilities. The condo she staked being one of them.

Was the priceless vase inside? Someone was paying a lot of money to find out.

The address itself didn't have much information to offer. A search of property titles showed the owner as a corporation. A shell that led to another shell and another.

Always a good indication of shady dealings. But she wasn't here to bust anyone's chops. Her mission was to get inside the property and locate the stolen artifact, then extract it if possible. Not her usual kind of mission, but for the money it would pay...seemed simple enough.

Of course, there was a reason the client hired pros. Getting in wouldn't be easy. The security was tight. Even if Audrey managed to pass the doorman, then the guard, the main elevator didn't go to the penthouse suite. The top floor had its own cab, and the access to it appeared severely restricted.

Legs crossed on her motel bed, she perused the safeguards. The penthouse elevator required express permission. Should someone gain access and try to use it, the elevator would simply shut down, locking the person inside.

As to other points of ingress, the rooftop appeared too secured, patrolled at all times by two armed guards along with motion sensors attached to an alarm. Disarming them would prove difficult given half of them weren't on a network, meaning she couldn't hack in and turn them off.

Suction cupping her ass up the side of the building was something they only did in movies. So what did that leave?

She'd need to find a way to get invited inside. Having already perused who was given permission in the last month to enter, she'd already spotted a possibility.

Tomorrow night, she'd exploit it. As for the rest of this evening...

She tuned in to the wireless transmitter embedded in Harper's diaper bag, which tapped into Hood's home camera network. Because his paranoia didn't extend to just windows and doors, but inside, too. Still, it suited her purpose. She had eyes inside his loft. She didn't think of it as spying, more like ensuring the safety of her daughter.

As she flipped through the lenses, she stopped at the living room. She couldn't help but smile at the man asleep on the couch, a baby sprawled atop him.

Enjoy it while you can. Because once the mission was done, he'd never see Harper again.

CHAPTER SIX

OVERNIGHT BAG IN HAND, EDITH KNOCKED AT THE LOFT door bright and early the next morning. When Mr. Hood flung it open—shirtless, hair standing on end, his eyes bloodshot—she tried not to smirk.

"Good morning," she chirped.

He growled. "Not really."

"Rough night?"

"What gave it away?"

"Don't give me attitude. You only have yourself to blame. You could have had me start last night."

"I foolishly believed the expression 'sleep like a baby.' It's a lie," he announced, stepping aside to allow her entry. "Babies don't sleep. But they sure can holler."

"Where's Harper?" Edith asked as she entered and set down her stuff. "I don't hear her crying."

"Not now, she isn't." He sounded quite indignant. "She's sleeping."

"Still?" The sun had risen over an hour ago. And most babies tended to rise with it.

"Not still, more like finally. Thought I was doing pretty good. She went to bed at like seven last night, then she was up at eleven and wanted to play. Then she cried and didn't go to sleep until around three." He sounded so disgruntled that Edith had to bite her lip lest she smile at his misery.

"Your first mistake was putting her to bed at seven."

He bristled at her rebuke. "She's a kid. I thought they needed to go to bed early."

"Did she have an afternoon nap?"

"Yeah."

"Then you needed to keep her up later. Probably until at least nine or so. Didn't the mother leave you any instructions?"

"Ha. As if that unfit bi—er, woman would do something so smart."

"Are you sure?" Edith passed by him, ignoring the naked chest as she beelined to the diaper bag. She went through the main pocket first, then the side ones, finally emerging with a sheet of paper. She waved it. "Found it."

"Give me that." He grabbed the typed instructions and groaned. "Her bedtime is nine thirty, and she's only supposed to nap for two hours max in the afternoon."

"Now you know."

He shoved the list back at her. "Don't you mean, *you* know? I hired you to take care of Harper. I have to get ready for work. I'm already late."

"What do you do?"

"Real estate agent."

A surprising job for a man built like an underwear model. Edith couldn't help but watch as he stalked towards the bathroom, his track pants hanging low on his hips, his back as muscular as his front.

Sigh. He was quite handsome; however, sleeping with the boss wasn't part of the job. Harper was. Since the baby slept, Edith bustled around, noticing the playpen, the fact that there was one of his shirts in the pen with the baby—who cutely enough held it tucked under her chin. A package of diapers was torn open, and a few scattered. There was more baby powder sprinkling the place than left in the bottle. He'd also gone through just about all the wet wipes.

Edith made a mental list of things she'd need to grab when she and the baby went out. In the meantime, she washed bottles and hung them to drip-dry. She tidied up the pillows on the floor and straightened the chairs, all the while keeping a closer eye on the bathroom door than the baby. The baby would give her warning when she woke, the man...he had a way of walking lightly, more predator than real estate broker.

It made her wonder if he'd done boxing or some other kind of sport before he turned into a yuppie. He obviously worked out because no one got that kind of physique pushing paper all day.

Upon seeing the door to the bathroom crack open, she whirled, pretending to be busy at the counter rather than be caught staring.

"Do you need a rundown of my place before I take off?" his deep voice asked from behind her. Closer than expected. Turning, she saw him standing by the massive island—the butcher block a gleaming hunk of wood that obviously hadn't seen too many chopping knives.

"I should be fine. It's not like you have many places to hide things."

For some reason, that made him smirk. "You'd be surprised. Here's my number if you need me." From the jacket pocket of his slick gray suit, he slid a business card. *Bad Boy Inc.: Specialists in international realty.* The logo was cute. A James Bond-esque fellow with a gun inside a bullseye.

"I'm sure Harper and I will be fine. I could use a key, though."

"Why would you need a key?" He frowned. "You aren't going to leave the baby alone are you?"

"Of course, not. But we might want to go for a walk. Or to run errands."

"Speaking of errands, remember that baby sh—stuff you said I needed? Mind grabbing it if you go out?" he asked. "Gonna need more stuff for Harper. Toys. Clothes. Food."

"I thought this was only temporary." For some reason, she couldn't help but tease him.

"Probably, but in the meantime, I'm gonna need more than diapers. The powdered milk and I kind of had an accident last night. I don't have much left. And Harry was saying I should get a teething thing for her to chew on. He says it will make her happy."

"I can do that, but it will take money."

"No problem. I'll leave you my card. And here's a key." He opened a kitchen drawer and tossed a key with a plastic fob marked FRONT. "The alarm code can be disabled with PITA."

"PITA?"

"It stands for pain in the ass. I had it created for my buddy to keep an eye on my place when I go out of town."

"Nice friend you are."

"The best. The type you can call to hide the body." He winked.

"When will you be back?"

He shrugged. "Depends on how my day goes. Got a new client, and he's a bit of a prima donna. Good news is I've got nothing out of town for the next little bit."

"So home by dinner at the latest then?"

"Yeah."

"And am I staying the night to help you with Harper?"

For some reason, the question made his nostrils flare. "No. Not tonight, at any rate. But I might need you later this week. I've got an evening open house scheduled."

"Sounds good. Have fun at work."

She waved, and he again got the strangest expression on his face, a look that softened as he peeked into the playpen at the sleeping baby. More surprising, he reached in and stroked Harper's cheek. Someone was getting a little more attached than he wanted.

Then he was gone, and Edith sighed in relief. There was something about having him so close that frazzled her nerves. A bad thing since she couldn't afford to be frazzled.

She had a job to do.

The morning was spent doing simple domestic things like washing some clothes—mostly to ensure that Harper had some clean things since her bag showed no spares left. When the baby woke, after a feeding—and a poop that made the eyes water—Edith bathed her and dressed Harper in the now clean clothes.

Done, Edith looked around. The place was tidy. The baby fresh as a daisy and ready to go out.

"Oopsie, baby girl. Looks like someone forgot to leave us his credit card." Tucking the baby into the chest sling with an extra blanket tucked around her to keep warm, Edith pocketed the key and the business card. She then grabbed her shoulder bag before leaving the loft.

Time to pay Mr. Hood a visit at his office.

CHAPTER SEVEN

THE MURMUR OF VOICES DIDN'T DRAW DECLAN'S attention from the screen. He was going over his new client file. But none of it involved the specs on the condo listing that had landed in his lap. He was digging into the man himself. The owner.

Name of Suarez—which he'd bet was an alias given the lack of history. The man only began to exist on paper a few years ago. Didn't go public until the purchase of the condo, which had been the dormant property of a shell company for over a decade.

Too many shady things going on at once. Not that Declan told Harry of his suspicions. His boss would blame him for being bored. Would assume the lull in missions had Declan looking for conspiracies that only partially existed.

His boss would be right. Declan just bided his time until his next real job. In the meantime, it never hurt to hone his skills and maybe discover something that should be handled before it caused a problem in his town.

Suarez wasn't all he seemed. Deep digging hadn't yet revealed any other names, nor could he find him associated with anything, and that in and of itself, raised a red flag.

From the records he could access, Declan knew age—thirty-seven—which matched the man's appearance. Five foot eleven inches with tanned skin, a bleached-white smile, aquiline nose, and dark hair. A good-looking bloke who'd not been associated with any women, or men. Yet he had a cool confidence that should make him a magnet. The lack of companionship was especially surprising for a man who believed in dressing sharp.

Suarez always wore white, collared shirts and dark suits, from a smoky gray to pure black, all custom-tailored fits. He topped it off with matte-black leather shoes. The man oozed wealth from the things he ate—prepared by a chef, and with names mere mortals wouldn't recognize—to the cars he drove or which were driven for him. Bullet-proof, of course. The man took no chances with his safety, which meant he relied on background-checked staff. All his people went through a vigorous screening, and he paid them well to be loyal.

From what Declan could discern, Suarez kept a chauffeur on staff, along with a housekeeper, chef, personal trainer, and a cadre of bodyguards—who resembled Russian gorillas in suits. Suarez hired them big. It, and the security measures in his home and office—which he rarely visited—spoke to a deep paranoia. Paranoid people usually had a reason to believe someone would harm them. Guilt had a way of riding someone's back.

Despite not working for any branch of government, by all appearances, Suarez was closely linked to a few offices. Since appearing on Declan's radar a few days ago, he'd managed to get wind of two lunch meetings, one dinner, and several government-labeled sedans visiting the condo.

Now, some people would say if Suarez were crooked, then why not just kill him? A simple solution that would only destroy the head of the snake. Like a hydra, another would take its place. Ending a criminal empire took more than the death of just one man. Declan needed to dismantle the operation.

So much fun, and what a stroke of luck that Suarez had approached Bad Boy Inc. to act as his realtor. Then again, BBI's cover as a prestigious realty company was actually true. They did big property deals around the world. It gave them an excuse to travel. Also, the amount of zeroes on the commission checks that he declared to Uncle Sam and paid a shit ton of taxes on made him smile. Not bad for a kid whose only prospect once upon a time was avoiding jail before he turned twenty-five.

Now, he kind of did well. While BBI provided services that some might consider extreme, there were some that Declan was quite proud of. Missions to discredit dictators. The removal of a drug lord breaking a chain of supply—for a while at any rate. The drug trade always came back.

They got evidence on big corporation owners hiding money not only from the government—not paying their share—but also from their shareholders and employees.

Times like those, Declan's name proved apt. *I am Mr. Hood, taking from the rich and spreading it around.* After lining his pocket first.

His pockets were getting pretty full. BBI ran a slick business with Harry at the helm.

Surely, Harry wouldn't protest too much when Declan

took down Suarez. Especially if Declan sold the condo first and collected their fee.

Five percent of fifteen million equaled lots of zeros.

Declan flipped through the tiny file on Suarez and frowned. So little to go on. He needed to dig up more dirt. At least having Suarez as a client gave Declan access to Suarez's home. Not that he'd been able to search it yet. They'd signed the contract in a restaurant and done only a single walk-through of the place. Since then, they'd only communicated by email and phone.

But there is the open house coming up. Maybe he'd get a chance to snoop a bit.

Another thing that bugged him was why Suarez was even selling. Not for money. By all indications, the man had a bottomless well of it. He'd owned the condo for a year. Appeared to really like it, and now wanted to sell it? No mention of moving away or downsizing. Just a simple command to, "List it for fifteen million and be advised I won't take one penny less."

On arrogance alone, Declan wanted to take the guy down a notch. But for that, they'd have to meet. In the meantime, he planned. He worked on a way to disable the security cameras inside the condo. Hard to search when eyes watched. He'd yet to find a way into the network to disable them.

Later this week, he might get a chance. He was supposed to hit Suarez's condo to discuss details of the open house, an event that Suarez had insisted on and took way too much interest in. During that meeting, Declan planned to take pictures for the listing. He'd be getting more than that, though. His camera didn't just take regular images, but thermal, electronic, even sound waves. By the time he was done and had it all analyzed, he'd know how many spiders lived inside the walls.

Declan flipped through the file, making mental notes of things to check when Ben popped his head into his office and yelled, "Boo!"

"Fucker!"

Ben, the office joker, who stood taller that most football players with a dark complexion and wide smile, grinned at him. "You should thank me. You've been sitting too long. Need to get that blood pumping, especially now that you need to keep up with a kid."

"How did you...?" Declan groaned. "Harry."

"Don't blame the boss man. Wasn't him that spilled the beans, bro." Ben jerked his head. "Your baby momma is here with the kid."

"What?" Jumping from his seat, Declan vaulted over his desk and lunged to the door. He glanced down the hall and let out a gusty breath as he saw Edith, her brown ponytail bobbing. For a moment, he'd thought the real mother had made an appearance. Which led to a quick feeling of relief—and, oddly, disappointment. Despite the sleepless night, the kid had her cute moments. Like when he'd held her, and she'd patted his cheeks before chewing on his chin. "That's not the baby's mother. It's my nanny."

"She's hot. I can see why you hired her."

Yeah, he'd noticed. "I hired her because she was the best qualified." And the only one available without skeletons in her closet. Which in retrospect seemed strange.

"Sure she was," Ben said, nodding, a placating grin on his face.

"Just because you hired your last contractor because he

looked good in jeans and a toolbelt, doesn't mean everyone makes decisions based on looks."

"Don't disparage the methods, bro. He looked even better with *only* that toolbelt on." Ben winked and leered.

"And how is that kitchen reno going?" Declan asked with a smirk.

That brought a scowl. "The new guy says I'm about a month away. They had to tear out most of what Adam did."

"Next time, before you seduce the help, make sure they finish the job."

"Says the guy who forgot to wear a rubber."

"I wore a rubber," Declan yelled. Only to flush as Edith suddenly appeared behind Ben.

"Am I interrupting? The lady at the front said you weren't busy."

"He's not. I was just leaving," Ben announced.

Edith stepped inside, and Declan noticed that she was missing something. "Where's Harper?"

"The receptionist at the front insisted on holding her."

"Wendy? Charles won't like that. She's been bugging him to pop the question."

"Is that the guy with glasses and beard? Because he's been playing peek-a-boo with the baby for a few minutes now."

"Actually, that sounds like Mason." Who would have thought their resident single guy would show an interest?

Edith moved closer to his desk. "So this is where you work? It's nice."

It'd better be given the cost of the remodel a few years ago. But even he had to say it was worth every penny. The feature wall had dark wood panels set horizontally with floating shelves that displayed framed images of properties he'd sold. The floor was carpeted in a dark mosaic that hid the dirt well and added a hint of color to the space. His desk was the same wood as the wall, big, rectangular, and contemporary with none of the weird curlicues and frills that adorned some furniture. The window at his back was almost floor-to-ceiling and offered a great view of the building across from them without allowing anyone to see in. The mirrored glass kept it private.

"Is that real wood?" She leaned over his desk, the top of her shirt gaping, giving him a view of her pert breasts encased in a white lace bra. She traced the grain, and he couldn't help but wish she traced something else. He looked away. "Why are you here?"

"You forgot to leave me any funds to go shopping for those baby things you wanted."

Shit. He had. Blame a lack of sleep for his brain not working. "Sorry about that." His coat hung on the back of the door. He scrounged in his pocket for his wallet and pulled out a black card. When he turned around, he saw that she'd opted to move his phone and park her ass on his desk.

It made a man think really dirty things. Things you saw in movies that involved sweeping everything off and legs wrapped around his waist as he plowed into her sweetness.

"There's a perfectly fine chair right there." He jabbed.

"Guess there is." She slid off the desk and snared his phone, sliding it back to its spot. She turned to face him. "Is that better?"

No, because he still could picture her sitting there. With fewer clothes.

He gritted his teeth. "Here." He held out the card. "Passcode is 2020."

She snared it from him, and for a second, he held it tight enough that she had to tug. "Thanks. Any price limits?"

He snorted. "No. But let's not go crazy."

"Sounds good. Other than baby stuff, you need me to grab anything?"

Could she buy him some control while she was out? "I'm good." Not really. His cock ached, and he thanked the fact that his tight briefs and loose slacks hid the evidence.

"You got a busy day lined up with clients?"

"Not really. Because we're high-end, we only handle a few at a time. I'm actually dealing with a new guy who's kind of high-maintenance."

"High-maintenance in what respect?"

"He wants me to be at his beck and call."

"To sell his house?"

"Condo."

"How hard can that be?"

He smirked. "Harder than you'd think. He wants fifteen million. Which means curating the people who come to see it to ensure they're legit clients who can afford it and not gawkers."

"I can't even imagine what a place that expensive looks like inside."

"Ridiculously bland," was his reply, whereas confused was his state of mind. This idle chitchat felt odd to him. "I really should get back to work."

"Of course." She moved around him, on the narrow side, brushing by him and the coatrack, wrapping him in her scent. "I'll grab Harper and go."

Speaking of going, he had to wonder. "How'd you get here?" he asked as she pulled on the knob of his door to leave.

"We took a bus."

"You took my baby on public transit?" He almost yelled. Almost. The idea of his daughter riding with the masses appalled him. Forget how he'd grown up, this was his daughter.

"Exactly how else did you expect me to travel?"

Actually, he'd not thought about it until she appeared. "You carried Harper all the way?"

She shook her head. "I used the chest sling I found in the diaper bag."

Was that the contraption with the straps? "How are you going to buy the baby things?"

"By going into a store."

"Don't be a smartass. You know I meant how are you going to get them home?"

"Probably an Uber. Don't worry. I'll make sure I bill the cost to the card, too."

Put herself and Harper at the mercy of a stranger? "Screw the cab. I'll take you."

Declan wasn't sure who was more surprised, him or her?

She shook her head. "You don't have to do that. I didn't mean to bother you at work."

"It's fine. Quiet time of year."

"What about your client? The one with the boring condo?"

"He'll call me out of the blue, I'm sure, with some ridiculous last-minute request for his open house."

Edith scrunched her nose. "Isn't that weird, having a

bunch of random strangers show up to look at a place?"

"Not all strangers. We get more brokers and agents than clients, usually. The very wealthy don't always have time to visit every available property."

"Fascinating stuff."

Why did it feel as if there were a hint of mockery in her tone? "Let's go buy some baby junk." Quickly so that he could then get rid of Edith and flagellate himself for putting himself in torture's way. "My car's downstairs."

"We don't have a car seat."

"You didn't care when you wanted to Uber."

She smirked. "I would have hired one with a seat. You can make special requests, you know."

Actually, he didn't know. Declan preferred to be the one driving.

"You're not taking an Uber. We'll buy a car seat."

"They're expensive," Edith noted.

"Your point being? Nothing's too good for my kid."

Her mouth rounded.

A quick search on his phone brought up an address within two blocks. "We can get most of the stuff nearby."

"But—" Edith appeared at a loss for words, and he wanted to fist pump. He certainly counted it as a point in his favor. Finally. He didn't think speechlessness happened often with Edith.

"I'll be right there." He shoved her into the hall and grabbed his coat, the weight of it reassuring.

The rest of the office, who'd apparently found a reason to mill in the reception area, didn't even attempt to hide their smirks when he emerged with Edith.

"I'm taking the afternoon off. Call my cell if you need me," he told their receptionist. With Sherry out sick, their evening girl, Wendy, was the one manning the desk. Which meant that, for once, their office would have regular hours and close at six rather than its usual 11:00 p.m. International deals didn't care about time zones.

As he glared at the people he worked with—Ben who made a sizzling gesture, Charles who held the baby while Wendy beamed, Calvin who smirked—Edith grabbed the harness and slid her arms into it.

While she was his nanny, it struck him as wrong to make her carry the baby. Harper wasn't exactly light. "I'll take that." He tugged the harness from his now gaping nanny and shoved his arms in, got twisted, needed help, and mouthed, "*I'll kill you*" to Ben, who snickered while Edith did something behind him to attach the contraption to his body.

Ben took a picture. Declan gave him the finger. It would probably end up on a montage at their Christmas party.

The straps around him tightened. Edith gave the harness a firm tug and declared, "It's ready for the baby." With some help, he tucked Harper into the strange contraption. The baby faced inward and flailed her hands, exclaiming happily.

Ben still held up his camera and cooed, "That's a good girl. Bounce for Uncle Ben."

"Uncle Ben?" Declan asked.

"Is that your grumpy daddy?" cooed Ben.

"Go to hell, Benny."

"Language," snapped Edith.

Ben erupted laughing, and he wasn't alone, as Declan glowered.

Paying no mind to his expression, Edith draped a blanket around Harper. "We're ready."

Off they went: a man, his daughter, and his nanny. A surreal moment.

The elevator was silent but for the music. The baby, having managed to get a chubby fist around his tie, chose to suck on it.

"How was the walk?" he asked in the most male lame attempt at casual conversation.

She glanced at him. "It was exercise."

"I usually hit the gym." Said the suave conversationalist.

"Most yuppies do," was her retort as the elevator doors opened and she sauntered out.

He ogled her backside. Yuppie? *She thinks I'm a yuppie.* It made the mercenary inside bristle. What an insult. What a credit to his cover. He still scowled, though, as he trudged after her out of the building into the not-quite-so-fresh air of the street. While traffic flowed rather smoothly, it left a haze of exhaust in the air.

"Which way, boss?" she asked.

Rather than reply, he set off at a brisk pace, which she matched. After a few strides, she was the one who went for idle chitchat. "How long you been working for those guys?"

"About seven years."

"Did you always want to be a realtor?"

"No." He laughed at the word. Far from it. Once he'd aspired to be a petty thief. All that had changed after his recruitment. "After I graduated high school"—which sounded mundane compared to the reality of his education at a private academy which didn't cost him a penny—"I spent a few years abroad doing odd jobs." Mercenary gigs that he had picked up freelance before Harry recruited him after a particularly crazy job in Istanbul. He still had the scar on his ass from the bullet that had grazed him as they raced for their lives, only barely making it across the border to safety.

Good times. It was after they'd shared a few drinks in a dingy, smoky bar, that Harry explained who he was, and how he knew what Declan was. Harry then asked him if he'd join Bad Boy Inc. The man offered job security, more thorough intelligence—which would have alerted him to the fact that the harem of women were all trained killers—and toys. Declan said yes. He'd been with Harry ever since.

"Seems like a good place to work."

"The best," Declan agreed.

A kid whizzed by on a skateboard, and Declan grabbed Edith's arm. "Watch out."

She shot him a startled look. "Thanks, Mr. Hood."

Way to make him sound old. "Call me Declan."

"If you insist."

The conversation fizzled as they arrived at the store. According to the sign, it was a baby emporium. Entering, he almost turned around and walked out. The place was a warehouse-sized showroom full of baby gear. Strollers. High chairs. Car seats. To the left, he saw rack upon rack of clothes. To the right, it was toys. And everywhere he looked, pregnant women and babies.

He didn't realize he was hyperventilating until Edith slapped him on the back. "Calm down. Those kids aren't yours. You're safe."

"I wasn't scared," he lied.

"Says the man who almost passed out." She snorted.

"Say hello to the consequences of putting your weewee in a hooha."

"Way to make it sound gross," he muttered.

"Having intercourse comes with responsibility. One screw-up can change the course of your life," she said, her eyes taking on a pained expression. "I'm sure you're wishing you'd doubled up on condoms."

Given Harper snoozed on his chest, head lolling to the side, a warm, wet spot forming where her mouth lay open and slack, he should have agreed. Instead, he found himself saying, "Not all mistakes are bad."

He then proceeded towards the stroller of all strollers. He stopped by it, admiring the sleek chrome, the cup holder—

"You are not seriously looking at that beast," Edith exclaimed.

"It's got Bluetooth." He pointed. "And a solar-powered navigation system in the handle."

"It's almost five thousand dollars. And huge."

"Yeah." He almost beat his chest at the manly size of it.

"How big is the trunk of your car?"

He eyed the stroller, thought of his trunk already packed full of stuff, and his shoulders slumped. "It won't fit, will it?"

"Nope." And thus began their shopping, him eyeballing the biggest and most expensive, her mocking him and showing him the more cost-effective and efficient version. They were standing at the checkout, Harper nestled in her new car seat/stroller combo, him eyeballing the bib printed with a baby Vader that said *Sith in training*, when a guy entered the store waving a shotgun.

"Don't move or I'll shoot!"

CHAPTER EIGHT

AT THE FIRST YELL OF "DON'T MOVE OR I'LL SHOOT!" Edith found herself shoved to the floor. Before she grasped what was happening, the car seat with Harper strapped in it landed beside her.

"Stay down," her boss ordered as he crouched behind the counter at the checkout.

The brief glimpse she'd gotten of a man entering with a weapon meant she understood why he barked. However, being huddled on the floor meant that she was blind to what happened next. Edith couldn't see a darned thing, she could only hear. Not exactly reassuring.

"Give me the baby," the gunman yelled.

Edith instinctively hunched over the car seat. Like hell.

Seemed Declan agreed. He stood. "No one's giving you anything. Put the weapon down."

Was he nuts? She rose high enough to peek over the counter.

The man with the gun stood just inside the door, his

face florid, his plaid shirt unbuttoned over a T-shirt. "Who the fuck do you think you are, man?"

"I'm the guy who's going to make you regret scaring all these people in this store." Spoken with masculine arrogance.

"Big threat from a pussy in a suit." Snicker. "What you gonna do? Sic your tailor on me?"

"What are you hoping to accomplish?" Declan asked, his tone calm and conversational.

"I want the baby."

Edith couldn't help but glance at Harper. The baby, oblivious to the drama, grabbed at her feet.

"No one is giving you a baby," Declan clearly stated.

"You're not in charge here, asshole." *Boom.* The shotgun blast echoed loudly amidst the shrieks of the people still in the store. Edith half expected to see Declan riddled with holes, but he stood tall and untouched. He was also suddenly armed.

If Edith hadn't been watching, she would have missed it the move was so smooth. One moment, Declan's hand was empty; the next, it emerged from his jacket holding a gun. How he'd managed to keep it hidden, she couldn't have said. The result, though? Declan was armed, his grip steady.

"Oooh, the man has a gun." *Chuck-chick.* The slide action of the shotgun sounded loud. "So do I, asshole. Now get the fuck down before I put some holes in you."

"Larry," a woman shrieked. "What are you doing?"

Larry pivoted to bellow at the orange-haired woman stalking to the front with a stroller. "Coming to get my baby, Kiera. Thought you could just walk out and take her?"

"Larry. You're acting nuts. Stop it. You're going to get arrested."

"Better I go to jail than live without you and the baby," Larry declared.

"Oh, Larry."

Edith could have gagged at the softened tone. She saw Declan rolling his eyes.

The distant sound of sirens had someone saying in a tight voice, "Thank God. The police."

Yes, the police came and arrested Larry, who swore up and down he wouldn't have hurt a fly. They led him away in handcuffs with Kiera, baby in her arms, following and promising to wait for him.

Declan paid for their stuff while an officer took statements. They spent the most time with Declan, making him pull out his wallet with his identification and his concealed-carry permit. Since there were no actual injuries, and cameras had recorded Larry's actions, witnesses weren't held long. Once the officers questioned them, they were allowed to leave.

It was a quiet walk back to the parking garage, Declan insisting on pushing the stroller, his face rigid. She could understand his tension. The moment in the store had been sobering. What if Larry had chosen to shoot at Declan rather than the ceiling?

And what man stood there still as a statue almost daring another to shoot?

Arriving at the car, she was surprised to see a four-door Lincoln, and a spacious one at that. Then again, as a realtor, he probably had to drive his clients occasionally. Edith showed him how to hook the car seat securely.

Sliding into the passenger seat, they still didn't speak.

The man was probably shaken up by what happened. Or was he?

Edith couldn't help darting looks at Declan as he drove. His strong profile. The big hands on the wheel. The nonchalance he displayed. Not just here, but when confronted by a crazy man.

He flicked a glance at her and caught Edith staring. "Something the matter?" he asked.

"Back at that store..." She hesitated because it sounded crazy to even say aloud.

"What?"

"You acted like some kind of action hero. Telling us to get down on the floor. Trying to talk sense into the guy."

"That wasn't heroic. But someone had to do something to stall Larry and give the cops a chance to arrive."

"How did you know they were coming?"

"Wild guess. A guy wandering around with a shotgun tends to draw attention."

Plausible. Yet... "You were so calm."

"As opposed to what? Having hysterics? Crying?" He snorted. "I might wear a suit, but that doesn't mean I lack balls."

"You carry a concealed weapon."

"Doesn't everyone in the city these days?"

"No." Especially not yuppie, suit-wearing, white-collar guys.

"Well, I do. I was mugged once. Decided I never wanted it to happen again."

Again, the answer sounded right. But something niggled. "Do you actually know how to use that thing?"

The gaze he shot her was smug. "Yeah."

"How come I didn't see it when you had your coat off at the office?"

"Because I don't walk around with it hanging out. I have a special harness inside my jacket."

"How do you secure it when you're at home?"

"I don't. Gun isn't much use if it's locked away and bad company comes calling."

"As if they could get in. Your place is locked tighter than Fort Knox."

"And? A determined home invader won't let that stop them. They'll find a way."

"To steal what?" she scoffed. "Your television? It's nice but not that nice."

"What if they want to harm me?"

"Why would someone want to hurt you?"

He shrugged. "Don't know. Don't intend to find out."

"Having an unsecured gun lying around is dangerous."

"For would-be criminals, damned straight it is."

Her lips flattened. "You have a curious baby who is mobile. You can't be leaving loaded weapons lying around."

"You really think a baby can get up onto my bed, go scrounging under my pillow, lift this gun, flip the safety, plus have the strength and coordination to pull the trigger?"

He had a point, yet she couldn't help but shake her head. "Do you not listen to the news? Accidents involving young kids happen every day."

"Are you one of those paranoid people who think every single thing you hear can happen to them?"

"No, but I do believe a bit of prevention goes a long way toward averting potential tragedies."

"What do you want me to do?"

"Get a gun cabinet."

"Kind of defeats the purpose of owning a weapon for protection."

She rolled her eyes. "Then get the kind that opens the moment you slam your hand on it."

"What if I'm across the room?"

She eyed him suspiciously. "Hold on. Are you implying you have more than one weapon stashed at your place?"

"If I say yes, are you going to yell at me?"

She gaped. "Idiot."

"Cautious."

"Your neighborhood is not that dangerous."

"Maybe not, but the business I'm in can be cutthroat."

She couldn't help but blink at the inane statement. "You have got to be kidding me. It's real estate."

"High-end real estate, the kind that fortunes are made or lost on. People can go a little crazy when that kind of money is involved."

The very idea that his job was dangerous had her snorting. "Is your job that dull that you need to imagine dangerous conspiracies?"

"I don't need to imagine. Speaking of jobs, what made you decide to become a nanny?"

"I like kids."

"Some people choose to marry and have their own, rather than babysit others."

"Maybe I don't want to get married."

"I thought all women had marriage as an end goal."

"Maybe the ones you know...or sleep with," she added slyly.

"Actually, the ones I sleep with usually just want a repeat."

She practically choked at his reply. "That's so—so—"

"True?" Declan supplied.

"Conceited was actually the word I was looking for."

"Can I help it if they love me?"

"Don't you mean lust? Takes more than one night of sex to form something meaningful."

"Speaking from experience?"

"I don't think my personal life is any of your business."

"And yet you seem to think it's perfectly within your rights to question mine."

Her irritation grew as he flipped the conversation around. "I'm trying to ensure that you keep Harper safe."

"Harper's safe. Safer with me than a hell of a lot of other people, I can guarantee you that."

"I have my doubts."

"Which you're welcome to. I know what the score is. I can take care of Harper. Speaking of which, I think I'm going to be staying in tonight, so I won't need your services. Where should I drop you?"

"Are you sure you don't want some help with Harper?" she asked.

"Now that I know about the napping thing"—he peered in the rearview mirror at the baby babbling and batting the toys dangling from the handle of her seat—"I will make sure to keep her wide-eyed and entertained until her actual bedtime."

"I don't mind helping."

"I'm sure you have things you could be doing other than watching me put on a diaper lopsided."

She did, and yet she found herself loath to leave him. "You can drop me off at that theatre close to your place. I think I'll catch a movie."

Which was how she found herself standing on the sidewalk, watching his taillights disappear up the street. Wondering if he truly could handle the baby on his own.

Wondering if he'd admit defeat at some point and call her.

She checked her watch. Six o'clock. She had some time to kill before the evening entertainment began. She grabbed dinner. Best to eat now in case it turned into a late night.

CHAPTER NINE

TEN O'CLOCK. AUDREY OBSERVED THE OFFICE BUILDING from her hiding spot across the street. In order to blend in with the upscale neighborhood and shadows, she wore a dark trench coat over a wool sweater and slacks. The perfect getup for a businesswoman working late. Except the building she targeted didn't have her employed in any of its offices.

With her hand wrapped around her phone, she entered the vestibule, the smoked glass windows hiding the inside lobby from the world passing by on the sidewalk. Not that there was much pedestrian traffic this time of the night.

Upon entering, she took quick note of the janitor, his floor washing machine whirring as he swung it side to side, cleaning the daily grime from the tiles. Stocky in build with longish, dark hair and tanned skin, he didn't look once in her direction.

The reception desk was manned by a single guard in a uniform consisting of a white shirt with a sewn badge and dark slacks. A young fellow, his brush-cut appeared fresh, his cheeks smoothly shaven. His gaze very alert. He stood at her entry.

"Can I help you, ma'am?"

"Yes. I'm here to deliver something." She waved a manila envelope.

"I can handle that for you." He reached out a hand, but she shook her head.

"Sorry, but I've been instructed to deliver it myself to ensure it gets to the right person."

"Then you'll have to come back tomorrow. Everyone's gone for the night."

"Not according to the text I received from Mr. Jackson. He said to meet him here around ten."

The guard frowned. "I could have sworn Mr. Jackson left hours ago."

"He returned to meet with me. I am only in town for a few hours on a layover."

"Then you made a wasted trip. He signed out before my shift started."

"Are you sure about that? Perhaps you missed him returning. Check your sign-in logs," Audrey prompted.

The guard leaned down and tapped on his computer. Audrey pretended nonchalance as she leaned against the desk, idly watching the cleaner, his head bopping in time to the music she could faintly hear coming from his headphones.

"Hunh. Looks like Mr. Jackson buzzed in from the garage about ten minutes ago but didn't call down to let me know."

She faced him with a smile. "Now that we've ascertained his presence, if you would kindly allow me entrance, it would be much appreciated."

"Rules state that after-hours meetings require me to call ahead first."

She sighed. "If you must."

The guard picked up the phone and held it to his ear. Meanwhile, the hand in her pocket, once again clutching the phone, pressed firmly.

"Mr. Jackson, it's Malcom at the front desk. There's someone here to see you."

She didn't hear the reply, but the security guard nodded as he replied, "Yes, sir. Right away, sir."

As he hung up, he returned his attention to her. "You can go up now, ma'am."

"Thank you." She pasted on a smile and sauntered away from the desk to the elevators. Idiot. Today's security put so much stock in their fancy electronics that they'd forgotten some of the basics. Or had no idea of what today's technology could do. It was easy to fake an entry from the garage and to simulate a phone being answered.

So why didn't she use said garage to enter the building? Because it would have meant bringing a vehicle. If she had to leave in a hurry, then she didn't want to have anything of hers left behind. Not to mention, it would have required co-opting someone's identification, always a much harder gig to pull off.

Hence why she opted for the front door and entered as a guest, the short, blond bob wig she chose masking her real hair, the contact lenses changing her eyes, just like the application of makeup in layers with shadowing changed the contour of her face. The cameras might catch her, but they'd never recognize her once she peeled off the persona she wore.

The elevator doors closed behind her, and she leaned

against the mirrored wall, knowing she was watched. She went to the floor expected. Walked right in, her phone slipping the electronic locks. Yet if anyone looked at the logs, it would appear as if Jackson himself did it from his office.

In the reception area—because she knew she was still observed—she slipped off the coat and then unbuttoned a few loops on her sweater. She adjusted her boobs, knowing what the guard would think—late-night tryst at the office, something Jackson had done before—and entered the private office, coat over her arm.

Jackson didn't allow cameras in his inner sanctum because of his extracurricular activities.

Yet, his office, even the man himself? Not her actual target. Once inside, she immediately went to the bookcase. While the public blueprints displayed the expected layout, a bit of digging had shown that there was a second secret set of prints which the architect kindly kept on a server that ran out of her home office, a server Audrey had hacked.

The plans showed a layer of secret passages amongst the floors. Hidden routes between the walls that could be used in the event of an emergency.

Or when, say, a hired retriever of classified documents wanted to raid a certain office two floors above for info that couldn't be retrieved otherwise.

The bookcase slid out and over without even the slightest whine. The mechanism kept in great working order. Kicking off her heels, she entered, and from memory, began to weave her way among the secret passages, the locked doors with their keypads in her path no match for her. These were meant to keep the casual interlopers at bay, but someone with her skills knew how to rip off the covers and hotwire the locks, causing the doors to release. In the process, she probably set off some kind of silent alarm, which meant she had to move fast.

She had to disable two such doors before making it to where she wanted to be. She spilled out into the lobby of the company she sought, the dull glow of an overhead light set to dim, enough to guide her steps.

She made it to the reception desk and the computer sitting on it. Since it probably used the same network as the other offices for the company, she plopped herself in the seat and tapped the keyboard to wake it up. She began typing. The login screen taunted her with its message.

Enter your username. She typed it in.

Enter your password. Tap, tap, tap.

Incorrect.

Audrey frowned. She must have spelled something wrong. She'd gotten the info just today, so it wasn't as if it were old or expired.

Again, she typed.

Incorrect.

Had she misjudged the company? Did they roll their passcodes in order to prevent hacking? That seemed rather extreme given their business. But, then again, paranoia abounded when money was at stake.

She tried one more time. Bad idea.

The screen went black.

She heard distant thuds that didn't click until she saw a metal screen come slamming down over the main doors into this office.

Oh, shit. Rising, she dove over the desk and ran to the opening to the secret passage, knowing she wouldn't make it in time. She grabbed a chair in passing and threw it. It landed in the doorway in time to stop the metal shutter from sealing off her exit.

This level of protection wasn't in the blueprints—public or private. This company was obviously more than it seemed. Which meant those who'd handed her the mission hadn't done their homework. Someone would hear about this screwup when she got out.

If she got out. Reaching the chair, she knew better than to yank it out. She'd never manage to get through without getting sliced in half. Instead, she had to wiggle through the gaps left behind, grunting and swearing and sweating as she squeezed herself back into the passageway. She worried as she ran to the stairs and the door she'd already wired open that it, too, would be sealed shut. However, the extra protection only seemed to cover the office itself. Hitting the stairs, she went down one landing and was halfway down the second on her way back to Jackson's office when she heard voices.

"I see her coat and shoes, but no sign of the woman," said the security guard.

"Tell them she knew about the secret tunnels," said another voice.

Tell who? They obviously reported to someone. Didn't matter.

There was more said, but they must have moved away from the door because she couldn't make out their words. But, more worrying, they blocked her exit. The staircases alternated every two floors instead of being one long version going down. To make it to the next set, she'd have move past the office. She could handle two men, but what if reinforcements arrived while she was dealing with them?

It would have helped if she'd brought a gun, but she knew the front desk might screen her, so she'd opted to go weaponless—except for the leather wrap bracelet that could double as a garrote. But, no gun. Which seemed stupid in retrospect. Her excuse? She hadn't expected this level of security.

Hesitating was costing her time. Rather than wait for them to find her, she went on the offensive. She crept up to the hidden doorway into the office. Waited until the guard stuck his head in the passage for a look, grabbed him, and kneed him in the face. Before he hit his knees, yelling, she'd vaulted over his back and confronted the floor cleaner. Except now, he wielded his mop like a weapon, his stance that of a fighter.

What was this place? Who were these people?

"Get out of my way. I don't want to hurt you."

He sneered. "Ain't no way I'm moving. And you aren't leaving. There are people wanting a chat with you."

"Too bad for them."

She feinted left, then ducked and swept her foot, aiming for his ankles. But he was fast. Faster than expected. The mop came down, and she barely rolled out of its path. She flipped to her feet and ducked his next swing.

He kept her at bay, seemingly not concerned about taking her out. Because he was waiting for something. Instinct had her ducking as the guard, who'd revived, tried to grab her in a bear hug. She spun and snared the gun in his holster.

With his weapon in her hand, she aimed for his thigh. Then cursed when she saw the dart sticking from his leg. Tranqs. Brilliant really. It meant no nasty messes that might involve law enforcement, and keeping a possible subject alive for questioning. In her case, it meant the guard sank to the floor. Ducking, she avoided the swing of the mop handle, whirled, and shot the janitor.

As he wavered on his feet, he slurred, "Fuck me, I should have brought my piece."

Implying that he usually had a gun, too.

Stranger and stranger.

But not her biggest problem right now. She still had to escape. Throwing on her coat, she left the heels behind. She might have to run. She headed to the elevator, only to see the numbers on it climbing.

Shoot. The cavalry had arrived.

She bolted to the red sign at the far end of the hall. According to the building plans, that exit had stairs. Since down probably meant more people to fight, she opted to implement her backup plan. Because Audrey hadn't come here with only one way out. Smart and long-lived spies always had a secondary escape route.

She sprinted up the stairs. Given she was already close to the rooftop, it didn't take much time.

The door at the top warned her that an alarm would sound if she exited. Kind of late to worry about that. She slammed into the bar and emerged onto the roof, the immediate scream of warning missing only a strobing, red light.

The wind at this altitude whipped at her, pulling at her wig, flapping her coat, sucking at her breath. It stole the heat from her body.

The gritty surface of the roof bit into the soles of her feet, the thin layer of the socks she wore no real protection.

As she neared the edge of the roof, the door slammed open, and a voice yelled, "Don't move."

Rather than obey, she sprang to the lip of the building, spinning to see who'd found her.

A black man in tight, leather pants and an open V-neck shirt faced her. He held a gun, a really big one. His face was familiar.

I've seen him before. He works for the company. The fact that he carried a weapon was not in his file.

A part of her was tempted to confront him, to find out more about his office because it was becoming obvious that Bad Boy Inc. dealt in more than just property. However, her bosses wouldn't appreciate it if she blew her cover—and theirs—because of curiosity. So, instead, she waved before jumping off the building.

CHAPTER TEN

WHERE THE HELL IS SHE? DECLAN PACED AS HE WAITED for Edith to arrive.

When the call came saying there'd been an attempted break-in at the office, he'd been tempted to bundle the baby and head over right away.

But he didn't need Harry's, "Come in as soon as you get a sitter," for him to realize that might not be safe. Someone whose motive remained unclear had gone through a great deal of trouble to get into BBI's office. This same person possessed the skills to not only take out the front desk rookie but also Diego, a retired Marine. Although, the way Declan heard it, Diego had fucked up, leaving his piece in his locker. The man went after the intruder with a mop of all things.

He'd be lucky if he were still allowed to wield one once Harry was done with him.

Then again, to cut Diego some slack, he wasn't a trained mercenary. Hell, he didn't even really know what Bad Boy was. Only the inner circle at BBI knew the secret.

Everyone else saw what they expected. A successful real estate company.

The real question was: which secrets was the woman after?

Declan wanted to be on the scene, helping his team find out. As a man used to only being responsible for himself, it burned to wait.

My own fault. I should have taken Edith up on her offer to spend the night and help me. But where would he put her?

His bed was big enough for two...

Beep. Beep. His mind went into warning mode. Steer away from that direction.

She wouldn't be sharing his bed because his couch turned into a pullout. Which would work short-term, but if Edith had to stay on because Harper became a permanent fixture...

Declan stumbled as the very idea hit him and he realized he didn't mind it. He and the little diva had done better this evening. He'd gotten more food in her than on him. He'd managed a diaper on his first try. Not thrown up at the contents of the dirty one, and rocked her to sleep on his shoulder by nine fifteen. He'd even spent a while longer sitting with her cradled on his chest, her warm body and soft breaths more soothing than expected.

It didn't last.

The moment his phone buzzed, he'd slid Harper into the playpen and become what he truly was. Not a daddy or a drool-collecting rag. But a killer.

The knock on his door arrived almost twenty minutes after he'd called Edith, who'd answered sounding rather out of breath, making him wonder exactly what she'd done after the movies.

And with whom.

He pretended his irritation wasn't jealousy.

For a man who wasn't jealous, he eyed her closely, noticing her hair scraped back in a tight tail, her cheeks flushed with exertion. The scarf at her neck hiding possible marks.

If she has any, then it's none of my business. Actually, if she had a boyfriend, even better. Declan never messed with another guy's girl. His logic being that if she messed with him while with someone else, she'd probably do it to him, too, at some point.

Her being off-limits made it easier to open the door when she knocked. It didn't curb the terse, "Took you long enough."

"That's how you answer the door?" She glared. "Excuse me for not being at your beck and call. Some of us had to get dressed and find a taxi. Those kinds of things take time. Let this be your I-told-you-so moment. Because this wouldn't have happened if you'd had me living in as I offered."

The woman dared to rebuke him. He hated to admit that she had a point. "Yeah. About the live-in part. We might need to discuss that when I get back."

Glancing around, Edith shook her head. "The live-in thing won't work unless you're planning to move. Having spent half the day here yesterday, I am well-aware of the limitations of this place. A single bed for one."

"The couch pulls out."

The look on her face said exactly what she thought of his offer.

He didn't have time to deal with this. "Listen, we obviously need to hash some things out. But I gotta go. We'll discuss it later." Because he was sure delaying would magically create a second bedroom.

Removing her jacket meant that Declan noticed her form-fitting shirt tucked into leggings. Form-fitting, as well. He averted his gaze too late. Her lithe, athletic shape remained in his mind.

Edith asked, "Where's Harper?"

"Sleeping in the playpen. You might want to get some sleep, too. I'll be gone a few hours at least."

He slipped past Edith, his sharp sense of smell noting the tang of exertion, and, at her hairline, he saw traces of makeup, the foundation smeared along the edges. The rest of her face appeared freshly scrubbed.

"Bye."

He needed to leave, so of course she found her chatty side. "You're in a rush. Something big going down in the real estate world?"

"Yes." How to explain that a femme fatale had broken into their offices, tried to steal valuable information, and took out several of their guys before vanishing in the night. "Someone put an offer on a property in Australia. Time zones. You know." Lame. Totally lame.

But she bought it. "Hope you make the sale."

So did he. The listing they were shopping would put a minor fortune in the company's pocket. But that wasn't the real reason for sliding out of there and racing to the office. A simple tap of a button on his dash flipped the timing on the lights, giving him green all the way.

Parking underground, he was more cautious than usual. He had his briefcase in one hand, a stun grenade and a revolver within it. His holster held his usual piece. He could yank it quicker than a blink.

He scanned the concrete space. Well lit. Not a single bulb dark. No sound but the soft scrape of his own shoes breaking the thick silence. He recognized four of the six cars parked. His friends were already here.

The elevator opened, and he waved upon entering, knowing someone would be watching. He went straight to the BBI floor, the doors sliding open to reveal a deceptively calm reception area.

Harry stood at ease, leaning on the counter. Ben paced to his left. Calvin stood to the right. Jerome lounged behind the counter, watching over Mason, who sat in front of the terminal, typing.

Lots of testosterone in one place. They used to be more balanced. It was weird not seeing Kacy among them, the fiery Latina having followed her husband as he went through a senior version of the academy, wanting to bring his skills up to par with his new wife's so they could do jobs together.

Too much sausage. Even Declan knew they needed variety. Harry was doing his best to find some female operatives. He'd put out feelers, but finding the right kind of operative to join their tight-knit team proved a challenging task.

The elevator door slid shut, and Declan strode towards the group.

"About time you showed up," Ben teased. "Kid slowing you down already?"

"Fuck off. I had to wait for my sitter."

"Might be time to put you on desk duty." Ben just couldn't help himself. If he weren't careful, Declan wouldn't be able to help himself from putting a fist in Ben's face.

Declan ignored Ben to speak with his boss. "Do we know who broke in?"

"We haven't identified the intruder yet," Harry said. "But we've got video footage. Ben had her cornered on the roof."

"Her?" Declan queried. "Are we sure it was a woman?"

"Yes, it was a woman, or a very convincing man," Ben grumbled.

"How did you lose her?" Declan asked, having gotten only the barest details of the break-in.

"We were on the rooftop. I didn't expect her to jump."

"Shit. She killed herself?" murmured Declan. "That's hardcore."

"That's just it, she's not dead," Ben exclaimed. "Damned chick brought toys. She rappelled down the building and then disappeared."

"How the heck did she manage to tether a rope on our roof with no one noticing?" Mason asked.

"She didn't do it ahead of time." Harry shook his head. "The intruder came prepared."

Ben's hands slashed the air. "Prepared? Understatement. She was like Batgirl. She shot out a rope from somewhere on her body, anchored it, and moved faster down that building than Jerome when happy hour starts."

"I doubt she's faster. Wave some Krispy Kremes and he's quicker than lightning," Mason noted.

"Damned straight, I'm fast," Jerome boasted. "I might not be able to beat you in a footrace, but I am an ace at flying." An injury had left Jerome with a bum leg, but that didn't stop him from being an asset to the company. Harry wasn't the type to put men out to pasture. There was always something for everyone.

"Have we figured out what the thief was after?" Declan asked.

Harry shrugged. "Don't know. She tried logging in to the computer." He waved a hand. "The fail-safes kicked in when she flunked three times. What's worrisome, is if it weren't for the fact that we roll the passwords daily, she would have gotten in. Hell, two minutes earlier, before the daily roll, and she would have."

"How did she get the codes?" Calvin asked, silent up to this point. "Have we been compromised? Is there a bug in the office?"

"Good question. Jerome?"

"I swept the place this morning. Like I do every morning. Nothing. But I'll check again." He moved to his office where he kept his sweeping kit.

"Can we see the footage of this person?" Declan asked.

"Sure. But I don't think it will do much good. Whoever she is, she used a disguise. Ben found a wig in a dumpster two blocks from here."

"Gonna run it through forensics for DNA?" asked Mason.

Harry didn't treat it like the dumb question it was. "Already bagged and waiting at the lab, but I doubt they'll get much. She poured lighter fluid all over it. I think she meant to burn the whole thing, but the flame she lit only got part of it before extinguishing."

"Wonder what she wanted?" Declan mused aloud as they moved into the Bad Boy war room. Which looked as cool as it sounded. The windows had a dark tint and were rocket-proof glass. It could be turned into an impenetrable command room at the touch of a button or a yelled command.

The massive, gleaming black table reacted to touch and projected a hologram over its surface for the presentations with visuals. There was a wall that was entirely comprised of a screen. Blank for the moment, but once they sealed that door, the surface would fill with all the facts they currently had on hand.

Taking their customary seats, the padded, leather chairs deep and comfortable, they all stared at the big screen, watching the spy's entrance into the building, listening to her discourse with Malcom at reception.

Appearance-wise, she didn't ring any bells. She looked like a businesswoman, from her perfect blonde bob to her elegant way of moving. The envelope in her hand added a nice touch, too. She did nothing in the elevator, not even glance at the camera.

Mason whistled when she stripped off her coat outside Jackson's office and adjusted her boobs. "She knew she was being watched. This is all a show."

She never once looked at the cameras. Just acted as if she truly were there to meet Jackson for some late-night office nookie. Except Jackson spent the evenings at home with his wife and never even knew his log-in and office were used. Malcom swore up and down that he called the office and talked to Jackson, whose raspy voice was rather distinctive. But that didn't mean shit. In these days of smart AI's, running a program to simulate a person on the phone wasn't that hard. Hell, Declan and the boys had used that trick themselves on missions. The fact that it had been used to infiltrate their office was disturbing.

The footage from the Bad Boy floor was murky, the night-vision camera giving the intruder a greenish cast. Still, they could see how she moved with assurance to the desk. How quickly she reacted once she triggered the alarm.

"Brilliant," Declan muttered as she tossed the chair to save herself an exit point.

"Holy shit, why isn't she working for us?" exclaimed Mason as she wiggled through the narrow gap.

A better question was, who *did* she work for? Because her preparation and skills weren't that of an amateur.

The rooftop footage proved most fascinating of all as it showed her standing without fear on the edge of the building. And then diving off.

"Damn." That seemed to be the universal reaction.

"Can we watch it again?" They rewound it over and over, stopping it and enlarging sections to get a better look at her face.

"Does she show up in any databases at all?" Calvin asked.

Mason and Declan were both scouring databases, each having their own methods for finding a person. Mason's being more about facial recognition. Whereas, Declan...he felt as if he'd seen that face before. Something about it nagged at him.

"What are you looking at?" Harry asked, leaning over.

"Academy graduate images." Declan swiped through the files.

"You're not supposed to be able to browse those. You know student records are secret to keep them safe," his boss grumbled, to which Declan shot him a look.

"Then don't tell your friend I was looking." The academy owner, Darren, was a long-time friend of Harry's. But while Declan knew the man, he felt no special loyalty to him. Darren's dad, however...—the man who'd recruited Declan at a time in his life when he thought he had nothing left to lose and was contemplating a life of crime—that man he would have done anything for.

"She's not academy trained." Harry paused the video and pointed. "No way would the Sarge have condoned that kind of sloppiness." Sloppiness in Harry's world being the fact that she'd left her shoes behind.

"I assume the shoes ended up with the wig in the lab," Declan mused aloud. Something about that chewed at him. It did seem odd that she'd intentionally grabbed her coat and yet, just as intentionally, left the shoes behind. Then again, way he heard it, running in heels sucked. So why wear them on a mission like this at all?

The shoes made no sense. Leaving them behind nagged at him. Especially since she'd tried to eliminate the wig. Did her best to rid any trace evidence, and yet...

A lightbulb went off, and Declan exclaimed. "Shit. Call the lab and tell them to put the shoes in a containment unit."

"What are you talking about?" Harry's eyes widened. Even as he dialed, his phone beeped. He stopped pressing buttons to read the notification that flashed on his screen. Then growled. "Something in the lab just exploded."

"Anyone hurt?"

"No. But the shoes, the wig, plus the other stuff we'd sent in for analysis are toast."

"Fuck."

And yet, brilliant. Who was this new player working against them?

It was Calvin who noted, "She could have killed them but didn't."

"What are you talking about?" Declan raised his head to pay attention.

"Diego and Malcom. Look at the fight." Calvin slowed it down. "Here. She could have throat punched him and ended it. Instead, she hit him in the diaphragm and knocked him out. As for Malcom, she had his gun."

"Which she fired."

"Into his leg. She didn't go for a kill shot."

"She was shooting tranquilizers."

"Are we sure she knew that? Because her face is shocked when she sees the dart. She also doesn't break their necks when they pass out. Hell, on the rooftop, rather than jump, she could have taken out Ben."

"Like hell, she would have," Ben hotly retorted.

"The point is, she didn't really hurt anyone," Declan mused aloud. "Which means, BBI employees weren't the targets, something in this office is."

"She's interested in one of our clients. But which one?" Harry asked the next most pertinent question.

And, even more importantly, was it a Bad Boy realty client she was after? Or one of their specialty assignment ones? A pity she'd failed to log in. At least then, they would have had an answer.

Jerome entered and held up two bugs.

"Where did you find them?" Harry asked.

"Reception desk, pinned to a stem of the plant in the vase. And Declan's office, on his phone."

Every muscle in Declan's body froze. His office was bugged. Call him officially staggered.

"Who had access to it?" Harry asked. "Let's get a list."

It would be a short one because very few people came to Declan's office. He usually used the meeting room when seeing clients. Other than himself, other BBI employees could have gone in there, but none would have bugged him. There was the cleaning staff, but security watched them closely when they did their early morning pass. Who else did that leave?

How about the person who visited him today and sat on his desk? Touched his phone, too.

Surely, he didn't suspect Edith?

A woman home alone with his baby.

Who did nothing during the store attack today.

Who gave him shit for owning a gun.

It seemed ludicrous, yet while the other boys ran their own investigations online, and re-watched the videos a hundred times, Declan reran Edith's background check. Her perfectly clean, *too* clean background. He sent a request to have it run against Interpol's database. It might take a bit because Interpol had recently cracked down on access, making it harder to hack for information.

While that cranked away, he flipped to peek at his loft, the cameras inside showing it dark and quiet. The door log showing no one entering or leaving since his departure. Zooming in on the playpen, he saw Harper sleeping, butt in the air, fist in her mouth.

Perfectly normal. However, now that he'd thought it, the idea refused to leave. Was Edith a spy?

He didn't tell Harry of his suspicions. It sounded crazy. Or was it?

The intruder was a woman. Edith was a woman.

So were a billion others.

While the woman escaped, Edith showed up to babysit.

Showed up more than twenty minutes after he'd called.

Could the woman who spider-monkeyed down the building have had enough time to change and make it back to his loft?

Only one way to find out. At the crack of dawn, as a few of them left yawning, Declan tested it, timing himself from the spot where they found the wig. He hopped into his car and sped to his loft. He made it in fourteen minutes.

It didn't mean his nanny was the intruder. But the bug in his office... He couldn't help but recall her sitting on his desk. The phone shoved to the side. Was that when she planted it? Or had the bug been there for days already?

Jerome would have caught it. The man swept the office every single day.

The questions whirled around in his head.

What if Edith were the intruder? How could he find out for sure? Accusing her outright would backfire if she were innocent. And how exactly would he broach it?

"Did you try and cat burglar my office tonight then jump off a roof?" Crazy shit.

However, he didn't have a choice but to try and find out because what if Edith were some kind of undercover operative? What if he had a killer hanging with his daughter at this very minute?

How should he handle it? Confront her right away, or see how long she kept up the charade?

Since he returned home in the wee hours, he did his best to be quiet, easing the door open, wincing at every click of the locks. Entering, there wasn't a single sound. The phone in his pocket, set to vibrate if the motion sensors triggered, remained inert.

He left the lights off, seeing enough by the ambient

light spilling in from outside to guide his steps. Declan stripped as he headed for his bed, leaving only his boxers. He was all too aware that Edith slept on the couch. Although he did find it odd that she'd opted to not pull out the bed. Her back, not his, would suffer in the morning. Pulling back the covers, he slid in with a deep sigh. He tucked his arm around his pillow and rolled onto his side, splaying his leg out and—

Touched someone!

CHAPTER ELEVEN

DECLAN MUTTERED A SHOCKED, "WHAT THE HELL!" HE was either the world's best actor, or he'd honestly not realized that Edith slept in his bed.

Technically, she wasn't sleeping. Edith woke the moment Declan stepped in the door. Mentally debated making her presence known, especially since she'd eschewed the couch for the bed. Who could blame her? When he'd left the evening before, she knew he'd be gone for a while, and her body could use something soft to sleep in. Especially given her less than stellar quarters the previous two nights.

Hence why she quietly scooched to the far side of the mattress, a king-sized bed which possessed more than enough room for two, unless a man chose to sleep smack dab in the center. Escaping unnoticed proved impossible when he flung out his leg and encountered her.

What she didn't expect was to find herself so quickly pinned under his half-naked weight.

"What are you doing in my bed?" The words were softly growled.

It seemed obvious, but still. "Sleeping, until you accosted me."

"I'm protecting myself."

"By caging me with your body?"

His lip quirked. "Not my fault you're small enough for it to work."

"This is really inappropriate."

"If you were worried about that, then you shouldn't have been sleeping in my bed."

"The *only* bed," she pointed out.

"The sofa—"

"Is uncomfortable, and you know it. You were gone. The bed was empty. I don't see the problem."

"The problem is you're in *my* bed."

The second problem she noticed pressed against the vee of her thighs. Perhaps she shouldn't have been surprised by his attraction, and yet she was. She'd done nothing overt to flirt with him. On the contrary, they clashed at every turn. She'd assumed her attraction to him was one-sided.

Wrong. It became blatantly obvious, and it didn't help —or hurt—that they were in bed, Edith wearing a T-shirt and panties, him in his boxers and nothing else.

Their skin touched. Neither of them moved. The moment was fraught with tension.

Shove him away.

But his weight felt good.

You're not in the right place to get involved with anyone.

Would there ever really be a right time?

His gaze smoldered, yet his words were gruff. "I knew having you spend the night was a mistake."

"Only because you think it's okay to molest me in my sleep. You could have stayed on your side."

"I'm not molesting you."

"Says the man still lying on top of me." Heavy and sexy and making her girly parts take notice.

"You took me by surprise. I reacted to protect myself."

She arched a brow. "Because so many burglars hide half-naked in your bed."

"I might have overreacted."

"You think? Care to move away now?"

"Not really."

The admission surprised her. "I work for you." She should have learned her lesson from last time.

"I know." Said with a sigh.

"Still waiting for you to move."

"Even in bed you're bossy," he grumbled. He began to shift, moving his weight away from her using his arms. The loss triggered disappointment.

How long since she'd been this close to a man?

The answer? Not since her ugly breakup. Since that debacle, she'd felt no desire for any kind of intimacy. Until now.

And now was the wrong time.

"How did that thing at your office go? Did you make the sale?"

He didn't immediately reply, tucking his hands behind his head. "Not yet. The real reason I went in was because there was a break-in."

"Oh no. Was anything taken?"

"Nope. Security chased them off before they got anything."

"Were the police helpful?"

"Totally," he said. "They got several good fingerprints. Shouldn't be long before we get a hit."

"If nothing was stolen, why bother?"

"Can't have people snooping around. Bad for business. Can you ask me a zillion questions later? I'm tired."

He rolled over onto his side, and she gnawed her lower lip. Before5:00 a.m. wasn't a good time to be awake. She settled back down. Stared at his back.

Rolled over and faced away from him. Sighed. Held her breath at how loud it sounded. A good thing she had no air because when he shifted, a heavy arm came over her. Tucked her back into his body.

"Mr. Hood?" she whispered.

He said nothing, his breathing soft and even. His body warm. Somehow, she fell asleep, only to wake smothered by a body. The arm over her ribcage had been joined by a muscled thigh over her legs, his face in her hair, and a hard-on pressing against her backside.

Oh, dear.

She wiggled in an attempt to escape. He mumbled and squeezed.

"Do you mind?" she exclaimed.

His body went rigid a second before he melted away from her. "Sorry," he muttered.

Funny thing was, she was sorrier he left. "I doubt your girlfriend would like you groping someone else."

"No girlfriend." He peeled open an eye. "Your boyfriend, he the jealous type?"

"I'm not dating." Ever again.

"Of course you're single." He sighed as if defeated. "I am so screwed."

"Why?"

He opened both eyes to fix her with a stern glare. "Because you're hot. That's why. I know you're the nanny. And I know I'm not supposed to be attracted to you, but dammit, woman, you're really not making this easy."

For a moment, she gaped at him, his admission startling. Sexy.

She rolled closer. "What if I like making it hard?" And yes, she meant that every bit as dirty as it sounded.

"What are you saying?" He eyed her with suspicion.

She reached for him, placing a hand on his chest, feeling the rapid beat of his heart. "We're both adults. Right?"

A wary expression entered his gaze. "Yeah. And?"

"This job, it's temporary?"

"Very. What are you getting at?"

Rather than reply, she leaned in to kiss him. Pressed her lips to his and then paused to see how he'd react.

He froze. They both did, with their mouths touching. Her heart raced at her presumption. Her cleft tingled in anticipation.

He kissed her back.

More like devoured her. His mouth slanted over hers and took her with a passion that caught her by surprise and stole her breath.

He caressed her lower lip, sucking on it. He nibbled the upper one and slid his tongue between. As their mouths explored, he shifted until his body sank atop hers once more, the hardness of him pressing, rubbing.

Her hands stroked the firm muscle of his back, feeling

the ridge of scars. She wondered about them, but they didn't stop her from touching. From gripping his firm buttocks and grinding herself against him.

Their breathing grew ragged, and only a thin layer of clothes separated them. Her fingers hooked into the waistband of his boxers, tugging them down.

She wanted him inside her. Wanted him—

"Waaah." With the strident cry came a dousing of the passion and a return to reality.

What was she doing? And with this man. A man who had secrets.

Hadn't she learned her lesson before?

Don't get involved. Especially not at work.

They sprang apart, his eyes as wide as hers. Edith quickly left the bed and went to the playpen to grab the baby and cuddle her. When he would have risen, too, she waved a hand at him. "Get some sleep."

"Sleep, she says." Declan snorted. "As if that's going to happen now."

Given her skin was still flushed from passion, she could understand his grumpy tone.

She turned from it, though, and bounced the baby. "Who's a pretty girl?" she cooed. "Let's get your butt changed."

"I need a shower," he grumbled. She didn't let herself look as he flung back the covers and stalked to the bathroom.

Looking might melt her resolve.

She used the respite to dress herself and change the baby. Then wondered what she'd do when Declan emerged. The man needed sleep. She needed time to clear her head and remind herself of what she was doing here. A walk would do her and the baby some good.

She quickly made a bottle and grabbed some baby cookies before she popped Harper into the stroller. She was heading out of the loft when the door to the bathroom opened.

"Where the hell are you going?" Declan snapped.

Turning her head, she saw him, a towel wrapped around his hips, upper body bare and glorious. Still damp and lickable. She needed to leave before she quenched her thirst. "Taking Harper for a walk so you can get a few hours of sleep."

She exited quickly and slammed the portal shut before he could say anything else. What was there to say?

You're fired. After what she'd done. Tried to seduce him then left him blue-balled instead.

He couldn't fire her yet. She needed this job.

"Ready for a walk, sweet pea?" She pasted on a false smile for the baby as they rode the elevator down. She used the descent to put herself in a Zen place where perfect abs and a smirking smile wouldn't make her panties turn into a puddle.

I will not sleep with my boss. Maybe if she repeated it enough times, she'd listen.

Someone coming into the building held the door open for her and the stroller. She emerged into a cloudy day, the kind to tug spirits down.

"Which way, Harper?" She could use some breakfast and a place with Wi-Fi. She wanted to check her emails. She'd not taken two steps when a large SUV came barreling down the street and screeched to a halt in front of the building.

That wasn't good.

Edith took a step back, knowing she wouldn't make it inside in time. She stood in front of the stroller as a thug spilled out of the black Suburban with its smoked glass.

The big dude, wearing a leather coat and sporting a goatee but no hair atop his head, smiled, showing off a gold tooth.

"About time you came outside." Leaving her with no doubt that he was there on purpose. The following words, though, were what chilled her most. "Grab the baby."

CHAPTER TWELVE

THE COLD SHOWER DIDN'T HELP DECLAN'S ERECTION. His hand managed some relief, but the main problem remained.

I'm attracted to my nanny.

And the attraction was mutual.

It was utterly wrong, even if it felt so right.

The passion between them was explosive. If it hadn't been for Harper waking, they would have fucked. It would have been glorious. Then he would have had to fire her. Probably with a huge severance package.

Or would he have to kill her? Was she the enemy? He still hadn't answered that question.

The very idea that she was the intruder seemed ludicrous now that he'd seen her again. His nanny, with her big eyes and trim figure, wasn't the same woman he'd seen in the video.

He'd totally convinced himself of that, yet when he exited the bathroom and saw her slam the door, claiming to go for a walk, he hurriedly dressed. Did he trust her enough to leave with his kid?

The answer? No.

And after what had almost happened in bed this morning, he had to fire her. Now. No waiting and making excuses not to. Declan needed to pull off the bandage and get it done. Rip at those painful hairs. It was the only way to handle it before something unfortunate—like them orgasming in his bed—happened.

He eschewed the slow elevator to skip down the stairs and spilled into the small lobby of his building, the glass doors to the outside showing a commotion.

He slowed his step as he tried to comprehend what was happening. It took a moment since it made no sense.

Edith was out there on the sidewalk, fighting off a big man, blocking punches, ducking in ways that defied science, her body bending back and then rapidly snapping upright to throw a jab of her own. She was handling herself like a fighting pro. That wasn't why he ran for the door, though.

Another guy was trying to lift the stroller, the baby strapped within, into a Suburban.

Oh, hell no.

"Get your fucking hands off my kid, asshole," Declan yelled as he barreled through the doors, sprinting past Edith and only partially seeing the roundhouse kick she managed to land. He grabbed the shoulder of the guy trying to kidnap his daughter and spun him around far enough to land a punch to his face.

As the stroller jostled back onto the sidewalk, Harper started to cry. Edith yelled, "I'm coming, sweet pea!"

The guy Declan fought pulled a gun, and they grappled

for control. Declan immediately grabbed the man's wrist to aim the weapon overhead. He slammed the guy against the truck. Hard enough that the hand holding the gun loosened and the weapon fell to the curb. The window on the vehicle rolled down, and he noted the muzzle of another gun poking out. He dropped down with a yelled, "Duck!"

Boom.

The weapon fired, Harper went into hysterics. Declan kneed his guy and wished he'd not run out of his place without his own firearm. But, no, it was a useless hunk of metal in his loft.

Pop.

Another weapon fired. Not the one from the truck. With a last punch that sent his guy sinking to the ground, Declan whirled to see Edith, her lower lip swollen, holding a gun on her bald thug whose fingers squeezed his arm but didn't quite manage to stem the flow of blood.

She shot a man!

And she didn't look one bit apologetic about it. "Get the baby," she ordered Declan, her cold gaze and aim never wavering from her target.

Declan snared the stroller, retrieving the fallen gun at the same time, and moved the yelling baby behind Edith.

The driver still held his weapon pointed, but he didn't fire.

A standoff.

Sirens wailed in the distance.

"Who are you?" she asked.

"Who do you work for?" was Declan's question.

But the thug didn't reply. Just smirked. He toed his groaning companion on the ground. "Get in the truck."

Edith snapped, "No one said you could move."

"You won't shoot," said the bald guy, his tone smug. "Too many witnesses."

Declan wasn't so sure about that. Edith looked pissed. Beyond pissed, actually. She just might do it. He put his hand on hers and pushed the gun down. "He's right."

"We can't just let them go. They tried to take the baby."

"I know. But if you shoot them, the cops will have too many questions."

As it was, they might have a hard time explaining.

The gun lowered, the would-be kidnappers piled into the Suburban and fled, tires screaming, the license plate covered in mud.

But Declan had marked their faces. He'd have a composite sketch done and circulated by the end of the morning. First, though, they had to give a statement to the cops about the random drive-by.

They didn't stay on the sidewalk. Fleeing for the loft, they hid the evidence so that when the cops came knocking, they could show their empty hands and exclaim with wide-eyed innocence that there was no gun. The 911 caller was mistaken.

With no one truly hurt—and only a hole in the building for damage—the police, with better things to do, took off, chalking up the incident to just another random act of violence.

His jaw set tightly, Declan locked the door when the police left. Turning, he saw Edith standing by the couch, the baby sleeping in her arms.

He'd not said one word to her about what had

happened. Not a single thing other than, "There was no gun. Some guys accosted you, and we fought them off."

Now, though, they were alone. He waited until Edith put the baby in the playpen to ask, in a voice his enemies knew meant business, "Who the fuck are you?"

CHAPTER THIRTEEN

A KILLER.

Imagine if she told the truth. Explain how she was a spy. An expert in international espionage. What would he say?

Why did she even contemplate it?

She stuck to innocence. "What do you mean?" Edith blinked at Declan, noting the tense lines of his body. She moved away from the playpen, giving herself room in case he attacked. No mistaking the anger vibrating through him.

"I mean, you're not a nanny."

She uttered a laugh that hopefully didn't sound too false. "Don't be silly. You've seen me take care of Harper. I am utterly qualified." More than he knew.

"Nannies don't know how to take down street thugs or carry pieces."

"Like you said the other day, one can never be too safe." She might have smiled as she tossed his own words back at him.

"You're also the woman who gave me shit for having a gun."

She cocked her head. "No, I gave you heck for not having it secured while at home."

"You're splitting hairs." Walking over to the stroller, he reached under and took her gun from the place where he'd hidden it. Pulling out his camera, he took a picture of it.

"What are you doing?" she asked.

"Sending it to a friend to run the serial number."

Her lips quirked. "He won't find it."

"Is it stolen?"

"Not exactly. More like unlisted."

He placed the gun on the coffee table and crossed his arms. "How does a nanny get her hands on an unregistered weapon?" Before she could reply, he barked, "Because you're not a damned nanny. Who are you? Who do you work for?"

"I could ask the same of you." There was no point in pretending anymore. Her secret unraveled the moment he came across her on the sidewalk taking on a guy almost twice her size.

"Don't you turn this around. This isn't about me. This is about the woman who lied her way into my home and planted a bug in my office."

They found that rather quickly. She lifted a brow. "Since when do realty offices sweep for bugs?"

"Not going to deny you put it there?"

Edith shrugged. "What would be the point? I admit I bugged your office. I don't suppose you'll give the microphones back? They're not cheap."

"Are you seriously asking me to return your spy equipment?"

"You could just say no. I don't know why you're being so rude about it. If you were a regular realty office, you would have never known it was there. What is Bad Boy Inc., really? Are you a front for drugs? Money laundering? Must be something hardcore given your security. The panic doors were a nice touch."

His gaze narrowed. "The only way you'd know about our security is if it *was* you who broke into our offices."

She tossed her head. "You can't prove it."

"You just admitted it."

"And?" She smiled. Teasing. Coy. Meant to drive him a little over the edge. "What are you going to do about it? Call the police? I think we've ascertained that neither of us is keen on that option. I didn't steal anything. No harm done."

"How about the fact you used me?"

"I did." Said with a hint of smugness.

"Why? What did you want?"

"Nothing you need to know." And, obviously, she'd miscalculated when she thought she could use him. Mr. Hood was more than he appeared. More than her research on him had shown.

"Is that why you were so insistent I hire you? To get close to me and steal company secrets?"

"I thought about sleeping with you for information, but the nanny gig worked out better."

He moved quickly, and yet she could have stopped him from grabbing her arms and shaking her. "Stop acting as if this is a joke."

"I wasn't laughing." Smirking, yes. Outright giggling, no.

He gripped her tighter, yanking her up on her tiptoes. "What are you hiding? Why are you spying on me?"

She could give him at least this. "It isn't about you."

"Then who?"

"Who do you think? One of your clients." It didn't take a genius to realize why she'd target a realty company. Perhaps he'd be willing to give her the info so she wouldn't have to hurt him.

"Which one?"

"If I tell you who I'm interested in, will you share what you know about him?"

"Like fuck. I'm not giving you shit."

"That's not nice."

"I stopped being nice when I found out you were two-faced."

Her lips pursed. "Insults? That will cost you."

"Like hell, it will."

"Language."

"Fuck your language rules. You're not the one in charge here, lady."

She couldn't help but laugh. "What makes you think you are?"

His grip tightened. A manly move that she totally expected.

She smiled as she slammed her foot down on his instep, brought up her knee, ramming it into his lower stomach. The rapid strikes loosened his grip enough that she twisted and broke free. A dive to the side meant she got her fingers on her gun. She aimed it at him. "Weren't you ever taught to never ass-u-me anything, Mr. Hood?"

"Ha. Ha," he said without mirth. "Very subtle. Ass out

of you and me. Not exactly the most original taunt. I'm not too proud to admit you fooled me."

"If it's any consolation, I was also guilty of assuming things. You are more than you seem, as well, Mr. Hood. A realtor with an office that is strongly guarded? A man with guns all over his apartment."

"You found them?"

"Last night after you left. Given what happened at your office, I grew curious." So interested that after her cursory search, she dug deeper. Found false bottoms in cupboards. Knives inside a window frame that folded away. The grenades he kept in the toilet tank. "Home security is one thing, but you have an Uzi inside your box spring."

Ignoring the gun she pointed at him, he flopped onto the couch, bracing his arm over the back of it. "What can I say? I like my toys."

"The stuff you've got lying around here is more than toys. You own electronics that even the government doesn't have. Military-grade weapons, some not available for sale because they're supposed to still be in development."

"I have connections."

She took the club chair across from him, gun dangling from one hand as they conversed. The strangest conversation ever. "You are an arms collector who stayed cool as a cucumber when faced with a gunman. You knew how to defend yourself against kidnappers. For an upstanding man of the community, you have no problem lying to law enforcement."

"I hate unnecessary paperwork."

"Don't play coy with me, Mr. Hood. You have secrets."

"I do." He wasn't even ashamed at having been caught.

"You don't know the half of it, Edith." The slow grin that stretched his lips did things to her lower half. Dirty things. With just a look. "And what's with the 'Mr. Hood' thing? I thought we were on a first-name basis, *Edith*. You're also one to talk. You're not a nanny."

"If I admit I'm not, will you admit you're not a realtor?"

"Oh, but I *am* a realtor."

She arched a brow.

"A realtor with a second job."

"Which is?" she asked through gritted teeth as he dragged this out.

"What if I told you I'm a mercenary for hire, and that the realty gig is just a cover?"

She snickered. "I'd say you watch too much television." And yet... She frowned. It would explain a few things. Except for one. Why hadn't her handler—the one she'd sent reports to about her lack of progress on the mission—warned her? "Why would a mercenary bother with a day job?" She knew why she had one. Mothers couldn't be full-time spies. Someone had to take care of the kids.

"Only an idiot doesn't have a real job. You need one to maintain your cover. Something Uncle Sam can tax. Something you can tell your neighbors. A paper trail to make you legit." He leaned back, the height of relaxation. Meanwhile, she felt her nerves stringing tight.

"So, you're saying the realty thing is all a fake?"

"Yes, and no. I really do sell real estate. However, Bad Boy Inc. is a front for a shadow company. We're actually a group of international problem solvers. Industrial espionage, information gathering on a rival, the maneuvering of government and law enforcement officials, bodyguards, acquisitions specialists. And, oh yes, assassins." He said the last with a cold smile.

"Are you trying to tell me that everyone in your office is some kind of American version of James Bond?"

"Not quite. We're not government-run or owned. We're independent."

"You're delusional."

"Why?"

"Because a real spy wouldn't be spilling his secrets."

He leaned forward. "Did you miss the part where I said I was an assassin? You assume you'll leave this room in a position to actually tell anyone."

"Are you really going to threaten the woman holding the gun?" She aimed it at him.

"You mean the one with no bullets?"

Her lips flattened. No use checking because the smirk said he told the truth.

"You won't kill me," she said.

"Says you. I, on the other hand, am mightily disturbed by the fact you weaseled your way into my home and used me to infiltrate my office."

"So fire me." She leaned back in the chair, displaying the same nonchalant confidence.

"I thought that was a foregone conclusion after what's happened."

"Is that so? Then I guess I'll be packing my things."

Except it wasn't her bag she prepped, it was the baby's.

"Those aren't your things." He prowled around the kitchen table strewn with baby gear.

She kept stuffing them into the diaper bag. "You're right. They're not. And yet I bought most of them."

"With my money."

"On the contrary, you clueless man." She held up a stuffed giraffe, worn smooth in spots by gnawing slobber. "I bought this, and I'm leaving with it. And Harper. Because you were right about one thing. I did manipulate you into hiring me." She dropped a grenade of her own. "To take care of *my* daughter."

CHAPTER FOURTEEN

Sometimes it wasn't a straw that broke the camel's back, but the realization that your baby's momma had super-duper lied that made a man go a little nuts.

Declan wasn't one to manhandle women, or hurt them unless they were shooting at him first. But the fact that Edith, or whoever this stranger was, threatened to leave made something in Declan snap.

He lunged for the woman, and she fought him.

Fought him dirty, too. Her knee connected with the soft tissue between his legs—*argh, she broke my balls*—and punched the air out of him. Her fists pummeled at his body, leaving bruises. However, Declan hadn't spent four years at the academy knitting tea cozies. He could take a hit. He could also subdue without leaving a mark.

The Vulcans had the neck pinch. A jab in the right spot could do the same thing.

Mid-yell, Edith's eyes rolled back, and she flopped into his arms. He didn't let her hit the floor, even as he wanted to shake her and ask her why. Why had she dropped the baby bomb on him out of the blue? Why all the subterfuge? Who was she looking to get information about?

But most important of all, was he the baby daddy, or was that a lie, too? Because the thing was, he didn't think he'd ever slept with her. Surely, he'd remember.

Even if he weren't Harper's daddy, there was the mystery of what Edith wanted and who hired her. Until he could find out, he had to keep her somewhere he could watch her. Somewhere safe.

The kidnapping attempt outside his building did show one thing. His loft was obviously compromised. Which meant he needed a place to take Edith and Harper until he could get the answers he wanted. Where could he go with decent security, where people wouldn't ask questions?

The answer proved easier than expected.

Ben brought over the keys within the hour.

As a realtor, Declan had access to many vacant properties, not all of them for sale. Some of them for rent fully furnished. The condo Declan chose in the downtown high-rise offered impeccable security, and best of all, no one but Ben would know where he was.

Ben, however, did ask questions. "Any reason why your nanny is handcuffed in the trunk?"

A passenger in his friend's car, Declan grimaced. "Remember how I said on the phone that I found out some stuff about the break-in, but I needed you to keep quiet?"

"Yeah."

"My nanny is the one who did it."

Ben shot him a look. "No, she's not. I saw that woman."

"I know what we saw. And I'm telling you, it was my nanny. Except, she's not really a nanny."

"Then what is she?"

"Not sure. However, it turns out she's Harper's mother."

"What?" Ben swerved as he took his eyes off the road to exclaim his shock.

"But she's more than that. I think she's an agent. When those thugs tried to take Harper, she pulled a gun. An unregistered one. And she can fight. Dude, you should have seen her taking on that beast. Then there's the fact she bugged our office and broke in."

"Looking for what?"

Declan shrugged. "Fuck if I know. But I aim to find out."

"Going to torture the mother of your kid?"

Could he do that? "I'm hoping it won't come to that. And, again, really doubting I'm the father." Which caused him more of a pang than he'd expected. Shouldn't he feel relief at being off the hook?

"Do you have a plan?"

Hell, no. But that didn't stop Declan. Arriving at the condo, they borrowed a flatbed dolly and heaped luggage around Edith's body before covering it with a layer of coats. To the casual observer, it would seem as if he were moving in.

While Ben maneuvered the cart into the elevator, Declan handled the car seat with a babbling baby in it.

Are you my daughter?

It bothered him to realize that he very much wanted

her to be his. This sweet child with the slobbery grins and the warm hugs made him want to be a father. Not something he'd ever imagined. Something he'd feared.

Yet now, he was more scared of losing it. With the lab being cleaned up from the bomb, the original swabs destroyed, there was no way to get a quick answer.

The condo was on the fifth floor with no balcony. Each floor had a security camera. As did the elevator, the lobby, the parking garage—which Ben was handling to ensure no one watching the footage even saw them enter the building. A round-the-clock guard watched the front entrance. Another patrolled the area at the back.

The condominium complex catered to the rich who didn't want to be disturbed, which suited him fine. He didn't need any more surprises.

It didn't take long for him to set the stage for his captive.

Ben shook his head when he saw the preparations. "Are you sure you know what you're doing?"

No, but he didn't let his doubt show. "I got this part of it covered."

"I'll dig and see if I can find out more about your baby momma."

"Run her fingerprints in every database you can find." Not just the DMV and police databases. He wanted FBI, Interpol, everything.

"Didn't you run it already?"

"Yes. But I must have missed something."

"You sure you don't want me to take the baby?" Ben asked.

No, because the baby was part of his plan.

A devious plan that she wouldn't expect.

When she finally snapped out of her unconscious state, she looked around and barked, "What the fuck is going on?"

Being a smartass, he shook his finger at her and said, "Language!"

CHAPTER FIFTEEN

REGAINING CONSCIOUSNESS WHEN THE LAST THING SHE remembered was fighting Declan put Edith in a bad mood. Being chided for her potty mouth meant she glared at the man who dared rebuke her language. "Where's Harper?"

He pointed at the floor behind him. Harper sat in a saucer type baby thing, hopping and bouncing as she tugged at the bright, plastic toys attached to it. "The baby store delivered it just as we were leaving my place. She seems to like it."

"Where are we?" She looked around and noted the lavish space with its crown molding, floor-to-ceiling windows, and ornate furniture, including an expensive-looking, cream-colored leather couch—that she'd drooled on before waking.

"Somewhere a little more private than my place."

Sitting up on the couch, she was surprised to find herself unfettered. Her gun sat on the table.

He noticed her glancing at it. "I reloaded it, and before

you freak on me about leaving it lying around, I will point out that Harper is contained, and the safety is on."

"Why are you telling me this?"

"Because it's yours. Go ahead. Grab it."

"You're giving me my gun?" She eyed him askance.

"Seems only fair since I've got mine." He lifted his arm, showing the bulge from the harness he wore. "Wouldn't want either of us to be caught unprepared again."

Her hand whipped out and grabbed the weapon. She aimed it at him. "You knocked me out."

"Hardly knocked. More like squeezed. Then perhaps administered a sedative to ensure a smooth transition."

"You kidnapped me."

"Relocated for our mutual safety."

"Making it sound fancy doesn't improve what you did."

"Fine. I knocked you out and kidnapped you. Is that better?"

"I'm leaving." She stood, keeping her aim steady despite the fuzziness in her head. She couldn't afford to wobble.

"You could. But then you'd hardly get what you came for." He swept a hand behind him, indicating the dining table, a laptop with its lid open on the surface.

"What is that?"

"Access to my client files. It is what you were after, correct? There they are."

Disbelief colored her next words. "You're just going to give them to me?"

"Not exactly give. More like let you browse."

Suspicion narrowed her gaze. "Why would you let me do that?"

"Because you're going to tell me who Harper's daddy is."

"You are." She said the lie quickly, but he caught it.

Declan shook his head, but not before she noticed a hint of disappointment. "No, I'm not, and you just confirmed it. Who is her real daddy?"

"No one you know. He's not a part of our lives."

"Does he know about the child?"

Her lips flattened. "Unfortunately, yes."

"Care to elaborate?"

"Nope. Let's just say our relationship was a mistake. He's not a nice man, and it's best if Harper is kept far away from him."

"Doesn't seem right keeping a child from her father."

"I don't need you lecturing me on how to raise *my* kid."

The emphasis made his nostrils flare. "That wasn't cool, making me think I was the daddy." She expected the anger in his tone; it was the disappointment in his gaze that brought the guilt.

"You said yourself during the interview that you didn't think she was. It was only supposed to be for a few days. A week or so at the most."

"Long enough for you to use me to get to a client. Seems rather elaborate for a simple espionage job. Wouldn't it have been easier to leave her at home with a sitter?"

"It's what I originally planned. However..." *My nanny turned out to be a kidnapper, my house blew up and...* "I didn't have much choice. My babysitter plans fell apart, and I needed somewhere for Harper to stay while I worked."

"And you chose a stranger."

Not a stranger by the time she was done. She had his

name because he was associated with Suarez. How to explain she'd run all of Suarez's accessible staff through all kinds of checks. Declan emerged the cleanest. No sign of an abusive personality. No large bills for alcohol or bar tabs. His internet browsing was for online shopping, and the only porn he watched was the movie variety with actresses over the age of twenty-one. He was considered benign enough that when she ran the possibility of seducing him, her handler sent her a message. *Good plan. Go ahead.*

"I made sure you hired me as a nanny."

"And if I hadn't?"

She shrugged. "Then you wouldn't have kept Harper."

"You're not from around here. Where do you live?"

Considering she'd left her house a smoldering ruin? "Nowhere at the moment."

His phone buzzed, breaking the staring match between them.

He pulled it out of his pocket and frowned at the screen. "I need to take this. Feel free to get started on your peeking. I already logged into the machine and all my client files are sorted in folders on the desktop screen."

He wandered off to the kitchen area, the phone to his ear, his voice too low for her to grasp what he said. He gave her his back.

She glanced down at her gun. *I could shoot him.*

Which seemed extreme since he'd not actually done her any harm. Still, the man hadn't yet explained anything about himself.

She debated her next move. Grab Harper and run?

Which would accomplish nothing. And where would she run to? Under the circumstances, she knew she could call in, and they'd extract her. She and Harper would be shipped off to a safe location with new identities, and the mission would be shifted to someone else. A failure on her record.

Through no fault of her own, but still...

After everything her boss had done for her, everything KM gave her, she owed it to them. Owed them to at least try. Especially since Declan had handed her the access she needed.

Tucking the gun into the back of her pants, she stooped over her daughter and gave her a kiss atop her head. "Hey, sweet pea. You being a good girl? Mommy's gotta do a bit of work."

"Gaaa."

Which she would take as a yes given Harper flailed her chubby fist at a rubber button that beeped when smashed.

Edith slid into a dining chair and placed the gun beside the laptop lest Declan suddenly change his mind. She still didn't understand his plan. Why was he being so nice to her? Why give her access?

And who was he, really? Surely, his story about being some kind of mercenary was a lie. What were the chances that she'd run into another specialized operative? And not just one, but an office full.

None of her intel had mentioned a group of that kind working in this city. Her handler hadn't said a word when Edith announced her plans to use Declan to get in. Shouldn't her handler have known?

Which reminded her...where was her phone?

Declan exited the kitchen, a bemused expression on his face.

"Bad news?"

"Hmm." He appeared startled and shook his head. "Not exactly. Did you find what you needed yet?"

"I haven't even started looking," she snorted. "Where's my phone?"

"Probably still in your bag." He grabbed her satchel from a console table by the door and dropped it on the table.

She dug inside and pulled out her cell, only to wince at the pile of messages. She quickly thumbed through them. All from one person.

He glanced over her shoulder. She didn't worry about him reading because they were in code.

The first one... **How's the vacation going?** Meant, *What's your status on the mission?*

Thinking of putting the house for sale. Real meaning, *Did you have anything to do with the realty company break-in?*

Hello?

Hello?!?!

Then her handler stopped even trying to code. **When were you going to tell me your house blew up?**

Where the hell are you? Why aren't you replying? Do you need help?

She quickly tapped back a message. *Am fine*.

"Everything all right?" Declan asked.

"Just my mother checking on me and Harper. She worries."

"Does your mother always freak out when you don't reply right away?" Declan didn't even try to pretend he wasn't reading. "I saw the message asking about your house. Did it really blow up?"

"Accident with the gas stove."

"You're homeless." Said flatly.

"Temporarily." When she noticed his expression, she quickly added, "It's not a big deal. Houses come and go."

"It is a big deal when a body is found in it and the mother and child have gone, or had you missed the news reports?" Declan swung the laptop his way and tapped into an internet search box. In moments, he'd pulled up an article.

She skimmed it, the basics of it being that a woman's body had been found in the home. When she read the neighbor's witness statement, she growled. "I did not tell her I'd kill her and bury her where no one could find her." But she'd thought it so perhaps it counted.

"Who was the woman they found?"

"How did you find this?" she asked.

"Why are you avoiding answering?"

Because how could she explain? "This isn't your business."

"You made it my business when you dropped Harper on my doorstep."

"I had no choice."

"Why not leave her with your mother?"

Another thing she couldn't truly answer. She opened her mouth to give an inane reply just as her phone buzzed.

You can trust them.

She frowned and typed back. ***Trust who?***

The reply was just as confusing. ***We've formed a temporary alliance with BBI.***

"Your mother sent me the link."

Edith froze mid-reply. "Excuse me?"

"Your mother. Harry gave her my number. Seems they know each other."

"My mother?" Code name for her handler.

"Forget about your mom for a second. I still want to know why they found a body in your old house." Declan drummed on the table with his fingers.

"I didn't kill her. Someone sent a fake nanny to kidnap the baby. She failed."

Declan's fingers froze. "Why is someone trying to kidnap Harper?"

"I told you, her father wasn't a nice guy."

"Why wouldn't he take you to court then? Who the he —heck kidnaps their own kid?"

"He does."

"Were those his goons trying to grab her outside my place?"

She shrugged. "Could be. But I don't know how. No one knew I was staying there."

"Your mother does."

"She wouldn't betray me." Of that, she was certain. However, there was no doubt they'd been very specifically looking to nab Harper. She eyed Declan. "Could it be one of your enemies?"

"Possibly." He rubbed his chin. "Someone might have thought they could use my daughter to blackmail me."

"You associate with people who would do that?" She couldn't help sounding shocked. Guns, secret identity, and now criminal elements? She really knew nothing at all about this man.

"What part of 'I'm a mercenary' did you not get? And don't act so high and mighty with me. You're not that innocent, Audrey Edith Marlowe. Because that's your real name, not Edith Jameson."

Audrey smirked. "And Marlowe's not my real one,

either." Only Audrey was original to her previous life. Soon, she'd dump it for a new incarnation. One that probably wouldn't let her keep the names she'd been born with. She'd hoped she could keep using her grandmother's maiden name and a new date of birth as her cover, but... staying hidden was more important.

"You've been a few people, apparently." He held up his phone and began reading. "Previous to that, you were Audrey Janet Edison. But that one didn't last long."

The gig in New York to take down a drug runner got too hot, too quick. Mother moved her before Audrey got swept up in a massive sting.

"Before that, though, you were in witness protection."

She froze. "You're mistaken." He couldn't know about that.

He ignored her and kept reading. "You were sent there when you blew your mission working undercover for the FBI."

Her mouth went dry. "Who told you that?" Those files were supposed to be buried. Was this what Mother meant when she had said Audrey could trust him? Had she spilled all her secrets?

"I have my sources. And some pictures don't lie." He flashed an image of Audrey at her Quantico graduation. "You were FBI."

The *were* aspect still stung. She'd been so proud of what she'd accomplished. As a child in foster care, she'd been neglected, beaten, and ignored. But most of all, people always assumed she'd never amount to much because of her dead, druggie parents. She'd proven everyone wrong, graduating in the top ten of her class and working her ass off to get into Quantico. She was a good agent. A great one. Until that case. A case that would forever haunt her.

Anger caused her to blow up. "Did your sources tell you that I blew my mission because I screwed my target? That, as a result of my actions"—which her superior encouraged so she'd get close to the target—"the entire operation was compromised, and he walked free while I got booted."

"I don't have all the details. Just the bare facts. They say all the evidence you gathered was thrown out because of your bias."

"My bias?" She snorted with disdain. "The facts don't mention that I was more or less ordered to sleep with the enemy." Not that she required much encouragement. He was everything a girl could want: handsome, self-assured, powerful, and strangest of all, attracted to her. As it turned out, he'd played her all along. "Do the facts mention that my boss intentionally threw me under the bus so that the case would get thrown out because he'd been bribed?"

Declan looked at her instead of his screen. "That's not in the file."

"Because no one knows. I found out about his involvement afterwards."

"What did you do?" he asked.

"What makes you think I did anything?"

His head tilted. "Because what your FBI boss did was a dick move. If it were me, I'd have taken revenge."

Her smile was colder than a shark before dinner. "He paid." The pictures of him snorting coke ensured he got tossed out of the FBI. The hooker that called to let him know she had syphilis ensured his wife left him. And all the cases he'd ever worked were being gone over with a fine-tooth comb as the bureau uncovered the depth of his corruption. Word had it, he now lived in a hostel, a broken shell of a man. He deserved every minute of disgrace.

"After the FBI relieved you of your position, you disappeared." It appeared that Declan had more questions.

Speaking so openly of her disgrace felt strange. She'd kept so much bottled up. Had to because she had other things to worry about. She peeked over at Harper, who happily gnawed on the plastic edge of the saucer. She'd been hiding for so long because of her daughter. Hiding who she was.

But Declan wanted the truth. Ugly as it was, it felt liberating to discuss how she'd been wronged. There was no point in hiding it; he already seemed to have the answers.

"I had to disappear because, despite the fact that the case was tossed, my safety became an issue." She knew things. Things that could still take Mendez down.

"Where did you go?"

"I went south at first. Worked as a security guard for a business." Which was a slap in the face to someone who'd once worked for the prestigious FBI. The bills didn't care she'd lost her dream job. They needed paying.

"But?" he prodded.

"Someone tried to kill me. Twice." Which was when a different FBI agent took an interest in her and her story. Agent Piper was the one who began unraveling the corruption that Audrey was caught up in. In exchange for protection, Piper wanted Audrey to testify. "For a while, I was in witness protection, which they really should rename witness targeting." It took a few months but, eventually, someone took a bribe, and Audrey's location was divulged.

"He found you," Declan stated.

"His goons did. I barely escaped." She still remembered that terrifying flight from the hospital and the men who had attacked her there. Men who thought nothing of going after a pregnant woman.

"Why are you still hiding? According to the files I have, Jose Mendez disappeared at sea almost a year ago. Went sailing one day and while his boat was found, he was not."

"I doubt he's dead," she said with a snort. "More like he reinvented himself." He was good at that. Good at hiding what he was. He'd fooled her completely. Made her believe in his innocence.

"Let's say he is alive, do you think he's still looking for you?"

"Without a doubt. Don't tell me you haven't figured it out yet." She glanced at Harper and Declan let out a noise.

"Fuck me, she's his daughter."

"She is, although he didn't know about the pregnancy until his goons came after me in the hospital."

"You escaped."

"Yes, and no." Dead bodies had a tendency to draw attention. But no one knew what to do with the pregnant woman who was attacked. "After the hospital incident, I knew he wouldn't stop coming after me." He wanted the child she carried. *His* child. Audrey would only live until she gave birth. Her options boiled down to hide or die. "I was desperate by that point."

"Did you kill him? Were you on that boat?"

Laughter barked from her. "I wish. Then I'd know for sure he was feeding the fish. Alas, I wasn't even in the USA at that point because I'd been recruited."

"By who?"

"By the *Inuattik Anânak*." At his blank look she grinned. "It's Inuit for Killer Moms."

"What are they? Like some kind of gang?"

"More like an agency, an international one. Run by a woman for women. Mothers to be specific." Those with nowhere else to turn.

"You're a spy?" His turn to look shocked.

"A Canadian Spy."

At that, he burst out laughing. "Canada doesn't have spies."

"Not many, true, but I don't work for the government. Northern Manitoba is where I trained." One of many camps all over the world. "Given my safety issues, they smuggled me out of the country. Furnished me with a new identity." A new purpose, and more training. They taught her things Quantico would have been appalled at. Taught her how to retake control of her life.

"So they recruited you, and now you spy for them."

She shrugged. "Spy. Steal. Whatever they need."

"Kill?" he queried.

"Only if necessary. I'm not an assassin."

"Says the woman who took on that huge thug."

"I know how to defend myself."

"And rappel down buildings." He shook his head. "How did I ever really believe the nanny story?"

"You're gullible."

"Excuse me?"

She couldn't help a sly smile. "Well, you did believe that a baby left on your doorstep was yours."

"Which I'm still peeved about. That's a cruel thing to do to a man."

"I'm sorry."

She could see the words took him by surprise. Worse? It was true. She did feel bad because she could see he'd come to care for Harper. Why couldn't someone like Declan have been the real dad instead of Mendez?

"Enough about me. Your turn." She knew she should be taking this reprieve to peruse the laptop but given the strange turn of events and Mother's insistence that she cooperate with BBI—which had to stand for Bad Boy Inc.—she wanted to know more. Who was Declan Hood?

"What is there to tell? I already told you, I am a super mercenary for hire." He closed one eye, pretended to aim an imaginary gun and smiled.

"Who do you work for?"

"Bad Boy Inc. Like I said, the realty thing is a front, and a good one. It allows us to travel around the world on various jobs. We can even write them off on our taxes since we usually wheel and deal some property at the same time."

"You really sell property?"

"The big money is made with our shadow missions, but the real estate gig does pay some nice commissions."

"What kind of missions have you done?" Since working for KM, she'd mostly done espionage. People didn't pay attention to the vapid interior designer they let into their home and office.

"More like name a job I haven't done. I've been at this a long time."

"Have you killed?"

"Yes." Said without even batting an eye.

"When you found out I lied, why didn't you kill me?"

He leaned back in his chair and managed a shrug. "Can't question a dead person."

"What about once you get the answers you're looking for?"

"If you're hinting around to see if I'm planning to kill you then the answer is no. Got no reason to, and there's no profit in it."

"Do you only work for profit?"

"Is there any other reason?" He arched a brow. "Don't tell me you work for free."

"The group I belong to pays us, but the missions we are given aim to improve the world. We help rid it of the corrupt. Correct wrongs. Return that which was stolen to the rightful owner."

"Sounds to me like you're vigilantes."

Her lips pursed. "In a sense, I guess we are, except many of our missions are condoned and paid for by governments."

"And what is your current mission?"

She paused and glanced at her phone again. Mother said she could trust him. Said to work with him. Since when did KM partner with other agencies? Then again, she'd been with them only a year. It could be this type of thing happened all the time.

"I am supposed to locate, and if possible retrieve, a stolen piece of art."

"All this subterfuge over art?" Declan snorted.

"You laugh but, apparently, the piece in question has the potential to cause widespread issues given its contro-versial nature." Religious etchings—and their interpreta-tion—had been known to start wars.

"You think one of my clients has it."

"I believe," she corrected, "that one of your clients was last to see it. The artifact had a tracking device that we were able to follow until it was disabled."

"If you know where it is, then why not send the cops in after it?"

"Did you miss the part about it being controversial? The client doesn't wish for anyone to see it. Would in fact prefer if it was destroyed before it was made public."

"Seems kind of extreme."

"I'm sure you've had missions that you thought odd but accomplished anyhow."

"Yeah. I have. Which I guess is your way of telling me to shut up. So, let's get down to business. I'm guessing since you spilled your guts that your boss told you to cooperate with me."

"Mother said I could trust you."

"Mother is—"

"The name of my handler."

Declan snickered. "And what's your code name? Baby?"

"Actually, it's Frenemy Mom." She held her chin up high. "And I wouldn't laugh." She held up her phone to show the text she'd received about him, detailing the specialties he'd mentioned plus his code name. "Sagittarius. How original given your last name of Hood."

"I am pretty accurate with a bow, too."

"Which I'm sure comes in real handy." She rolled her eyes.

"I'll have you know shooting arrows takes skill."

"And it's so practical," she mocked. "Because no one remarks on a grown man walking around carrying a great big bow and a quiver of arrows. Do you wear green tights, too?"

Some men might have snapped at her mockery; he laughed. "Do I look like the altruistic type to you?"

"Don't try and pretend you're some badass killer now. I've seen you with Harper."

"She's a cute kid."

"The best." Speaking of whom, Harper rubbed her eyes. Naptime had arrived.

Before Audrey could grab her daughter, Declan had Harper on his shoulder. He bounced her as he walked; the man who'd treated the baby like a live grenade only days before now putting her to sleep like a pro.

The sight of them created warmth inside Audrey, and a longing. A longing for a life where she had a partner to be a father to her child, a husband to stand by her side, and a lover to hold her at night.

A lovely fantasy that would never be a reality. Given her lifestyle, what kind of man could she get involved with? She could never tell her secrets. And what if she had to flee in the middle of the night? What then?

I wouldn't have that problem with Declan. For one, he understood what it meant to live a double life. She wouldn't have to hide from him.

What am I thinking? She barely knew the guy, and what she thought she knew wasn't even the real him. The reality was even better.

Sexy.

Strong.

Capable.

Distracting.

She had a mission to do, and now she had the means to do it. Turning her back on the man who made her heart ache for something more, she peeked at the laptop. The entire screen was covered in folders, each one labeled with a last name and address. She knew the address, but the name took her by surprise. "Suarez?" The information trail she'd followed, sparse as it was, had the object being delivered to a Malcomson.

Declan, having laid the baby in the playpen he'd brought from his loft, moved closer. "What about Suarez? Is he the guy you're interested in?"

"Actually, I thought the fellow was named Malcomson, but this is the right address. Have you been inside his place?"

"I have."

"Can you get me in?"

"Not easily. But that might change."

"Why do you say that?"

"Because the condo we're in? It's in the same building."

She whirled in her seat to find him behind her, still standing, which put her face at the level of his groin.

The groin was covered, yet for some reason, it instantly brought to mind that morning. In bed. With him rubbing against her.

The more she stared without speaking, the more the fabric only inches from her face swelled.

"Um, Edith."

"Audrey."

"Audrey, we should probably be working on the case."

"We should," she agreed. Yet she didn't move. He did, dropping to his haunches, bringing his face in line with hers.

"It's probably not a good idea for us to get involved."

"You're right. It's not." She whirled. "As you've learned, I have a terrible track record when it comes to that."

"That's not what I meant."

She opened the file rather than look at him. "It's true. I let Mendez fool me into thinking the FBI had him pegged all wrong. I let him seduce me." The wine he'd plied her with had helped. "I let him feed me all kinds of false information that compromised the investigation. I won't let it happen again."

Declan slammed the lid to the laptop shut, almost catching her fingers. She shot him a glare.

"I think I gave the wrong impression. You're attractive."

A comment that warmed except it came with a huge "but" attached. "But we're co-workers, and fraternizing isn't allowed."

"It's not encouraged, perhaps, but given that my boss fell for his partner, Harry is lenient about it happening so long as both parties are mature about it."

"Afraid you can't handle sex in a mature manner?" She baited him. The sting of rejection choosing her words.

"It's not the sex that's the problem. It's the mushy shit after. You deserve something more than just a casual hook-up."

She blinked. "Are you saying I shouldn't get laid because I should wait for Mr. Right?"

"Exactly."

The fact that he didn't think he was Mr. Right wasn't what bothered her, it was how he ignored the fact that she had needs. Why shouldn't her needs be fulfilled? "You do realize that in this day and age, women are sexually liberated creatures fully capable of deciding who they'll sleep with and when. Not only that, if a woman, or I, choose to screw a guy, once, on a whim because it feels good, then I'm allowed. I don't need your permission."

"I never said you did."

"You just did."

"I only meant—"

"I know what you meant. You think if we have sex I'm going to turn into some clingy thing that you'll have to remove. For your information, I don't cling. And secondly, what makes you think I even want to sleep with you?" She did but that didn't mean she wouldn't make him squirm.

"Er, well—"

She stood from the chair so that she faced him. "If I wanted to have sex with you"—she grabbed the fabric of his shirt and yanked him close—"I would, and it wouldn't even be hard. All I'd have to do is kiss you." She brought her mouth close. "Kiss you like I did in bed this morning. And you'd *fuck* me." She used the dirty word on purpose, and he shivered.

His hand cupped her waist, his mouth moved in close, and he almost managed a kiss.

Almost.

She shoved him away. "Good thing I agree we shouldn't get involved, though. Now, if you don't mind, I've got some research to do."

CHAPTER SIXTEEN

Mind?

Why should Declan mind the fact that she'd roused his hopes, hardened his dick, then punctured any optimism he had?

And the worst part?

He'd done it to himself. Hearing her story, he'd felt himself softening towards her. This woman with the dual personality was both fighter and damsel in distress all rolled into one, which made her sexier than hell. Even when she spat the angry parts of her story, he'd seen the vulnerability. Wanted to hunt down the bastards who'd dared to harm her and do bad things to them.

When he told her she deserved better than a one-night stand, it wasn't because he wanted to protect her. If he were honest, he was more worried about himself.

He was supposed to work with her, and yet he couldn't stop thinking of that morning. How she'd felt under him. How her lips tasted.

He was the one obsessed. The one who didn't call his

boss when he found out the truth. The one who hid her away rather than turn her in.

Not that it mattered. Someone had ratted him out. Harry had called and rocked his world with the words, "*She's an operative for a rival agency*."

Which he'd scoffed at until Harry texted him over the file. A file he'd skimmed that made him see her in a new light.

Then came the words, "*I want you to help her*."

He knew Harry meant with her mission, yet his heart wanted to do so many other things. Give her a home once he found out hers was gone. Give her protection because someone wanted to do her harm. Give her his body because he was sure she'd make better use of it than science.

"If you're done mooning over the fact you'll never have me, get over here so I can ask you some questions about your client."

He frowned. "I was not *mooning*."

"Good. Because that would be pathetic."

Was she intentionally being a bitch? He eyed her doing her best to ignore him and almost smiled. Why yes, yes she was being intentionally disagreeable. And he could only think of one reason why.

He sat down at the table beside her, then scooched his chair closer. Close enough that his thigh rubbed hers. She never glanced at him, but she couldn't hide the hitch of her breath.

"What do you want to know about Suarez?" Declan asked.

"Everything. The file I received from my handler was thin."

"Thin because he didn't really exist other than on paper until about a year ago."

She frowned. "You noticed that, too. No images. No public appearances."

"He's got a meticulous paper trail, though. Name on business charters, bank accounts, homes, even records of the schools he attended."

"But the online yearbook has no image. Just a blank spot," she observed. "No known girlfriends or family either."

"Do you know what he looks like?" Declan asked.

"Do you?"

"He's my client. We've met in person. I even have an image. Want to see?"

She whirled in her seat. "Yes."

It took Declan only a moment to pull up his file of Suarez images. Not very many, but enough to give her an idea of his appearance—and see if she recognized him.

Flipping the phone around first, he showed her. "This is Suarez."

Leaning forward, she studied the image. Shook her head. He swiped to show her a different one, and she shook negatively again. "Never seen him."

"Were you conducting surveillance on him?"

"Not hardcore. Given I need to care for Harper, I've only been able to stake out his place sporadically. Which is probably a good thing. If I skulked around too much, I'd get noticed. Suarez chose a good location to hide."

Her observation coincided with his when he'd first seen the condominium, towering amidst a green oasis. On one side, a park with only a few straggling trees. The older versions had succumbed to some kind of beetle, which meant few places to hide on the east side. A financial insti-tution filled the building on the west side and, given the sums of money sometimes flowing through, had a crazy number of cameras watching outside for suspicious activity or loitering. Cameras, he might add, BBI had hacked into in the hopes of catching Suarez doing some-thing. The man moved like a ghost. Which was funny given that, in person, he was anything but silent.

The other side of the building was comprised of a six-lane road and a movie theatre that wasn't tall enough to properly allow a peek inside Suarez's condo or avoid being seen on the rooftop.

The fourth and final side consisted of a bike path meandering alongside a river. A condo this price needed a view, and a water one fetched a premium.

"The security on this place is tight," Declan admitted. "It's one of the reasons I chose to bring us here."

"It looks like someone lives here."

"Fully furnished rental. Very popular with the business guys who need a crash pad for a few weeks or months but prefer something outside a hotel."

"Won't your client be pissed that we're staying here."

"We've got permission. Your situation provided a great excuse." He didn't explain that he got permission after the fact. At the time, he just needed a secure location.

Her lips pursed. "An excuse to whom? Who did you tell about me?"

He could see the unspoken words, how badly am I compromised. "I might have mentioned your fake nanny status to a few people."

"What?" she yelled.

"Don't worry. They were people I could trust. As to

those I couldn't be sure of, I gave them a great story." He leaned back in the seat, and his grin turned lazy and a bit naughty. Because he knew she wouldn't like what he announced. "Told them my hot new nanny was having ex-boyfriend issues and since my daughter took so well to her, I offered my help."

Audrey blinked, her lashes long and dark, without any need for mascara. She possessed a natural beauty that didn't require any help.

"You, of course, realize everyone you've spoken to will think we're sleeping together."

"Yeah."

She slugged him. Unexpectedly—and quite hard, too—in the gut. She then leaned close and hissed, "Not funny, asshole. The last thing I want is for Mother to think I'm neglecting my mission for a man."

Declan crossed his arms and arched a brow. "Exactly why would anyone assume us having sex makes you incompetent? Or is this your way of saying you think it would be so good you'd be mentally out of it. Because if that's the case, then I am truly flattered."

Her mouth opened and closed a few times before she sputtered, "You're unbelievable."

"Yes."

"Conceited."

His smile stretched wider. "With good reason."

"We need to keep this professional."

"I am. You're the one who turned a perfectly good cover story into us having a tawdry affair. We are two agents, pros. Or at least, I am. Surely, the people you work with are smart enough to know you will do your job."

"Speaking of job"—she turned back to the laptop

—"let's talk about the Suarez condo. More specifically, the layout of his place. Possible entry points that aren't his front door. Air vents. Maintenance conduits. Something along those lines would be good. A request at City Hall only gave me the basics. I wanted the builder's blueprint, but they didn't have one."

He intentionally brushed his hand over hers as he moved the cursor on the screen. "No blueprints because the city apparently lost them, and the builder didn't keep his copies."

"Odd coincidence."

"We both know that was intentional." He pulled up the listing, a more in-depth one than was available publicly. A property of that type of wealth had no need to be displayed online. It would see the right type of clients by appointment only.

She scanned the information. "Technically, Suarez doesn't own it. Files show a company bought the place almost a decade ago. It's been mostly vacant. Yet now you have that Suarez fellow trying to sell it."

"He's acting on behalf of the company, of which he is a majority silent owner."

"Why is he selling? Seems like a good investment to keep."

"It is. All reports indicate he's flush with cash. He has no need to sell."

"Must be nice to have that kind of dough," she mumbled.

"Does your agency pay you well for jobs?"

She spared him a glance. "I'd do it for nothing to thank them for saving me. Without KM, I'd be working minimum wage, struggling to make ends meet. Or dead in a ditch."

The reference didn't sit well. "While guilty of many crimes, the notes I read said Mendez was never suspected of violence."

She sighed. "Those reports are a sham. He has a dark side."

"And you still slept with him?"

"I didn't know about the dark side until after. He can be very charming."

"Charming?" He gaped at Audrey. "You were undercover, investigating him for embezzlement and fraud."

"White-collar stuff. And he was suspected. Not convicted at the time. Ever heard of presumed innocent? He had me fooled. You don't understand. He was a nice guy. Always pulled out my chair. Complimented me. Used to kiss my hand to say hello."

For some reason, the wry fondness ignited a burst of irritation. How could she have fallen for such smarmy tactics? "You got played."

Her lips twisted. "I know. Trust me, I know. Played by the best, which is why I felt triply stupid afterwards. I should have seen it coming a mile away. But at least one good thing came out of it." She cast a fond smile over at Harper, who awake from her nap, now played in her saucer. She used her feet to twirl the seat, her head back, grinning.

"Do you miss him?" He couldn't have said why he asked. Morbid curiosity. Why should he care if she mooned after another man?

"Miss being with someone who made me feel like the most important thing in the world?"

"So that's a yes, then." For some reason, that only irritated him more.

"Not him. I don't miss that two-faced bastard. He ruined my career. Then tried to harm me and the baby."

His brow tugged into a furrow. "Now I'm confused. You made it sound like you missed being with the guy."

"I don't miss him. What I meant was I miss being with someone. Not being alone. It's nice to feel as if you're part of a team."

"Don't you get that with your agency?" he asked.

She shook her head. "We don't work together often. We are more like sleeper agents. Called when something is happening that is close enough where we can slide in for a peek without drawing notice."

"Not a full-time gig then. What's your cover when you're not spying on rich dudes?"

"Interior design."

"Paint chips and hardwood floors?" he snickered.

"Don't laugh. It's good money. Better than I made when I was an official agent." She sounded defensive.

He hastened to calm her. "Don't get all pissy. I just think it's interesting the way we've got these cover jobs that no one would suspect."

"Yours does sound kind of cooler," she admitted. "Mine doesn't let me travel around the world. Not that I really could with Harper."

Hearing her name, the baby exclaimed, "Hap." And clapped her hands.

"Single mom traveling the world wouldn't fly, but a family could."

"You can't take a child on a mission."

"Not on the dangerous parts, but imagine the education they'd get from the immersion in other cultures."

"Until the parents got killed or arrested on foreign soil and she ended up in some horrible orphanage, abused and alone until some slavers bought her and auctioned her off to a child abuser." Audrey finished her tirade, chest heaving.

He stared at her before saying, "You've put way more thought into this than you should. And using the most extreme examples."

"It could happen."

"So can the flu. And car accidents. Given your thoughts on children on missions, how the hell did you ever convince yourself to let me have her?"

"Because you seemed like a decent sort."

"Then you didn't do a very good background check, or you would have seen I was arrested and charged with assault."

"I read the police report. You were protecting a woman who was attacked. The charge was bogus."

"That's what my lawyer argued." Whereas, the guy who'd actually started it all by dragging Celine into an alley had sued Declan because, as he argued in court, Declan had hurt him worse than he hurt the woman. "By that you assumed, what? That I was some kind of good guy?" He smiled. "Boy, were you wrong."

At that, she snorted. "Being a mercenary doesn't make you bad. Otherwise, I'd be screwed. You have a moral compass. That's the best thing you can ask for."

"So you left Harper with me, assuming I wouldn't completely fuck it up."

"Oh, I figured you'd fuck up most of it, which was why you hired me."

"You're sly, Ree."

"Ree?" she queried.

"I can't call you Edith anymore. That was my fake nanny. Audrey is your formal name. If we're going to be partners on this, then I need something short and quick. Since Aud, sounds odd, I think Ree is a nice choice."

"We're not friends."

"Never said we were. We're partners. For this mission," he quickly added. "Nothing more."

"Whatever you say, Zee."

Declan had to ask. "What's that supposed to be short for?"

Her smile was wide and mischievous, and the expression in her eyes was full of mirth. "Crazy."

The laughter startled Harper, and he was first to rise and grab the baby, snuggling her close, bouncing her until she calmed and tugged at his beard.

Looking back at Audrey, he found her staring at him, winsome longing in her regard. She turned away, but it remained burned in his mind. This time, he realized it for what it was. Not her missing Harper's father, but rather having a partner to help raise the child.

A sweet child, and an even sweeter mother.

The emotions he was starting to feel for Audrey seemed much too quick. Shouldn't it happen over time?

Or was this a case of The One? Harry had once spoken of it. Claimed that when he saw Sherry hiking up her skirt and climbing over a wall to join an embassy party in the Middle East, he'd fallen in love. They married quickly, barely knowing each other. Yet their affection for each other stood the test of time.

Could it happen to Declan?

Whoa. Stop with the crazy shit. She was right to call him Zee. Where the heck were these thoughts coming from? Declan was a single guy. Happy with the bachelor life. He wasn't looking to settle down with a chick, even a hot one, and become a dad to a ridiculously cute kid.

"Here." He thrust Harper at Audrey.

She snuggled the baby on her lap and continued to browse his file. She brought things back to business, which was just fine by him. They spent the next two hours discussing what they knew and studying what they had. She was frustrated by the lack of options to get into the apartment.

"Unless you can somehow pass yourself off as a potential buyer of his place, with the money to prove it, you can't make an appointment to see the inside."

"Why not? You're the realtor. Tell him I'm rich."

"First off, I'm the realtor of a super controlling client. He calls the shots, not me. Visitors must run through him first."

"He's checking out potential buyers? Why?" she asked.

"Paranoia."

"Because he's hiding something."

"Or he's just paranoid. Whatever the case, I can't just invite you in to take a gander at his place. If it were that easy, I'd have already detected it."

"How on earth are you supposed to sell that condo if you can't show it?"

"Luck?" He chuckled. "And it's actually easier than you'd expect. When people are at certain levels of wealth and power, they don't always have to see what they're buying. Sometimes, it's a matter of location or prestige. They also have the sense to know that if they don't like something about a place, they can pay to change it."

"Rather than explain to me how the rich suck, why don't you give me ideas on how to get inside?" Her tone was snarky with the implied words of: *because you won't.*

"The only thing that comes to mind is the upcoming open house."

"That's perfect." Her expression brightened as she straightened, her hand tucked around Harper, holding the snoozing baby in place.

"Not really. The open house is by invitation only."

"Then it's not an open house."

"No, but it is the one time I know when the security will be laxer. Maybe we can use that."

"Except if we're both there, then who watches Harper?"

"I'll bring her with me. Claim my nanny had a day off."

"You can't bring the baby."

"Why not? Suarez is a white-collar shithead. Nothing will happen to her. Or do you want to miss this opportunity?" Declan dangled temptation in front of her.

She nibbled. "You're not even sure you can get me in."

"Is that a challenge?" Declan quirked a brow.

"Yes."

"Let's say I do manage to sneak you in, what do I get?"

"Get?" she repeated. "I thought we were helping each other. I am not bargaining sexual favors for it."

"Never asked for any. But given you challenged, it seems only fair I receive a boon. I want you to make me cookies."

"You're kidding, right?"

"Nope. I get you into that condo, and you bake me cookies. Chocolate chip and nothing from a can or plastic package. I want them made from scratch."

"Cookies?" She sounded rather incredulous.

"Yup. I wanna smell them as they bake, and eat them warm from the oven."

She laughed, her body shaking, causing the baby to stir and grumble in her sleep. She settled down as Audrey held her breath. But her eyes still held a twinkle. "Okay, you're on. You get me in, and I'll make you cookies, but if you can't, I want you to make me bread. From scratch. And it better be fluffy."

"Bread is impossible to make."

"Not impossible, just hard. Which my job will be if you don't get me in."

"I'll get you in," he muttered.

And she'd be making him cookies.

CHAPTER SEVENTEEN

GUESS I'M MAKING COOKIES.

She had no doubt Declan would get her in. She'd just pricked his male ego. He'd go to any lengths to win.

A phone beeped. His. Rising from the chair, she stared at his butt. She really had to stop noticing how fine it was.

It didn't help that she now knew that fine ass belonged to a mercenary. A man who could take care of himself. A man who understood what she did.

A man who looked way too gorgeous when he held a baby in his arms.

Her poor panties needed changing.

The playpen creaked a bit as she laid Harper inside while Declan grabbed his phone. He didn't talk long before hanging up and returning to her side.

He chuckled, a low, rumbly sound. "Speak of the devil. Guess who wants a meeting?"

"Is that unusual?" she asked, rising and facing him.

"Not really. Suarez meets with little notice and at places of his choice. Says it's to keep people on their toes."

Reminded her of Mendez, except his reasoning was that it made it harder for people to track him down. "When and where does he want to meet you?" Could she use his absence from the condo to infiltrate it? With Declan entertaining him, she'd have ample notice to get out.

What about Harper?

They couldn't leave her alone.

"I can see the devious cogs of your mind churning, Ree. Might as well stop right now. I'm meeting Suarez at his place."

"That blows."

"Not really. I am going to bring my camera to do some interior pics. Maybe you'll see what you're looking for."

"I doubt he's got it perched out in the open."

"Never know. Guys like him are arrogant and convinced they can't be touched."

"I know the type." She made a face. "When are you meeting him?"

"Soon." He rubbed his face. "Guess I'd better hit the shower."

"That quick?"

"When the client says jump, you jump."

"When will you be back?"

The wide shoulders rolled. "No idea. So stay put and get comfortable. Maybe check out the apartment a bit. It might give you ideas for Suarez's place since they share the same designer."

She'd momentarily forgotten that they were in the same building. She didn't know if she should kiss him for making her job easier, or slug him again for having put Harper within reach of a possible criminal.

But was anywhere truly safe? Look what had happened at her own house. Her castle had been invaded. The princess almost snatched. Perhaps Declan had a point about taking the baby with her.

What am I thinking? I can't bring Harper.

Someone had to watch the baby while Mommy played spy. She slid her gaze to the closed door of the bedroom.

He'd actually gone to shower. Left her alone.

She could walk out that door with Harper. Ditch him.

Which would accomplish what, exactly?

Mother had told her to work with him. He was cooperating just fine if she ignored the part where he rendered her unconscious and brought her here. In his defense, he'd just found out that she wasn't whom he thought.

The man was willing to help her get into Suarez's condo. So why even contemplate leaving?

She knew why.

Because he makes me tingle.

Bad news.

The last time that happened, she got involved with the wrong man and paid for it.

I didn't know who Mendez really was.

She got the impression that Declan lived more openly. Thus far, his actions appeared exemplary. Especially considering the extenuating circumstances. He'd stepped up with Harper and continued to step up even after finding out the truth.

But did that mean she could trust him?

She made an irritated noise as she realized she no longer trusted herself to make simple evaluations. Her past now shaded how she dealt with the present. Second-guessing herself and the people she dealt with. Looking for ulterior motives. Except she couldn't see one for Declan. Helping her didn't really give him anything. The cooperation between their agencies was a courtesy thing. Mother would probably throw a little thank you their way if BBI actually helped. If not, so long as no one got in her way, they'd part amicably.

He gained nothing by aiding her.

Before she knew what she was doing, she'd made it to the bedroom door. The knob turned, and she entered the room, leaving it open only a crack behind her. He'd left the bathroom door ajar, and steam wafted as he bathed, the heated moisture landing on her exposed skin. She blamed it for the flush when she entered the bathroom itself.

She was just in time to see him step out of the shower, nude and glistening. She'd seen his upper body before but, this time, it hit her hard. Just how strong he truly was. Sexy. Tough.

The healed wounds struck her anew. She saw them for what they were. Battle scars.

He snared a towel and wrapped it around his waist. Unlike many men who probably would have said something crude or flirtatious at being interrupted while bathing, he said nothing. Just tucked the ends of the fabric around his hips.

Audrey wet her lips. "Why are you helping me?"

"Why wouldn't I?"

"What do you get out of it?"

"Cookies."

She waved a hand. "Please. We both know that's a silly reason. You're putting your reputation on the line. If your client finds out you let someone into his place to spy..."

"He'll fire me."

"Which is bad." Being in the housing industry, she knew how little it took to sink.

"For him, you mean. The rumors I'll spread about his prima donna ass will have me looking the victim and him the impossible-to-please client."

The reply had her blinking. "Retaliation by rumor?" She laughed. "That is devious and less violent than expected."

"Can't exactly go around killing or beating up clients that annoy me. I do live here, you know."

"Touché." The wry laughter surprised her, and as she relaxed, he moved closer. Close enough for her to reach out and touch beads of moisture pearling on his skin.

Hold on a second. She was touching!

She moved closer as he froze. Her palm flattened on his chest, feeling the rapid thump of his heart. She glanced into his eyes, saw a wariness in them. "Thank you."

"For what?"

"Everything so far." Because if she looked at things from the outside, this man truly had gone above and beyond.

"You don't have to do this."

"Afraid you'll lose the cookies?" She leaned up. "Don't. I'll still make them. This is something else." This was about her wanting to feel something other than worry. To feel as if she were real. Desirable...

One thing no one ever warned about after becoming a mother was the doubt that would assail her about her desirability as a woman.

Her body had changed. She'd changed.

Her hand curled around his neck to draw him in for a kiss. He didn't resist, his lips slanting over hers in a soft and slow exploration. Her body trembled. Desire coursed through her veins, engorging her nipples, moistening her cleft.

The tingles he could invoke multiplied. Brought along friends. And shivers.

His arm curled around her, dragging her against the dampness of his skin, leaving no doubt as to his own arousal as the hardness of him pressed against her lower belly.

He lifted her, placing her ass on the vanity. Her legs slipped around his waist. Her fingers tunneled through his hair.

In between harsh kisses, he managed to pant, "What happened to—"

"Shut up." She kissed him some more. Forget what she'd said before. She needed him.

He held her tightly to him, her legs wrapped around his waist, putting delightful pressure on her cleft. She rocked against him as they kissed, the layer of fabric separating their bodies an aphrodisiac.

He bit her lower lip, worrying the flesh, drawing sharp gasps. He let his mouth trail to her jawline. Then her neck.

The T-shirt she wore didn't stop him in the least. His mouth latched on to her breast, the lack of bra something she only noticed now. He took advantage, giving a wet suck of her nipple through the thin fabric. Her sex clenched.

The track pants she wore weren't her own, fabric on them loose, and his hand easily slid inside. Delved and then worked against her flesh, his finger stroking and rubbing her through the wet fabric of her panties. Driving her desire.

The moans erupted in jagged pants.

Her pleasure peaked as a mini orgasm took her.

The cold granite surface of the counter shocked the heated flesh of her ass. A small discomfort that barely put a dent in her lust.

She froze.

Lust. Out of control desire. The last time that happened...

She pushed away from Declan and hopped off the counter, struggling to straighten her clothes at the same time. She didn't look at him as she exited, saying, "I think I hear Harper. You should get ready for your meeting." She needed to leave before she finished what her aching body wanted.

Didn't I learn my lesson?

No, she hadn't. Because all she could think of was marching back in, tossing him on that bed, and having her wicked way with him.

Sex would be the ruin of her.

The lack of might also kill her.

She sat on the couch, knees tucked to her chest, hoping he'd come out and demand they finish. Ignored her disappointment when he didn't.

When he did finally exit, looking dashing in a suit, she sat on her hands lest she be tempted to strip him out of it. But she could have sworn he read her mind.

The wink he sent her with a mouthed, "*Later*," showed she'd not yet learned her lesson about business and sex. Because all she could think about was how long before she could peel that suit off him.

CHAPTER EIGHTEEN

IT USED TO BE THAT DECLAN THOUGHT HE UNDERSTOOD women. He knew what they liked. What they expected. How to treat them. Most of all, he knew how to get them into bed.

Which wasn't as crude as it sounded. Many men wanted to have sex with no attachments.

It was a worthy goal.

For a man.

But it came with only a few rules to ensure it worked.

Don't call her the next day. No man should ever appear too smitten.

Don't sleep over. Bed sharing involved cuddling. Cuddling led to expectations.

Most of all, don't ever, *ever* do it with someone you work with or who works for you.

Then he'd met Edith, slash Audrey, slash Ree. The spy.

As his nanny, he'd wanted to throttle her almost as much as he wanted to kiss her.

As Audrey, the Killer Mom agent, he wanted to clap at her performance...and kiss her.

As Ree, the woman who made him yearn, turned his dick rock-hard, and made him want something other than a bachelor life, he wanted to do more than just kiss her. He wanted to cuddle after.

If there ever was an after. They'd been going hot and heavy when she decided to break things off. Left him with an epic boner.

He managed to stuff it into his pants and dress, all the while hoping she'd come back to finish what she started.

She didn't.

She'd barely glanced at him from her spot on the couch when he exited the room. She'd curled up on the cushions, legs tucked under her, laptop nestled atop her thighs.

"I'm off to my meeting."

"Yup." Her only reply as he walked out the door.

No begging him to stay. No flirty eyes inviting him to do something else.

Not even a twitch as he shut the door. He ensured that it locked behind him before heading to the elevator. Despite being in the same building as his client, he had to go down to go up, which meant time to think about stuff.

Since he couldn't think about Ree without getting a hard-on, he concentrated on the fact that Harper hadn't sprung from his loins.

Which bummed him. Kid was cute.

Like her mom. A special-ops mommy, now hotter in his eyes than ever.

The pile of lies she'd pitched at him should have made him hate her. What kind of woman let a man get his hopes up about being a father? The same kind of woman who could throw a punch, use a gun, and break into his office.

So fuckin' sexy. He also had respect for a woman who devised a plan and saw it through. She'd created a devious scenario to get close to Declan and, in turn, Suarez. The fact that she didn't know he was a mercenary too was kind of funny.

Entering the elevator, he clicked the button for the lobby and noted the cameras watching. They'd be keeping an electronic eye on him the entire time he moved through the building. What were the chances that Suarez wouldn't know Declan came from within the building? Not that it mattered. Declan's cover story was a good one.

At the lobby level, he switched to the other elevator, having to press a button that scanned his features before permitting him entrance. Suarez controlled who visited.

Since there were no stops, the elevator zipped, his stomach getting that funny feeling as his body moved too fast. The doors swished open onto the penthouse foyer. Only one door to enter, and it was flanked by a pair of big dudes in suits wearing thick, dark glasses—that he'd wager had all kinds of electronics running through them that checked for possible weapons. The guards had their hands on the butts of their guns.

The one lacking any hair atop his crown greeted Declan. More like caveman grunts.

"Arms out." While Caveman One faced him with a stony expression, Caveman Two ran a wand over his body, checking for explosives, wires, anything that might cause their boss distress. A waste of time since he never arrived armed. Stupid, too, given that his best weapons were his mind and his fists.

The electronic frisk was only part of the check. Hands followed, patting him all over, touching him in places that he'd be embarrassed to show on a doll. Declan knew better than to bring anything out of the ordinary to this meeting.

He had to wonder what would happen if he did wear a piece. He also didn't feel a real need to find out.

Their check complete, Caveman One opened the door, and Declan entered, slipping off his shoes before daring to set foot on the thick, white wool carpet. No wood floors here. Everything in this condo was about plush comfort, from the covering underfoot meant to cushion, to the overstuffed sofas set in a semi-circle facing the panoramic view of the city.

Suarez stood by the fireplace, a glass of white wine in hand. His dark suit a contrast to the snowy interior.

"I expected you sooner given your new accommodations." The sharp rebuke put an end to the wondering if his client knew.

"Sorry. I didn't think you'd appreciate it if I showed up still wearing my workout clothes and sweat."

"Exercise." The man grimaced. "Who has time for that? You should invest in muscle stimulus therapy. It allows you to tone your physique while you sleep."

The newest and laziest way for the rich to remain trim. Declan would stick to the old-fashioned kind of exertion. "I'll have to look into that, sir."

"I'm sure you will, but I didn't call you here to speak about your inefficient use of time."

"What did you need?" Declan knew better than to tell this man he could have made his request by text or over the phone. When some people reached a certain level of wealth, they expected in-person service. The last time

Declan had come to the condo, it was so the client could revise the menu for the open house. As if whether they had Atlantic salmon or Pacific for the sushi really mattered.

"Booties."

Declan blinked. "I'm sorry, sir?"

"We need booties. To keep the carpet pristine."

"Don't worry. Any potential clients will be told to remove their outer footwear."

Suarez slashed his hand. His tanned fingers bare but for one ring, the stone of it a deep gray. "Not good enough. What if they are barefoot? Or their socks retain a stench? I want everyone wearing booties."

Utterly ridiculous request. Arguing wouldn't accomplish shit. Declan nodded. "Of course, sir. I'll order a box today."

"Excellent. I am not in the mood to renovate."

Renovate over a possible carpet stain? Declan clamped his lips.

"The wine, as discussed, will be white. The food to be eaten in the tiled kitchen area only."

"We'll ensure people respect your home." By *we*, Declan meant some of his buds from BBI who would be moving around the place under the guise of showing it to their rich clients. Meanwhile, they'd hopefully catch something he'd missed.

The evidence of wrongdoing Declan was looking for had to be here somewhere. It was the only place Suarez spent any amount of time.

"Speaking of respect, I hear you suddenly inherited a baby?"

Declan knew better than to ask how Suarez had

acquired the information. The man had his sources. "You heard correctly. My daughter kind of appeared out of the blue." And wasn't his. But no point in telling Suarez that right now.

"What's her name?"

"Harper."

The expression on his client's face was one of polite disinterest. "How unique. I also have a daughter." Suarez tipped his wineglass—the fluid in it clear as water—and finished it.

"I didn't know you had kids." His thin file didn't show him having been married either.

Suarez set the glass down. "She's my only child and is kept well-guarded. But you'll be meeting her soon."

Not if Suarez was in jail. Which would hopefully happen after the deal for the condo. He'd hate to lose out on the commission.

"About that open house, sir. You sure you want to hold it at night? The windows and natural light you get in this place in the daytime will be a huge seller." Night also made the streets less likely to have wandering people who could swoop in to help.

Suarez shook his head. "Ah, but the view after dark is unlike any other in the city. As someone who enjoys it nightly, I can assure you, it is a major selling point."

"Speaking of selling, I really should have some images of the place. To dangle in front of those a little reluctant to displace themselves who might be a good fit."

"No." Not even a hesitation.

"If you want me to sell this place, then I need to be able to give people who contact me about the listing something."

"You are capable of describing it, I'm sure, and if they are interested, they will see it in person. No images."

"If you insist." Although the strange persistence lent credence to the idea that Suarez hid something.

"I have another meeting in a few minutes. Leave." Suarez didn't see him to the door, simply dismissed him with a wave of his hand, expecting Declan to see himself out.

Only, this time, Suarez surprised him by ghosting behind him as he put on his shoes. "One more thing, Hood."

Declan froze and pivoted. "Sir?" He saw Suarez, his face in shadows, watching him, his expression not revealing anything.

But for the first time since meeting the man, Declan finally got a sense of menace.

"Bring your daughter to the open house. I'd like to meet her."

"I thought we discussed you staying away."

"This is my home." The words were low.

"It is, but having the owner around makes people nervous."

"If you say so." Suarez didn't sound convinced. "Bring the baby anyway. If you like. Let her see what her father does for a living."

"Probably not a good idea. I'll probably be too busy to handle Harper."

"Who's watching her right now?"

"The nanny."

"Excellent. Have her bring the baby."

Saying no again wouldn't achieve anything, so Declan nodded. An open house with at least a half-dozen BBI mercenaries in attendance would probably be one of the safest places for Harper.

You know what this means, right?

He entered the condo he'd borrowed with a huge grin, almost able to smell the cookies, only to exclaim, "Don't fucking shoot."

CHAPTER NINETEEN

AUDREY LOWERED THE GUN WHEN SHE REALIZED WHO was at the door. "Ever think of knocking?"

He shut the door behind him before snapping, "No, and before you say anything, don't you think it would look kind of weird to anyone watching if I knocked instead of using my key?"

"You think they're watching?"

"I'd count on it. Suarez is one paranoid bastard. He already knew I was living in the building."

"That's creepy."

"You haven't even heard the half of it. Did you know he wants everyone to wear sterile booties for the open house?"

"Sounds like he's a neat freak."

"He's a freak all right. He's worried about people leaving toe jam on his precious carpet, and yet he's ordered my daughter to come to the party."

"You can't bring a baby to a business function."

"Exactly what I said. To which he replied that I should bring the nanny, too."

Her expression turned thoughtful. "You know, that might actually work. While you're keeping the guy occupied, I can slip away using the baby as an excuse and spend some time looking."

"Have you forgotten the cameras?"

A snort escaped her. "Please. If your agency is as prestigious as you claim, then you'll have the tools to disrupt them."

"That's the plan, but he'll also probably have guards around."

"I guarantee they won't want to follow a woman changing a poopy diaper."

His nose wrinkled. "No one wants to be near one of those."

"Good job on finding me a way in."

"You're welcome. And you know what that means." He rubbed his hands together. "Get the oven heating, Ree, because you owe me some cookies."

The man oozed cockiness and really deserved a slap. Instead, she pointed out the obvious. "You haven't gotten me inside yet. There are two more days until the open house."

"And?"

She wagged a finger at him. "Until I actually set foot inside, I am not making you anything."

"After I busted my balls to get you an invite?"

"I highly doubt you worked that hard." She snorted as she sat back down on the couch, having popped to her feet, gun in hand the moment she heard someone at the door.

"A deal's a deal, even if the result fell into my lap. I'll admit, I wasn't expecting the invite. Just goes to show you how weird Suarez is."

"Weird how?" Because there was one thing she'd learned since she began doing covert surveillance, people did lots of weird shit—from dressing up in giant teddy bear costumes, to smearing themselves in butter.

"It's a few little things. The way he won't have any mirrors in his place. Even had the ones in the bathroom removed. The hardcore screening to get in his presence. The guy is more protected than the President, I swear. Then there's his paranoia about getting shit on his damned carpet, and yet he insists I bring a baby—which are notorious for stains—to his exclusive open house party."

"Guess he likes babies more than people," she replied with a shrug. "You said exclusive. Does that mean I need to dress up?"

"Probably. You'll have to doll up diva, too."

"I don't know why you insist on calling her—"

"Waaaa."

From zero to full-blown pay-me-attention, Harper awoke and wasn't shy about letting them know.

Declan wiggled a finger in his ear as the baby continued to yodel. The princess was awake. "You were saying? Coming, little diva."

He popped his hands into the playpen, casual as you please, and plucked out Harper. The baby gurgled at seeing him, her hands reaching for his beard. Amazing how quickly a little person could get attached.

Big person, too. Only a few days, and already she found herself fond of Declan. Eager to spend time with him. The entire time he'd been gone, she'd listened for his return.

Wondered how his meeting went. Even worried a bit about his safety. No matter what Declan thought, Suarez was a criminal, and even white-collar ones could turn rabid if cornered.

With the baby handled, she returned to the open house and her attendance. "Friday's still a long way off," Audrey murmured. "Almost two days, and too much time. I don't know if I should wait that long to get in."

"You might not have a choice. The place is locked down tight."

"Says you. I say you just haven't found the opening yet. Do you have any more pictures of the interior?" She pointed to the laptop. "I only found a few. Several of them blurry."

"Because I was using a contact lens camera." He pointed at his iris. "Needs heavy lube to be wearable and unnoticeable.

"Eye cam?" She shuddered. "I tried wearing one of those lenses. They're uncomfortable."

"It gets easier with practice. And lube. Lots of greasy lube, which affects the clarity of the images."

"Why not use your cell phone instead?"

He adopted an incredulous expression. "You did hear me when I mentioned Suarez's paranoia, right? You really think he's letting me take pictures of his place? Phone is allowed inside, but it can't come out of the pocket. As for other electronic gadgets, his goons scan me each time I go inside. The eye lens passes because of the gel deflecting the scanner."

"I assume they do full pat downs, as well."

"Pat down, lift the coat, I've had my balls fondled a few times, too. You can't bring a weapon in."

"The open house will be busier and full of people just as rich and paranoid about security as him. No way are the guards going to be frisking as hard." The time frame to go in sucked, but it was looking like the most viable option. But that didn't mean it would be easy.

She really should have a plan about which rooms she thought most likely hid the art. Given its size, it would need a bit of space if displayed. If hidden, there were only a few places that would actually be feasible.

If the vase were still in the condo. There existed the possibility it didn't. Perhaps the tracker had been removed, and the treasure relocated.

Personally, Audrey thought the object remained in the condo. If Suarez truly were that private and arrogant, he'd be the type to want to see his prize. Gloat or jerk off to it. Another thing she'd seen all too often during her surveillance years with the FBI.

She skimmed through the blurry images. "I can't see enough to really get any context."

"These are stills of some of the clearer shots. If you want a sense of space and layout, I've got a sketch I did. Plus, we can put the footage into a video mode. It's a little dizzying, though."

He slid onto the couch beside her, easily slipping Harper from his chest to his lap. It appeared utterly natural. Harper even leaned her head against his chest. One perfect moment that lasted seconds. Because little girls liked to move around. Harper wiggled and twisted to get down onto the floor. Baby wanted to explore.

Audrey hopped to her feet and moved quickly, shutting all the doors, putting a chair across the access to the kitchen with its cupboards. By the time she was done doing a quick baby-proof, she'd managed to restrict Harper to the large open living space.

Upon returning, she eyed the club chair across from the couch where Declan sat. He took up a good chunk of the loveseat. Sitting beside him would put her awfully close.

He'd snared the laptop, and looked up from the screen at her, noticing her hesitation. "You going to sit back down? Here's a general map of the floorplan. It will give you an idea of what to expect Friday."

When she moved towards the chair, he snorted. "Kind of hard to see from over there."

Super valid point, except he forgot the part where sitting beside him might entice her into doing things she shouldn't. She couldn't stop thinking about the kiss they'd shared. The explosive attraction between them.

Remember what happened last time.

However, that was becoming harder and harder to use as an excuse because more and more this situation was nothing like it. Declan appeared to be open and honest. He'd not actually done anything to get her into bed. She was the one with the issue.

Or was that part of his devious plan? Drive her insane with desire until she mauled him.

Yes, mauled, because she wasn't feeling totally in control.

Ugh.

Get a grip, Audrey. He's a guy. Not a god. It's sex, not the end of the world. And not the fucking time to be worrying about it. Concentrate on the job.

Think of Harper. The baby was crawling around their feet. A witness if Audrey misbehaved. Good mommies didn't make out like felines in heat with their babies around.

Audrey perched herself on the couch, pressed against the armrest farther from him, feet on the floor, knees pressed together.

"You okay?" he asked.

Not really. Her prim pose proved uncomfortable. How dare he notice? "I'm fine," she snapped, drawing her legs back under her bum. She had to stop acting like a teenage girl crushing on a cute boy. As a grown woman, she could handle her hormones.

Declan began pointing out details in the fuzzy video, and she found herself paying more attention to him. The scent of him, soap and cologne, a musky mix that she enjoyed. She eyed his jawline, covered in a soft burr of hair, giving him a rugged appearance despite the white collar of his shirt and loose tie.

His lips moved as he spoke. She stared at them, recalling how they'd felt both firm and soft as they kissed her.

She threw herself off the couch. "I'm going to make us dinner."

It provided distraction. As did bathing Harper. Playing with her. But at the same time, she remained conscious of him at every turn. He oozed too much presence for her to ignore him.

It didn't help that he acted so damned normal. Talking about the case with her. Yapping about himself.

She learned about his rough childhood with a father that turned to hard booze once his mum died. How Declan went through a period of rebellion that almost resulted in him going to jail. His rescue and redemption by the Secundus Academy.

"A school for misfit boys?" she asked, pausing in her crawling after Harper.

"And girls. They took all the misfits they could find into the school, especially those on the brink of arrest, and redirected our interests. The academy gave us purpose. Enhanced our street-born skills."

"So you're a classic case of bad boy gone yuppie bad boy."

He stared at her, the corner of his lip twitching. "Yuppie? You do realize I've killed people for less."

"You can't deny it. I mean, think of the different classes of killers for hire. You've got your junkie who does it for a fix. He's usually sloppy in appearance. Why waste money on clothes when you could get high. Then there's your gangster with the lettered jackets and bandanas. The bikers—"

"Who have beards." He stroked his.

"You don't have a bike."

"Says who?" He winked. "I am a man of many toys, Ree."

"You're also a man with many suits." She'd raided the closet and found quite a few.

"Nothing wrong with looking sharp for work."

"You wear suits, Zee. With ties. You're a yuppie killer."

"You make it sound like a curse," he moaned. "Now I'm going to have to go shopping for a whole new wardrobe."

At that, she snickered. "Shopping for a look. The height of yuppiness."

He glowered. "I wouldn't talk, miss interior designer in suburbia."

If he thought he insulted, he was sadly mistaken. "I am proud of being a Killer Mom."

"Why the code name Frenemy, though?"

"Because a good chunk of my training was geared towards my being able to get real close to subjects. Befriending them so I could use them."

"Is that what you're doing with me?" Declan asked.

"I am using you. In case you'd forgotten, we're not friends." She turned from him at that point and put supper on the plates, the fridge having been stocked with some fresh, ready-made meals. She chose the quickly heated soup for their dinner.

Harper got mushed peas and rice cereal, which Audrey spoon-fed to her in between grabbing bites of her own meal.

Apparently, Declan wasn't done chatting. The distance she kept insisting on being ignored by a man who wouldn't respect boundaries.

"You never told me how you got recruited. How were you picked up?"

"Mother had a source at the FBI who told her about my case. She came looking for me and didn't care about what I did."

"So she recruited and trained you?"

"Yes, and no. KM did ask me to join their group. But I didn't require as much training as others. Most follow an intense two-year course. Given I'd already done my time at Quantico, I was better prepared than most." Even then, she'd had to learn the differences between building a case for a legal entity like the FBI and getting information any way possible, where laws and fair rights never entered the equation.

"And KM only recruits mothers, no men?" he asked.

"No men." Which could make for a challenging workplace at times as the different personalities—and offset menstrual cycles—caused some moodiness within the ranks. It was the main reason that once they graduated, they were immediately shipped to a territory to watch. "The group caters to mothers only, which is a wider group than you'd expect. We accommodate all ages." Some recruited very young from abusive situations who thrived with the chance to improve their lots in life. Others old, abandoned by husbands looking for younger wives. "KM doesn't give a hoot about race, size, religion, or even nationality. They recruit from everywhere." Because the turnover was high. Mothers would do anything to keep their families afloat. But after a few missions and the taste of an easier existence, some craved the normalcy of a real family life. Not everyone was cut out to be a spy or agent forever. But some thrived on the challenge and adrenaline. Like Audrey.

"An interconnected worldwide group. That's impressive. I'm just sorry you had it rough. That all of you had it rough. That shouldn't happen." He apologized for something he'd had no hand in. Felt sorry for her.

It should have angered her.

How dare he pity her? She'd survived.

However, she needed help. If not for the agency, she probably would have died, and Mendez would have Harper.

Perhaps it was the glass of wine she'd had with dinner. Or the fact that Harper pulled herself up using Declan's leg and drooled on him. Or maybe it was simply the need to tell someone her story that had her spilling what had happened.

And he listened.

THE FALSE CONTRACTIONS *stopped in the middle of the night, but the nurses wouldn't let her leave, stating a doctor needed to discharge her.*

Audrey was tempted to ignore them and walk out. She felt fine. At least, she did now. Earlier with her stomach stitching painfully, she'd worried the baby was coming early. At twenty-two weeks, the baby needed more time in the womb to have a fighting chance at life.

The cramping sent her to the hospital. The emergency room must have been quiet, because they admitted her right away, put her in a bed, and took her vitals.

Every test returned fine except for her hiccupping belly. Braxton hicks the doctor called the cramps. Normal, but they still kept her for observation. Just in case, they said.

Bored, and relieved it was nothing, she napped. Napped right through dinner and most of the early evening. She awoke just past midnight, well rested, wide-awake, and starving.

"What do you say we feed you, sweet pea," she said, cradling her belly. She already knew it was a girl. Unlike some, she'd asked for the results, wanting to feel that connection to the life growing in her womb.

She tugged the monitoring strips from her body, quickly pressing buttons on the machines to quiet them lest they draw disapproving nurses. Audrey had endured quite enough of disapproving expressions by this point. She could still see the faces of her superiors as they dressed her down, never outright calling her a whore for sleeping with the target but still implying it.

Worse, at times, she felt like a whore. She'd sold her dignity for the price of a few words and moments of pleasure. Flushed years of hard work down a toilet. And for what? A man who fed her false information and then one day called her into his presence—the same day she found out she was pregnant as a matter of fact— telling her he knew who she was. Laughed at her and admitted he'd known she was FBI all along. Then proceeded to smirk as he ruined her career and life.

The joke was on him. She never told him about the baby.

Never would. Her child deserved better than that man.

Problem was, he didn't take kindly to her determination to bring him down. She might not have her career—the FBI allowed her to quit rather than be fired—but she did have access to some secrets, things Mendez never knew she'd discovered.

Confidences that could get her killed, and which resulted in her being put into witness protection. Not exactly the most luxurious of situations. Alone and pregnant in a city she didn't know, living in a bleak apartment.

Grumble. Her tummy kept growling, and the room the hospital placed her in had nothing to eat. Only a pitcher of tepid water to drink.

Rather than wander the halls in her open-backed gown, she scrounged in the cabinet where the nurses had stored her things. Her stretchy pants fit over her growing abdomen, the sports bra barely contained her engorged breasts. She pulled her hair back into a ponytail before shoving her feet into sneakers. She had her wallet in hand when she poked her head out of her bedroom door, looking for a nurse.

She'd seen a vending machine by the waiting room. Chips would satisfy her craving for a crunch. She snuck out and was returning with her stash—two bags plus an apple from a basket left on a counter with a note to take one—when she noticed the door to her room open.

Crap. The night nurse must have decided to check on her. She'd probably get a lecture on leaving without asking permission.

Whatever. She was a grown woman. She could do what she liked.

Audrey took a bite of her apple as she sauntered towards the door. As she reached the threshold, she said, "Sorry, I went looking for a snack."

A man appeared in the frame.

A man with a dark leather coat, and flat eyes. One who didn't work for the hospital.

He barked, "Found her."

It didn't take a genius to realize that announcement didn't bode well. All too mindful of her pregnant belly, Audrey chose to avoid a fight. She dropped her snacks and whirled, pelting down the hall, expecting to get shot in the back at any moment. A cart left parked by a wall narrowly missed her hip, and she grasped at it, fingers scrabbling at the surface, looking for a weapon before shoving it back in the direction of her pursuer.

A woman screamed, and a man shouted in reply.

Pop. Pop.

Muted gunfire, softened by a silencer. The screaming stopped. These guys meant business.

Audrey ran faster and didn't turn to look back. It wouldn't have made a difference if she had. A hand clamped onto her shoulder, spinning her around. She stared at the big man with the menacing expression.

"Someone wants to see you." He began to drag her, his iron grip digging into her flesh. She didn't doubt that he'd hurt her if she refused to go with him. As for help...

A nurse cowered behind the counter, whimpering when the man barked, "Don't do anything stupid."

Another guy stood outside her room, holding a gun loosely in his hand, straddling a body on the floor. A nurse, judging by the outfit, not moving, the pale green fabric of her smock shirt turning dark and damp.

Don't go with them. It was all Audrey could think of, and yet, pregnant and without a weapon, how could she hope to escape? As they went past the trolley of supplies, she saw her chance. She grabbed the rim with two hands, swinging it into the legs of the man. A feeble distraction to hide the main event.

He roared and shoved the metal cart to the side, flipping it over with a clang, spilling the contents. He advanced on her, and she froze, standing in place as he got close.

The scalpel she'd palmed plunged into his gut. She gave it a twist, and it was his turn to gape.

She backed away from the man, the hot wetness of his blood on her hand. Blood she spilled. In all her time in the FBI, this was the first time she'd done harm.

Her stomach roiled. She felt sick.

The wound, while nasty, wasn't a killing blow. Her attacker didn't die. Not that she knew of, at least. He and his companion both escaped as she sank to the floor, hyperventilating. Stomach cramping.

The police questioned her in the hospital but didn't blame her for what happened. Cameras showed her to be innocent in the attack. But the cops wanted to know why.

Why go after Audrey?

She wouldn't give them a reply.

The doctors told the police to back off. They worried the stress of the attack would send her into premature labor. What they didn't grasp was the fact that them holding her as a virtual pris-

oner stressed her more. Mendez had found her, and there was no way the goons who escaped wouldn't tell their boss about her pregnancy. Or did Mendez know already?

She had to leave. Now. That very same day, when the police left, and the nurses changed shift, she fled the hospital, terrified at every turn that someone would attack her. As quickly as she could move, she hit her shitty apartment, packed a bag, ready to flee. To disappear to a place where no one would know her. Where Mendez wouldn't find her.

Screw witness protection. They obviously had a mole.

The knock at the door just about stopped her heart.

She stood, still as a rabbit in the field that'd spotted the shadow of a hawk above it. The knock came again, and a voice, husky and clear, female and firm followed.

"Mendez won't stop until he finds you. I can help you live."

Her world had changed the moment she answered and said, "How?"

Marie Cadeaux, code name Mother, didn't just tell her, she showed her. Trained Audrey. Gave her not only a second chance at life but also a future. As for Mendez? Mother had told her to not worry about Mendez. Said she'd handle him.

Audrey didn't ask how. Didn't want to know if she'd signed his death sentence.

Eventually, though, curiosity drove her to check in on Mendez. But there wasn't much to see because Mendez abruptly disappeared not long after Harper's birth. Audrey never knew if Mother had a hand in it. Nor if Mother was the reason the FBI had finally stumbled onto enough evidence to arrest him. Someone had tipped off Mendez. He vanished, as if into thin air. No one could confirm if he was dead or alive.

A few weeks passed, then months. Audrey graduated and left the KM training facility to return to the USA with Harper. She almost managed to relax, carved a home for herself and her daughter, began her new career as an interior designer. Was looking at a bright future with the occasional adrenalizing mission to break up the daily routine of being a mom.

It was a good life. A safe one. Or so she'd thought. The attempted kidnapping and her burnt-out shell of a home proved that she believed an illusion.

I never should have let my guard down.

She should have known better than to think Mendez was dead. Who else would go after Harper?

What she didn't understand was how they'd found her at Declan's? How long, too, before they tracked them to this new location?

I'll be done in two days. If she found the object. Two days of worrying that someone might come after the baby.

As for when this mission was over? Audrey didn't doubt that Mother would have a new home for her. New name and identity, too. She would start over. Again.

"That blows."

She'd almost forgotten that Declan was there. Didn't even realize she'd been speaking her inner thoughts aloud. He'd been so silent as she told her story. She shrugged in the face of his pity. "What happened with Mendez was my fault. I knew what he was going in. How I fell for his lies…" She shrugged. "My fault for not guarding myself more closely."

"You did not seriously just take the blame?" He scrubbed a hand through his hair, a sign of agitation that left it standing in floppy spikes. "What happened wasn't your fault. The guy set out to trap you by the sound of it. Then went after you."

"Because I got involved."

"You were told to go deep undercover. You did your job. You got close to your target, and none of them drew you back. Sounds to me like your team should have seen what was happening and pulled you out."

She gaped at him. "You're blaming them?" Such an odd idea.

But he seemed convinced. "A good team watches. Always. While the mission is important, so are the people. If a plan is going off track, it's better to halt it. Continuing with a bad plan is asking for trouble."

"They didn't know Mendez was on to me."

"Stop making excuses for them. If the roles were reversed, my team would have done anything to get me out of harm's way and take the guy out."

"The FBI doesn't just take people out."

He snorted. "If you say so."

"They put me in a protection program."

"They divulged your location, which almost resulted in your death." He stole the words out of her mind. "You got fucked."

"Language." Said without heat because Harper, asleep on his chest, couldn't hear him, and she could see the anger in his eyes. A righteous anger—on her behalf. "Don't act so pissed. My problems belong to me."

"What part are you not grasping? I'm saying you shouldn't have been going through this alone." He sounded so disgusted.

"What part of I messed up and paid the consequences for it don't you understand?"

"Consequences shouldn't include living in fear that this Mendez character will come after you or the kid."

"It is his child," she pointed out. "He has a legal claim to see her."

"If he was that keen on custody, he could have taken you to court. Kidnapping is never all right."

"Assuming it was him."

Declan gave her a look.

She sighed. "Fine. It's most likely him. But why now? He disappeared. Why surface now and try to abduct Harper?"

"Maybe he was waiting for the right time."

"Then he'll be waiting a while longer. He won't get her."

"Of course, he won't. We'll keep her safe."

We.

He said it so easily, and for a moment, Audrey let herself believe it. How nice would it be to not be alone?

Except the reality remained, this was only a momentary blip in her life. Once this mission with Suarez was over, she'd go back to being a regular ol' mom. A new place for her new life, but still one where she pretended to be someone she wasn't.

Sigh.

"You look tired. We should go to bed," he declared. "You take the master, I'll sleep out here."

She wouldn't argue the use of a big bed. But she did wonder at his choice. "Why not use the guest room? It's got a bed, too."

"I don't like its location. I want to be able to hear in case someone comes after you and the baby again."

The sweetness of his words brought moisture to her

eyes. She turned away before he could see. It also shamed her to realize that he'd thought of something she hadn't.

Sleeping in the master bedroom, far from the front door, she would never hear someone breaking in. The reminder that she had to be on her guard once more brought weariness to her mind, but a determined tension to her shoulders. "I'll sleep out here."

"Like hell, you will." He crossed his arms over his wide chest.

"I am because it makes the most sense." She angled her head towards the playpen. "Probably better off letting it stay put. Moving it might wake Harper up."

If anything, his stony countenance got even rockier. "I can handle the baby. Go sleep in a bed. I've got things covered."

The fact that he wanted to protect them melted something in her. There was a temptation to just say yes. To let a man take care of her. What happened the last time she'd let her guard down for a man?

She shook her head. "I don't need protecting."

"Because you can protect yourself." He rolled his eyes. "You think I haven't figured that out? I know you kick ass. Don't forget, I saw the bruises you left on Malcom. Watched the videos. You are badass. But, guess what, Ree, even badasses can use a hand sometimes."

She wanted to say something, but he'd left her without words. Here was a man who'd known her a scant few days, and yet he put himself out on a limb for her.

"What do you want in return?" What would he demand of her in payment?

"I don't want anything, Ree. It's as simple as helping out because it's the right thing to do."

"I didn't get the impression you always did the right thing." She used to be that way, too, once upon a time.

"Don't, usually." He shrugged, and his grin turned a touch mischievous. "Guess you bring out the good guy in me."

"A good guy wanting to protect a badass?" She arched a brow as she threw his words back at him.

"It's a classic love story." The moment the words left his lips, his eyes widened. Even his beard couldn't hide the tense shock in his expression.

Had he seriously said love story? "We are hardly a—a —" She couldn't say it aloud. She skipped the *L* word for something her tongue managed to spit out— "Cliché. I don't particularly care for you." Had there ever been such a huge lie spoken?

"Are you really going to throw shade at me after what we've been through? That's cold, Ree."

"You implied there was something happening between us." There totally was. There shouldn't be. She had to stop it.

He appeared determined to do otherwise. "There is totally something happening."

"Hormones. Nothing else," she said aloud not just for him. She needed convincing, too.

"It's more than that." He stepped closer to her.

Her nostrils flared, and she heaved in a breath. Jeezus, the scent of him. She wanted to close her eyes and just smell him. The sharp tickle of his cologne, and man... Hot hunk of man.

"I am not sleeping with you," she declared. Sleep. Ha. It would be passion and screaming all night long. She wished she could cross her legs and turn it off. The melting continued.

"I didn't realize I'd asked?" He arched a brow. "Go to bed, Ree. Alone. I promise if Harper starts hollering, I will wake you up. We can both be wide-awake and take care of her. Because that makes more sense."

"I'm her mother."

"And I was her fake father." A sheepish smile tugged his lips. "Let me pretend a while longer. She's cute."

So was he. "Wake me," she admonished.

"Yeah, yeah. Go to bed." He pointed down the shadowy hall to the bedroom. Not his lap. He didn't even offer her a goodnight kiss.

How disappointing.

She left the door open a crack and stripped down to her shirt and panties. She slid the gun under the pillow—after checking it again for bullets, astonished he'd actually given her a loaded weapon. What kind of crazy person did that?

Declan did. A guy sleeping alone on a couch, guarding.

She tried to sleep. Really, she did. Rest eluded her. Desire for the man in the other room not the only reason.

She worried.

Worried that Mendez was indeed still alive and actively hunting her.

Worried that she'd fail her mission.

Worried that she was turning into someone who hesitated because of a broken heart rather than grasp the possibilities life offered.

Why was she afraid to sleep with Declan?

He'll try and use it against me.

How?

What benefit would he gain from it? Nothing. Her boss wouldn't care if they had sex so long as it was Audrey's choice.

Sleeping with him, though, might affect her mission. Could she concentrate properly if distracted by him? She couldn't afford to have her mind turned right now. Not with everything at stake. Most especially a little girl.

At the same time, though, was abstinence needed to do her job?

An appealing thing about Declan was the fact that he knew about her. Knew her fall from grace, her shady redemption. Her baggage and greatest treasure.

And he was so good with Harper.

It made her wish things were different.

Made her wish he weren't in another room, so very far away.

CHAPTER TWENTY

So close, and yet so far away. Declan lamented his choice of the sofa, not because it was shorter than his body but because he wasn't in bed with Audrey.

The more he got to know the woman, the more he needed to know. He wanted to learn everything he could about her. Especially how she'd feel coming for him.

Keeping a cool lid after that scorching make-out session following his shower proved almost impossible. He could understand her hesitation over getting involved. He hesitated, too. She might not work for his office, but they were collaborating. It made them coworkers, in close proximity. They had to be careful to make things work. Yet, at the same time, the enforced living situation meant he got to know her more quickly than say a woman he met at a bar or had dinner with. They'd already spent hours together. Talking. Eating. Playing—with Harper, not each other, which created its own brand of closeness.

Because there was no mistaking he felt close to Audrey. Wanted to be closer.

He blamed that for the restless sleep he tumbled into. Dreams of chasing her, capturing her for a kiss, only to have her melt in his arms and lead him on a chase again haunting him.

A few hours were all he managed before a noise had him rising. He checked the door first. No one in the hall, according to the peephole. Which, he might add, he didn't put an eyeball to. Good way to lose an eye. He used the iris-cam in the peephole to look via the app on his phone.

He checked on Harper next. She slept, ass in the air, thumb tucked in her mouth.

The noise came again, a mumble, a rustle of sound that justified him lightly pushing open the master bedroom door.

Audrey rolled on the bed, grumbling in her sleep. The faint light from the bedside clock illuminated her face enough for him to see that her eyes remained closed.

The sheet had ridden down, displaying the flesh of her leg. The pale skin of her ribcage and belly peeked as her shirt twisted around her in slumber. Only her panties covered the essentials, and he allowed himself one heated look before turning away.

The disappointment was very real, but he knew it was wrong of him to watch her while she slept. Creepy, too. Only weird peeping Toms ogled women without their knowledge. He went to leave, but she mumbled again.

"Zee."

Probably wishful thinking made him think she'd said his nickname.

"I want to." The words were soft but distinct. "We shouldn't." She kept talking, and he couldn't help but listen.

"Oh, Declan." No doubt she sighed his name. Nicely. The kind of sigh that made a man harden.

She's dreaming of me. An erotic dream, apparently, given that he could hear the rustle of sheets as she squirmed.

Turn around.

He didn't. Looking now would be wrong. So very wrong. He needed to leave. This instant. He made it through the doorframe when he heard it.

"Declan?"

He froze. Did Audrey still sleep talk?

"Why are you in my room? Is Harper okay?"

Uh-oh.

He glanced over his shoulder to see her sitting upright, the blanket clutched to her chest. "Sorry, didn't mean to wake you. Heard something and was checking it out."

She went to swing her legs off the edge of the bed.

"Don't get up. Turns out it was a false alarm."

"Are you sure? If you heard something, we should check it out."

"Already did. "A grin tugged his lips. "Did you know you talk in your sleep?"

"Do not," she huffed.

"Do, too."

She frowned. "What did I say?

Pride filled his masculine reply. "My name."

"Probably giving you heck."

As if he'd let her off the hook. "Not the way you were saying it."

"You are imagining things." She leaned over and grabbed a glass from the nightstand.

Rather than leave, he moved towards the bed. "How

long you going to keep fighting what's happening between us?"

"I don't know what you're talking about."

He sat on the edge of the bed, and she froze, glass to her lips, eyes wide in the gloom.

"There's something sizzling between us. Don't deny it," he said with a slight shake of his head. "I feel it. You feel it."

"We can't act on it."

"You started it earlier today." He'd been thinking of it ever since.

"A mistake. It won't happen again."

"Why not?"

"My mission—"

"Has nothing to do with this." He reached out and ran a knuckle down the soft skin of her cheek.

"Us getting involved wouldn't be professional." The words tumbled out, high and rapidly.

"Jumping out of our skin each time we touch isn't good either. It's the middle of the night. Everyone is asleep. Except for you." He drifted closer. "And me."

"We could work on the case."

"The case can wait until morning. This can't." He slanted his mouth over hers, capturing and caressing it, swallowing the hitch of her breath.

He went slow, waiting to see if she'd protest or push him away. She didn't. She leaned into him, her fingers clutching at his shoulders, her mouth taking the kiss to the next passionate level, devouring him. Her tongue sliding in for a hot dance.

It took only a little nudge to have her lying down on

the bed, and him alongside her. He ran his hand up and down her hip and waist, content to take things slow.

She was the impatient one. She rolled him to his back, straddling him, her eyes glittering in the shadowy room. Snaring the hem of her shirt, she pulled it off in a fluid motion, revealing her handsful of breasts, the nipples large and inviting. He cupped them, feeling their weight in his palms.

As if sensing his urges, she leaned down enough so he could latch his mouth to one, sucking on that nub, feeling it harden. He kept tugging, slightly surprised by the sweetness he tasted.

He switched breasts, lavishing the other with the same attention while she moaned and squirmed atop him.

Despite his track pant bottoms and her panties, he felt how hot and wet she was. The dampness permeated the fabric. Made him eager.

He cupped her head with his hand, drawing her to his mouth. He wanted to taste her. "Strip off those panties and bring that pussy to me."

She gasped.

"Now," he growled.

The strip of fabric went flying, and he remained on his back as she straddled him and worked her way up his body. The narrow strip of hair at the top of her pubis was hypnotizing in the shadowy room. She didn't stop until she'd positioned her legs on either side of his shoulders and head. She held herself over him, a pink, teasing temptation.

He grabbed her around the thighs, pulled her down to his mouth. He tasted her sweet honey. Immersed himself in the heat of her. His tongue flicked at the slit of her sex, the wetness of her passion only increasing his hunger. He devoured her clit, latching his lips to that nubbin of pleasure. He teased her. Nipping. Licking. Worrying that button of flesh while she writhed and cried out. He opened his eyes to watch her. Saw her looming over him, her hands pressed to the wall to hold herself upright, her eyes shut, her lips parted, panting and wet.

She was so fucking beautiful.

Especially when she came. The ripple of her orgasm had him digging his fingers in as he let his tongue ride the wave of her pleasure. His hips thrust, his cock thick and hard. She did this to him without laying a hand on his dick.

Her writhing slowed, and she groaned. "That was so..." She didn't finish the sentence, suddenly moving instead, and it was his turn to gasp as she sat on him.

Sheathed his cock in one swoop that engulfed him in an inferno of flesh. He scrabbled to hold on to something. Her hips proved a nice anchor, holding him to one spot, gasping as she ground against him. Groaning deep when she bounced, driving him hard. Then huffing against her mouth, their lips meshed together as closely as their bodies. The rhythmic stroking, her body sliding hard against his, brought his pleasure coiling. He teetered on the brink.

When she came again, moaning his name, "Declan," he lost it.

Completely lost it inside her. Spilling his seed.

The condom still forgotten in his pocket.

First time ever.

He didn't panic.

Happiness wouldn't let him.

CHAPTER TWENTY-ONE

AUDREY LOST TRACK OF THE TIMES THEY MADE LOVE. Lie. It was three, with over five orgasms for her. A record. Her body felt relaxed. Pleasured.

Hungry...

Even after a night of sensual exploration, a night of insane bliss, she was greedy.

She wanted more.

And he would have given it to her, too. He stirred against her backside. He was a spooner. His body wrapped around hers. So nice. The heavy weight of him pure delight.

She would have totally gone for round number four if she hadn't heard Harper begin to squawk.

Before she could roll out of bed, he had, bouncing to his feet and yanking on his track pants. He muttered a brisk, "Stay in bed. I got this."

Like hell. Harper was her responsibility.

She had her legs thrust over the side when he reappeared with the baby.

"Say morning to your mommy?" He cradled her against his chest and had his head against Harper's putting them cheek-to-cheek. He held up Harper's hand and waved it before mimicking in a high-pitched voice, "Hi, Mommy."

Audrey gaped.

"Ma!" Chubby arms reached for her, and she took her daughter, expecting the sloppy morning kisses.

"I'll grab the bum stuff. Hold on," he announced.

Sure enough, he returned a moment later with a fresh diaper, wipes, and a sleeper.

"No pad?" she asked.

"Er."

Audrey snickered. "I'll manage this time."

"I'll be right back." He popped out again as she changed her daughter. The happy baby gurgled and immediately flipped for a crawl once Audrey had finished buttoning her into a fresh sleeper.

He reappeared, juggling a bottle and two coffees. The hot cups went onto the nightstand. The bottle he offered to Harper, who pulled herself to a sitting position and snatched it from his hands. She immediately tipped it back.

Declan slid into the bed, and Audrey couldn't hide from him in the dawning morning light. Nor did her humming body want to. No point in pretending that last night didn't happen.

"Coffee." He handed her a cup, carefully watching Harper, who'd flopped in between them to drink her bottle.

Audrey took the mug and sipped. "That was a fast coffee."

"Got to love a Keurig machine."

"You're getting good with a bottle, too."

"It's not rocket science."

Maybe not, but he'd taken the time to learn. "About last night," she said, still not sure exactly what to think about what had happened."

"Don't make this complicated, Ree."

What was that supposed to mean? She frowned rather than ask.

He grinned at her expression. "It means, let nature take its course. Don't overthink this. Let it happen."

"Easy for you to say." He wasn't the one who'd end up emotionally involved and heartbroken.

"Give this a chance."

"A chance to what?"

Rather than reply, he leaned over, gave her a kiss, and then slid out of the bed. "Gotta get ready for work. Suarez will have a hissy fit if I don't have his booties."

"About the open house... Do you really think it's a good idea for me to bring Harper?"

"Technically, it should be safe. Bunch of rich folks, tight security. No one's going to try anything there."

"I just don't know if I like it."

"Would you rather I found someone to babysit?"

A stranger watching her child? The idea didn't sit well, either. The last stranger she'd chosen turned out to be a killer. A sexy one who made her melt in bed, but still. She'd not exactly chosen well.

"How would you explain a nanny showing up with no kid?"

"We could always make you my girlfriend."

She blinked. She knew he meant fake girlfriend, and yet a part of her had a meltdown. "Me and you."

"Yes, me and you. I don't think Suarez will say anything."

"Can't you get me in as a client?"

He shrugged. "Possibly. But I'd rather not."

"Why?"

"Because it wouldn't look too professional if I kept trying to hold the hand of a potential client."

"I knew this would affect the mission." She jabbed her finger at him.

He rolled his eyes skyward and sighed. "Pay a woman a compliment, and she acts like I stabbed her with a fork. Fine. You want to come as a client and me to pretend I don't know you, then I'll pretend."

"Thank you."

He didn't reply. He headed for the bathroom stating, "Gotta get ready for work."

She made sure she was dressed by the time he exited. She handed him a bowl of cereal and a quart of milk. Breakfast of champions.

He checked his watch as he sucked back the last of his coffee. "Gotta fly. Mason's picking me up downstairs."

"Why not take your car?"

"Because I was gonna leave it for you. The keys are in the front hall if you need them. But I wouldn't recommend roaming around. The less coming and going the better for keeping you and Harper hidden."

She pointed out an obvious flaw in his plan. "Won't someone looking for Harper just stake out your office and follow you from there?"

He grinned. "Ah, Ree. We can only hope they're that stupid. If they're watching, we'll nab them. If they can follow Mason, I'll eat that disgusting jar of baby peas in the fridge."

"They're not that bad."

He shuddered. "Rather eat grasshoppers. Stay inside. Lock the doors."

"Yes, Daddy." Her turn to roll her eyes. "I'm not an idiot. I know how to stay safe."

"Keep your gun close by. And Ree?" He beckoned, and she followed him to the door, ready to bolt them in.

"What?"

He yanked her close for a kiss. A hard, bone-melting kiss. Then growled, "Try and stay out of trouble. I'll be back as soon as I can. Ben's around if you need help."

"You left me a sitter?" she huffed.

"I left you an extra gun in case shit happens. And the proper reply is 'thank you.'"

"Ohm," babbled Harper, having managed to reach them by the door. Audrey scooped her up. "Go. We'll be fine."

"You might want to get that cookie batter ready." He winked as he tweaked Harper's chin to the baby's chortling delight.

Then he was gone. The door bolted. She leaned against it.

Stay inside. Don't go out, even into the hall. Stay away from windows.

Blah. Blah. Blah. As if she didn't know this already. Their safety relied on being discreet.

Mother, however, didn't see it that way. "I'm pulling you out."

The words took Audrey by surprise. "But I'm not done

with my mission. I just need one more day. I've got a way in."

"You and Harper need to vacate the area. An extraction team will arrive by three this afternoon."

"I don't need extraction. The mission is going well. Declan's going to get me into the condo."

Rather than remark on that news, Mother's cold query was, "How come you didn't inform me of the kidnapping attempt yesterday?"

Audrey twirled a piece of hair around her finger. "I thought you knew about it. I mean, you did message me, ordering me to cooperate, after all."

"Telling you I've found us allies doesn't mean you don't report to me. Why didn't you let us know you and the baby were attacked?" It was a measure of Mother's worry that she let emotion heat the words.

"We escaped. Declan helped us to get to safety."

"Declan, is it?" The sly query put Audrey on the defensive.

"What do you expect me to call him?"

"Mr. Hood. That is his name."

"That's kind of formal seeing as how we've practically been living together for days." Had slept together, too. She knew things about him and his body that weren't on any report, she'd wager.

"You wouldn't have had to if you'd simply told me what happened at your house. If I'd known about the fake nanny and attack—"

Audrey cut her off. "You would have sent me somewhere safe. I know. Which is why I didn't call. I have things in hand. I'll be able to search the condo tomorrow during an open house Declan is hosting."

"No, you won't, because you'll be in Nebraska. Natasha Coxson, widow, relocating with her daughter for a fresh start."

The idea of leaving, starting over, had her gripping her phone too tightly. "You can relocate me after I've completed my mission."

"No. Too risky."

"What's risky is me going into hiding again. Listen to me," she cut Mother off before she could speak. "We thought he was gone." He, being Mendez. "The kidnapping attempts have proven us wrong. But more important, don't you see? There's only one way he could have known I'd be in this city."

It took Mother a moment before she cursed fluently in French, the rapid-fire Canadian kind. "We have a mole." Because how else would he have followed Audrey? Even the flight she'd booked was for a different city. She was supposed to land, check into a hotel, then slip out and drive to her real destination, faking a stomach flu that supposedly kept her in her room.

But Mendez had found her. Found her working for Declan, and only one person knew where she was.

Good thing she didn't suspect the woman who'd rescued her. Mother ranted.

"How dare someone betray a sister?" Because all the agents were supposed to be family.

"We don't know for sure it was intentional. Could be a hack."

"Damned computers. I knew getting on a network was a bad idea." Mother dropped into Italian for her next round of cursing. A former agent herself, Mother could not only kill a person with her bare hands without leaving a mark, she could also speak eight languages.

"Before you start shooting people and dumping wine all over the keyboards—"

"I wouldn't waste wine like that. Beer, though..."

Audrey laughed. "Before you destroy everything, make sure you've found the right culprit. If it is a hack, we need to find out who planted it."

"Given they went after Harper, it has to be Mendez. And here I'd hoped he died. They never did find his body after his yacht sank."

"So you did have something to do with that," Audrey pounced.

"No idea what you're talking about." The fake innocence was almost comical.

"Doesn't matter who tried to get rid of Mendez. He's back, and if he is determined to get his hands on Harper, then he's going to keep trying, even if I move to Nebraska in the next few hours. We have to solve our security leak before I do anything."

"What are you suggesting?"

"I stay here. For now, at least," she added hastily. "Let me finish my mission. My location is as secure as it's getting. Assuming that no one is tapping our phones."

"I've got us on a scrambler. If they can hack that, then we're just plain screwed."

"Declan's done some stuff to keep us out of sight, as well."

"Declan again. I guess a mission with a handsome partner is preferable to unpacking a new house," Mother said dryly.

"It's also safer. He's a trained killer."

"Men can be bought."

"So can women. Am I happy Harper's in danger? No. I'm not. But the truth is, she is as safe with me as anyone else." Especially since Audrey would shoot to kill. Besides, being separated would only increase her anxiety.

"You don't want to leave. Fine. Don't. But you're getting help. I already dispatched a team."

For some reason, Mother's determination to do something made Audrey think of what Declan had said. How the FBI had let her down. How her team let her fall.

KM, her family, they wouldn't leave her dangling. She knew whoever Mother dispatched would have her back. "I could use some extra eyes doing surveillance. Maybe we can lay a trap before the next attempt." Because she had no doubt there would be one.

They discussed a few more things they could do before Mother sighed. "I'm worried about you."

"Don't. I'll be fine. *We'll* be fine." Somehow. Someway, she'd come out on top. She had to. Because Harper depended on her.

She hung up with Mother and then spent time entertaining Harper and sifting through her thin file on Suarez.

Why hadn't she agreed to go as Declan's girlfriend? Would it have been so bad?

The knock on the door startled her.

She frowned, especially when the feminine voice said, "Yoo-hoo. Declan, honey, it's me. I'm back in town early. Your office said you were staying here."

Her first impulse? Anger. Her second, which occurred the moment the peephole app loaded, was astonishment.

She flung open the door to see one of her few friends, another secret agent with KM.

Carla.

But why was Carla declaring herself Declan's girlfriend?

Audrey flung open the door, then bit her lip lest she laugh as Carla met her with pouty lips. "You must be the nanny." Carla eyed her up and down. "I told him to hire someone older."

Carla sauntered past, and Audrey closed the door more slowly. Before she could fully turn around, Carla was hugging her.

"How are you doing? I heard about the house thing. What the hell happened?"

They spent an hour catching up, Audrey spilling all that had happened from fake nanny until now. Carla kept exclaiming. But at the end, it was her turn to admit why she was here.

"Mother said you needed to be removed," Carla replied when asked.

"I don't. I'm fine."

"Are you? Because I wouldn't be if my ex came sniffing around." Carla's ex was a gangbanger. High up in his circle, too. After he'd killed Carla's family—mother, two brothers, and a friend—she knew she had to leave. That she and her son, Nico, would forever be in danger if they remained. Carla left, and only returned once to her old stomping grounds. Apparently, her ex's funeral drew a decent crowd. They had to bring out a mop for the spit.

"Running means I'll forever be watching over my shoulder."

"So, what's the plan?" Carla tugged Harper onto her lap and bounced her.

"I'll complete my mission."

"I mean after that. You want to draw out Mendez, then

that means you got to stick around. Where you gonna live? Work?"

Audrey almost said Declan's name. Almost. The word so close she had to bite her tongue to stop it. The sharp pain made her think. *Why would I assume I'd stay with Declan?*

He'd alluded to it. Told her to relax and take each day as it came. But how many days would that be?

One? Two? A week?

Then what? He'd tell her so long and dump her on the street?

He won't do that if there's a danger to me and Harper.

What about when that danger was gone? What then? He'd have done his duty by her, and she'd be left...alone.

"What am I supposed to do?" Audrey asked with a hint of bitterness. "Go to Nebraska and wait for Mendez to find me again?"

"No, because you're right. You can't keep watch forever. So we'll stick around town."

"We?"

"Me and the girls." Carla winked. "Did you really think we wouldn't come to help?"

"What about your boy?"

"Auntie is with Nico. They'll be fine for a few days. Don't worry. We know what we're doing. It's not like this is our first mission."

"Where are you staying?" Audrey asked.

"A lovely dive in the heart of town. The others are supposed to meet me there."

Others meaning more Killer Moms. Allies. People Audrey knew. Women who didn't turn her head and make her yearn for something impossible. "You brought a car?"

"Does a taco have meat?"

"That is a stupid expression. "

"It's Nico's favorite right now. It is also sadly a step up from his last favorite expression, 'Does asparagus pee stink?'"

Audrey wrinkled her nose. "Does it?"

"Very." Carla laughed. "How do you not know that?"

Because asparagus was green, and Audrey didn't do many green vegetables. Lettuce was about the only thing.

"What's the plan?" Audrey asked, even if she could guess. Relocation.

"You can drop the face. I'm not here to pull you from the mission. Think of the girls and me as moral support. And babysitters." Carla winked.

"I know I shouldn't have brought her." The guilt hit Audrey fast and hard.

"Didn't have much of a choice the way I hear it. You're also not the first to do it."

Glancing at her friend, Audrey's eyes widened. "You took your kid on a mission?"

"They sent me to Orlando. Of course, I brought him. Only an idiot would turn down the chance to hit up the theme parks on the company's dime." Carla winked.

"So I'm not the most horrible mom in the world?"

"Never." Carla brought her arms around Audrey and hugged. "You did what you needed to keep your baby safe. And now, your sisters are here to make that task easier. We'll take turns at the motel watching the baby while we finish off the mission."

Motel? As in leaving the condo.

Leaving Declan...

"Leave? Is that the best idea? Declan might be able to get me into the Suarez place."

"I don't know if I'd trust that guy."

"Mother said I should." Her gut also insisted.

"Seems kind of weird Mother didn't warn us about him beforehand." A scowl pulled at Carla's lips.

"Yeah." So what ulterior motive could there be? Maybe she should stay and—

Why the hell was she looking for an excuse to remain? Common sense said to go with Carla. She knew her, and she'd probably know the rest of the team who was sent. Even if she didn't, they were all sisters in KM. Bonded by a common theme.

Looking around, Audrey hardened herself. "Give me a minute, and I'll pack up."

It didn't take them long to gather Audrey's and Harper's things, minus the bulky playpen. What took forever was the wait for the elevator and the ride down. Audrey couldn't help but feel as if eyes watched.

Carla, cool as ever, played the part. "I'm not sure how long this gig will last." She eyed Audrey. "I think we might require someone more mature for the job."

Catching on, Audrey replied, "I am very qualified. I've been doing childcare for quite some time now."

"Doing anything else?" An eyebrow quirked, and Audrey fought the heat trying to ride in her cheeks.

The elevator doors slid open, and she stepped out, pushing the stroller. Following Carla's brisk pace. Wondering if they had an audience watching.

They made it to the car, which Carla had just left on the street with a sign in the windshield: *On Delivery*.

"Don't tell me that actually works?" Audrey asked.

"Do you see a tow truck or a ticket?" Carla slid the cardboard off the dash as she got into the driver seat. In the back, Audrey did a few final tugs on the car seat.

"Good to go."

Which, apparently, were the words for drive like a bat out of hell, around corners, through alleys, zipping in and out of places no car should go until they arrived alive—barely—at their destination.

A place without Declan.

CHAPTER TWENTY-TWO

A CROSS TOWN...

Declan was about ready to pack it up and go back to the condo. He'd accomplished fuck all in the office other than stressing about leaving Audrey alone.

She claimed she was fine. He would know since he texted her every hour.

By the fifth time, she virtually snapped on screen. *No we're not dead. Relax.*

He waited two hours before contacting her again, still stuck at work, his damned client Suarez making him do a thousand little stupid things. Declan wanted to tell him to fuck off. He had better things to do than pull up yet another listing in the area for comparisons, but he didn't dare do anything to set the man off. The open house was tomorrow. He'd promised Audrey she would get in. He couldn't let anything stand in the way.

Audrey would get a chance to search that condo, and Declan would earn his cookies. Then maybe he could challenge her with something else. Anything to keep her close by.

Maybe he would be better off sabotaging the open house. The longer she couldn't get in to the condo, the longer she'd have to stick with him.

Which was probably some of the most selfish thinking he'd ever done.

Intentionally ruining her chance for success for his own gain. Wrong.

Bad.

He wouldn't do it. If Audrey decided to stick around, he wanted it to be of her own volition. With perhaps a gentle nudge from him.

Finally, as he prepared to leave, Harry chose to beckon him into his office. Declan sank into the club chair across from the boss's massive desk.

"You wanted to see me?" Declan did his best not to fidget, lest Harry notice his impatience.

"How's it going with the child?"

"Fine. She's not mine."

"So I heard. How are things with the mother?"

Explosive. He settled for, "Good."

"Just good." Harry shuffled some papers on his desk. "I got the impression that perhaps things had progressed a tad further than that."

"Anything we did was consensual and won't impede our ability to complete her mission."

Harry harrumphed. "I hope you're right. Marie—"

"Who?"

"Audrey's handler. The one she calls Mother. She's worried about Audrey."

CHAPTER 22 · 223

"I wouldn't hurt her." The hot exclamation almost had him lunging from his chair.

"Not intentionally. No. But you do realize she's not like the women you usually meet and sleep with. She's—"

"Special. You think I didn't notice?"

"What are your intentions?"

"What are you, her father?"

Harry's lips flattened. "No, but she is a mother. You can't toy with her like you would someone else. You can't insert yourself into that child's life unless you mean to stick around. It's not fair to lead them on. Either of them."

"Is this just going to be a lecture on how I'm not ready to be a daddy?" Because he'd thought he was doing pretty good. Harry seemed convinced otherwise, though.

"Never said that. Just said to be sure what you want because there's a lot more at stake."

Declan was fully aware of that. Aware that getting involved with Audrey and Harper would mean some life-style changes. No more knives under the bed. No turpentine and rags under the sink. No more spacious closet with only his shit. Or a counter that was free of long hair and makeup supplies. It also meant shirts with handprints, and ties with wet, slobbery spots.

All things he could handle if they kept making him feel... He didn't know how to describe it exactly, other than happy. Complete. As if they were a missing piece of his life's puzzle.

But these weren't things he could say aloud. Men didn't admit feelings. Especially to their boss.

What he could do though was explore more of those emotions with Audrey and Harper. Spend time with them. Once he got back.

Mason loaned his car to Declan. He took a very circuitous route to the condo. The fewer people who knew his location, the better for everyone.

Upon returning to the condo, the moment he opened the door, he felt the emptiness. The playpen still standing and yet all of Harper's things were gone.

He cursed and immediately texted Audrey.

Where are you and the baby?

With friends. The reply came right away.

Why? I thought we had a plan. A plan that involved one more night together. Maybe more if he could convince her.

Plans change.

What about the open house? It was what he wrote, yet what he really wanted to say was "*What about us?*" Because they were an us. After last night, the passion, the intimacy. This was her running away because she was scared.

I'm still coming. Just get me on the list of guests.

Where are you?

Because anywhere other than by his side felt wrong.

Where I should be.

At this point, the terse replies were pissing him off. Especially since he wanted to text so many things. Like, *are you really going to leave me?* But he'd have to turn in his man card if he did something so emasculating. It was becoming clear that what he felt for her wasn't reciprocated. He wasn't talking about the passion. There was obviously something electric between them, but beyond that, she remained all about the job.

The funny thing being, usually, Declan was all about the mission, too.

Given his boss had explicitly ordered him to help Audrey, he had his justification for loading a special app onto his phone. A tracker program he'd not thought he would need. He'd truly expected to find Audrey when he returned. Given the way she'd bounced without an explanation, he was damned happy he'd put that bug in the car seat, and the second in the stroller. Even her phone got a bug while she was asleep.

The app finished with its security measures, which involved a code plus a fingerprint before giving him a list of devices he could map. Hers were highlighted in pink. He clicked all three.

The good news? She was still in the city. The bad news? She'd left, which meant slinking to find her and being that guy who whined, "Why?"

He could have stopped himself.

He didn't.

Once he saw the shitty motel in the bad part of town, he was glad he'd come. Back in the seventies, for maybe a few months, this place had shone. The cutesy wood shingle roof, and the prime color plastic seats bolted outside the matching yellow, blue, red, and green doors. Now, the roof sagged, and the seats were faded by use and exposure. The signal for her phone led him to the ground level and a yellow door, scuffed and dented, the paint peeling in spots.

The curtain twitched. Someone watched.

He knocked.

A lovely woman with a tanned complexion answered. "*Sí?*"

"I am looking for Audrey and Harper."

"*No se.*" The woman went to shut the door, but he wedged his foot in.

"Listen, I know they're here."

The muzzle of a gun was aimed at his nose before he could blink. "Who are you?" The tiny Latina eyed him with cold resolve. "Better make it good, or you'll be fleshy slush on the sidewalk."

"Ask Audrey, she'll tell you who I am." He held his hands out to his sides, not doubting for a moment she'd shoot him.

He heard an exclamation. "Declan, what are you doing here?"

"This is the guy you made into your fake baby daddy?" The woman's lips split into a smile. "He's cute."

"That's not why I chose him," huffed Audrey. "He was convenient to the case."

"Telling someone they're a daddy when they're not is a shit move to make." The Latina took his side.

"Language, Carla."

The woman named Carla snorted. "Harper is bound to hear worse in her lifetime. Don't be so mollycoddling."

"I told her the same thing." Declan offered his most charming smile.

Carla lowered the gun. As if she hadn't just threatened to put a hole in his face, she said, "Won't you come in?"

Entering the shabby motel room, he spared only the briefest glance at the interior—the faded, textured wallpaper, the generic framed art, the heavy furniture bolted to the wall and scratched into antiquity. He only had eyes for Audrey, who stood on the far side, Harper balanced on her hip.

"What are you doing here?" she demanded.

"You left."

"Didn't you read the note?"

Note? He shook his head. "Nope. Just came to find you."

"Do you have news on the case?" she asked. The brisk tone at odds with the temptress he'd slept with the previous night.

"Nothing new. Just more crazy demands from Suarez. Oh, and good news. I got you in. A certain rich lady couldn't make it, and rather than cancel her invite, I'm going to present you in her place."

Carla moved around him and flopped onto the bed, gun by her side. "We'll need deets on the identity."

"Already got it." He waved an envelope. "Everything you need is right here."

"Hand it over." Audrey leaned in to grab the envelope, and the baby leaned out, cooing.

"There's my diva," he announced softly when chubby arms reached for him.

Even Audrey couldn't deny the baby a snuggle with her favorite guy, and he milked it. Hugging the sturdy body close, rubbing his beard on Harper's cheeks until she chortled.

Carla snorted. "Maybe you should have kept him as the real daddy. I can't tell who's more wrapped around the little finger, him or the baby."

While he seemed to have partially won over Carla, Audrey appeared less than impressed. "How did you find me?"

"Does it matter?"

"As a matter of fact, it does. Because if you did it that easily, then so can Mendez."

"So you're sure it's him?"

She waved the envelope as she gestured. "Who else would it be? You know a lot of other men who would try and kidnap my daughter after already failing several times?"

"I'm glad you are convinced it's all about you," he flung at her. "What if this is about me? What if my enemies were after my kid because, keep in mind, you might know the truth, but other people don't. Anyone looking in from the outside only sees the story BBI fabricated."

"If they're your enemies, then it's probably a good thing we distanced ourselves." Audrey crossed her arms.

"Distanced yourself?" He snorted. "You put yourself in the worst section of town. How is this"—he gestured around him—"safer?"

"I'm not alone," Audrey hotly stated.

"Don't drag me into this lovers' spat." Carla threw her hands in the air as she slipped off the bed. "I think Harper and I should go for a walk. Come on, chubby cheeks." Carla snared the baby from Declan and plopped her in the stroller.

He expected Audrey to protest, but instead, she eyed him.

"Are you going to just let them go?"

"No one knows who Carla is, and she'll shoot anybody who comes near Harper."

"Damned right, I will. Don't you worry. Auntie Carlita will waste anybody who hurts the sweet baby," the woman cooed as she backed out the door. It shut with a click.

"Another KM agent?" he asked.

Rather than reply, Audrey slapped his arm with the envelope. "Why are you really here? Is this about last night? Because while it was good, I don't recall making any promises or offering any repeats."

"I was concerned about your safety."

"I'm fine."

"Harper's safety, too."

"She's also fine. Now that you've seen it and dropped this off"—she waved the brown package—"you can go."

"Come back with me." Yes, that plea came from him.

"Why?"

He thought about naming off all the safety reasons why she should. Instead, he gave her the truth. "I missed you."

"You were gone all day for work. You didn't have time."

"Didn't have time?" He arched a brow. "I texted you."

She groaned. "I know. What the heck, Zee? Are you some kind of control freak?"

"I worried."

"I told you not to."

He shrugged. "Can't seem to help myself. I care what happens to you and Harper."

It took her a moment before she replied. "You barely know me."

"Funny you should say that because for me, it feels like I know you pretty darned well. Already, I know more about you than my last three girlfriends." Because, while not a fan of dating, he had made attempts.

"Exactly what do you think you know?" She crossed her arms. "Good stuff. Not something you can sic a tech goon on like my date of birth or height."

A smile ghosted the corners of his lips. "I know you hate sugar in your coffee. Wear full-bottom undies, cotton. Wrinkle your brow right here"—he pointed to a spot on her forehead—"when you read. Shave with my razor. Make a face when you change diapers, and hum a nursery song whenever Harper is upset."

"I am also a slob who hates ironing and doesn't like beards."

"You liked it well enough last night."

"I was lonely."

So was he, and he'd found someone he didn't mind shaking that loneliness off with. "Why is it so hard for you to admit you might like me?"

"Because my taste in men is faulty."

"A mistake with one man doesn't mean your taste is shit."

"You and I would make a terrible couple."

"Why?" He really wanted to know because when he saw Audrey, all he could think of were the ways she complemented him and his lifestyle.

"We're both stubborn for one."

"Fighting happens in couples. You can't always agree on things."

"Your job is dangerous."

"As is yours."

"Mine is optional. I could walk away now, and they'd let me."

"I call bullshit. We both know you have no interest in leaving the job or you would have called your boss and canceled this gig the moment someone tried to kidnap Harper."

Her lips flattened. "I've already got a new identity waiting for me in Nebraska."

"I can have another one created that has you staying here."

"With you?"

"With me, or if you'd like to take a step back, then you could get your own place."

"And do what, date?" She said it so incredulously.

"What's wrong with that?"

"What's wrong, is the fact I have a daughter, one who is already getting too attached to you. What if we date, and she continues to fall for you, and we break up? Then what?"

"You're assuming we'd break up."

"Because it happens. A lot. I don't want to see Harper's heart broken."

Harper's, or her own? "Does this mean you're going to...what? Never date again because there's a possibility it won't work out?"

"I don't know what I'm going to do." She paced. "A part of me wants to believe what we've got happening between us is real and doable. But..."

"Can't we ignore that pesky doubt?"

She shook her head. "No. Because that other part of myself keeps reminding me what happened the last time I let go and let my emotions make my decisions."

"Let me ask, if he'd not betrayed you, would you still be with him?"

"I hate him."

"That's not what I asked. I said, had he not done what he did, would you still be with him?"

"I'll never know because he did. Just like I have no idea if you're really this good guy you're making yourself out to be. What if that's also a sham? How long did your last relationship last?"

He shook his head. "This is where you're making the mistake. We can't compare what happened before to now.

What I feel for you is different than anything I've ever felt."

The words brought a flush to her cheeks, and she dropped her gaze, staring at the carpet. "That feeling will fade."

"Are you so sure of that?"

She opened her mouth, probably for another rebuttal.

He growled. Why wouldn't she give them a chance? He dragged her close to him and slanted his mouth over hers, stemming any more arguing. Reminding her of one of the ways they were so good together. So right.

If she'd pushed him away, he would have moved.

If she'd said no, he would have stopped.

He let his lips, and his lips alone, talk for him. Her mouth replied in nibbles, her tongue with sinuous grace, and her hands... Hot damn, her hands grabbed his ass and held him for dear life.

She kissed him as if she'd not seen him in ages. He kissed her as if he'd almost lost her and found her again.

They were wrapped around each other. Arms, lips, bodies pressed.

A shout interrupted. "Move the fuck away from me."

"Carla!" Audrey gasped.

Declan sprang into action. He yanked the door open and charged onto the cracked sidewalk outside. His hand around the grip of his gun, ready to shoot.

Kill if necessary.

Audrey pushed past him, and he let her with a shake of his head. Carla had no need of help. The fellow, wearing tattoos across even his face, knelt on the ground. Carla held a gun to his forehead as she ranted. "Is this how you treat women? Is this how you would treat your mother?"

Carla spat on the ground. "You are not a man." She dropped her aim to something lower, and the thug dropped his hands to cover his junk.

"I'm sorry," the tattooed thug replied.

Carla's hand pulled back, and he flinched. "Get out of here. Now!" Carla snapped. "Before I make sure you don't ruin the gene pool by procreating."

The big dude ran, the situation easily resolved.

But it gave Declan the argument he needed. He crossed his arms, projected the sternest look he could on Audrey, and said, "It's not safe here. You need to come with me." He didn't thump his chest, yet he might as well have given how tightly Audrey's face pinched. It was Carla who jumped in to save him.

"Man's got a point. Place is a shithole."

"You chose it!" Audrey pointed out.

"Because I'm cheap. But the baby deserves better." Carla eyed him. "I hear you got a nice loft."

Audrey finally unfroze enough to snap, "The loft is compromised."

"So you say. But as far as we know, that condo isn't, and it's got great security. How many bedrooms?" Carla asked.

"Two."

A smirk crossed the Latina's face. "Perfect. You two get the master, and I'll take the spare."

"We're not sharing a bed," Audrey protested hotly.

"Then fuck on the floor."

"Carla!" Audrey screeched. "Language."

However, Carla kept talking as if Audrey hadn't said a word. "You want me to change my language, then let's go somewhere that doesn't think the word 'fuck' should be present in every sentence."

"Why me?" Audrey sighed.

"I can sleep on the couch," Declan offered.

Audrey glared at him. "I should make you."

"Or you could stop being stubborn," Carla interjected. "Lighten up. The man is pretty. Take advantage of him."

"Pretty?" He made a face.

Audrey grimaced. "How exactly are we supposed to pull this off?"

"The same way I got in. You're the nanny, and I'm his hot and sexy Brazilian girlfriend."

Was it him, or did Audrey growl?

He certainly noticed a glower when she sat in the back of his borrowed car while Carla got in the passenger seat. As Carla reminded, the hired help always sat in the back.

Audrey's lack of conversation during the ride might have bothered him more if he didn't know the cause.

Jealousy.

And where there was a burning green fire, there was hope.

CHAPTER TWENTY-THREE

THEY ENTERED THE CONDO VIA THE PARKING GARAGE, Declan using the fob on his keychain to open the door to the underground lobby. Audrey felt naked as they exited the car, unpacking the baby and her stuff.

Audrey, in the role of nanny, cared for Harper, whereas Carla, Declan's fake girlfriend—who hung on a touch too tightly and smiled a bit too widely—clung to Declan, impeding his intention to help.

Grumbling about it meant showing it bothered.

Which it did.

Very much bothered.

What did that say about Audrey?

That I am once again falling for the wrong man.

Not that he'd done anything wrong. Yet. On the contrary, Declan did everything right. He said the right things, showed a bit of hesitation, but didn't let fear control his actions.

He didn't let trepidation interfere with his wants and needs.

Carla had mocked Audrey's hesitation earlier in the hotel room with a snorted, "If I had waited for the right guy to come along, I'd be eight years dry at this point. Do you want to turn into a spinster with cobwebs between your thighs, or are you going to live life knowing for every up there will be a down?"

Deep words from her friend, who went through men quickly, wasting no time dumping as soon as she realized he wasn't the right guy.

Audrey wondered how Carla protected her heart. She already knew that Declan would break hers.

You think Declan is the problem? her inner voice derided. *You're the one who wants to run away.*

Damned subconscious. It poked holes in her reasoning.

Can't know what will happen if I don't even try.

It kept her mind occupied as they rode the elevator, Audrey with her head tucked, hands on the handles of the stroller. Declan stood with Carla draped on his arm. Neither paid Audrey much mind.

It bothered her a heck of a lot more than it should have.

They made it to the apartment, and yet they didn't drop the act. Declan had warned them before arriving that they should run a sweep.

"What about the security?" Audrey asked. "Isn't it set to ping if there are issues?"

"I think we can all agree that security is only as good as the next hack. The times I've not been overcautious, new lessons were carved into my skin."

It brought to mind his scars, a few on his upper body, the puckered hole by his heart being the most worrisome. He was a man of action.

Could a man get any sexier?

Upon entry, Audrey pretended to fuss over the baby all the while triggering a bug detector in the stroller. Declan kicked off his shoes and announced, "I'm going to grab something from the wine rack." Which happened to be in the utility room—with the Wi-Fi router.

According to the plan, he would reset it, which would cause everything on it to disconnect. He'd then watch his app to see what signed on and lock out any signals outside this condo. No remote viewing would be allowed.

Lifting the baby, Audrey snared the blanket with the bug sweeper tucked inside. They wandered towards the living room area at first, Audrey humming to Harper, pausing in the middle of it, pivoting and doing a large turn before announcing, "Someone's diaper needs a change." Which was code that her watch didn't vibrate, the detector saw nothing. She was sweeping a new location.

Conscious that cameras maybe watched—and Declan hadn't given the all clear yet—she moved through the dining room. Shifting the baby on one hip aimed at the kitchen, then the other hip to clear part of the dining room and hall.

She didn't react at the slight tremble in her wrist. She waited to reach the bedroom before exclaiming, "Who's a smelly girl?" Code for "We have a friend listening." Harper tried to crawl away the moment she hit the mattress on the bed. Audrey grabbed her by an ankle and laughed. "Silly baby. Get back over here." Extending her arm to capture her escaping child, she could see the face of her watch. The second hand staying still and quivering. A mini compass for a signal.

While she took care of Harper, who did have a smelly

diaper, she listened. A distant murmur of voices. It roused a jealousy that she couldn't shake.

When Declan entered the bedroom finally, he startled her with his, "Took care of—"

Don't say it. Her wrist had also vibrated in the bedroom. She whirled and opened her eyes wide. Her lips rounded into the word *no*, but she said, "Mr. Hood, can I help you?"

"You most certainly can." He prowled towards her. Eyes alight with mischief. Sensual and sexy in his prowl.

Audrey might have taken a step back, except Harper chose to let go of her neck and reach arms for him.

"I think she wants you," Audrey managed to say despite a dry mouth.

"Oh, I think she does." He might have grabbed the baby, but his eyes, his words, those were for Audrey.

"If you'll excuse me, sir." She went to move around him, but he blocked her, still wearing that naughty smile.

"Don't leave. I've been wanting to get you alone. If only Carla hadn't decided to show up. I swear, we broke up."

Her mouth rounded. What game was he playing? "Didn't look broken up to me."

"I've told her I've fallen for you. She thinks it's just a passing craze. A male fantasy about a nanny."

This time, she fought not to smile. The idiot was playing. Playing as if this were a soap opera for anyone listening.

"Is it just a craze? I've seen Carla. She's..." Audrey dropped her head lest she snicker aloud. "So beautiful."

"You are a thousand times more gorgeous." He moved towards her, and she stepped out of reach, getting fully into the area on the other side of the bed. The watch didn't buzz.

She inclined her head. "You should leave. We can't do this. Not now." Her tone dropped, and she eyed him wickedly. "Not ever." She pushed past him, traversing to the other side of the bed, feeling the twitch in her wrist. Something with a signal was nearby.

Someone had entered the apartment.

"Don't say that. What you and I have, it's special."

"I bet you say that to all the girls." Did he? Because that would totally kill the warmth in her heart.

"Nope. You're the one I want."

He stepped towards her, and she backed into the wall. The baby squirmed to get down. He let Harper down at his feet. She crawled towards the hall and the main area with Carla.

She'd be fine for a minute while Audrey dealt with the bug. Where would it be? The nightstand didn't have much on it, not even a lamp. But her glass of water...

"I could use a drink," she exclaimed, reaching for it. Declan beat her to it, knocking it over just as her fingers fumbled for it. She stroked them over the underside of the cup. Found the tiny bug. They were so small these days. It made her wonder how many of them got eaten by accident and... You know.

She pinched it between her fingers, marched to the bathroom and ran it under a hard stream of water. She let it go and watched the water swirl. Conscious of the fact that he'd followed, his heat at her back.

He ran the edge of his knuckles down her arm, and she glanced into the mirror. Shouldn't have as her eyes locked with his. She saw his head dip as he nuzzled aside her hair and placed a soft kiss on her neck. "I do want you."

"Who planted the bugs?" She tried to ignore him.

"Don't know. But I've already texted Mason to pull all surveillance footage."

"It's not safe."

"Not safe would have been leaving someone behind."

"Someone tried to listen."

"The key word being 'tried' and you're avoiding me."

She ducked her head. How to explain? "I'm scared."

"I'll protect you." He misunderstood, and yet, for a moment, she wanted to believe in him. In them.

She turned in his arms and laced them around his neck. She didn't say anything, just hugged him tightly, her mouth finding his in a torrid kiss.

Why fight this? Why not take the pleasure as long as she could?

The passion abruptly halted at the yank on her pants by a chubby fist. She looked down and saw Harper using them both to climb to her feet, grinning wetly at them.

Nookie time would have to wait.

What torture it was to sit across from him, one eye on Harper, the other straying to him while conscious of Carla watching. Audrey didn't know how to act with him. The spying devices were gone, which meant he and Carla no longer played the happy couple. However, Audrey wouldn't exactly call herself and Declan a couple either.

She didn't know what they were, so she avoided him. Which only worked for a short while. When she'd left to fetch a drink, on her return, he snagged her and got her to sit beside him.

He had her at his side at dinner, choosing to feed Harper so Audrey could eat. Carla smirked between bites.

After dinner, Harper got to watch some children's shows while they went over the plan for the open house. Carla offered to go as his girlfriend, her impromptu act to get in the building the first time, screwing Audrey out of the chance to use that as a cover to get in.

Given someone obviously watched them, they'd have to maintain their guise each time they left the apartment.

The question was, who watched? And how brazen would they get?

Declan didn't think they'd come after them full force at the condo.

"Too public," he claimed. "This isn't a movie where the bad guys, with no regard for people videotaping, storm private residences, gun blazing. They've got to be subtler."

Audrey arched a brow. "How was trying to grab us off the street subtle?"

"That was a quick crime of opportunity that would have worked with anyone else." He squeezed her hand.

So sweet.

She took the plunge and did something bolder. Placed her hand on his thigh.

A moment later, his hand covered hers. Her stomach just about exploded with butterflies.

"Could it be Suarez who planted them?" Carla asked. "He knows you're staying here."

"Why would he be watching me? I'm just his realtor."

"Why wouldn't you assume he was?" Audrey said with surprise. "You keep telling me the guy's a control freak. Is it so far-fetched to think he might have had someone plant a few bugs to see what his employee is up to?"

"He's not my boss."

"But he is your obnoxious client. Who is criminal enough to receive stolen art."

"You don't know that for sure. You haven't found it yet," Declan countered.

"You're splitting hairs. We need to find out if Suarez is playing games. I need to get inside his place."

"Not as the nanny you're not. I don't want you bringing Harper anywhere near the party."

"You're forbidding me?" The very idea of it made Audrey laugh. "You can't tell me what to do; however, on the Harper front, I agree. I won't be taking her into possible danger. Which means, I need to go as someone else."

"I don't know if that will work. The file I brought might be better suited for Carla."

Her hand left his leg. "This is my mission."

"No one is trying to take it from you," Carla interjected. "We'll make whatever he brought work."

Declan eyed her and grinned. "Good thing you're handy with a makeup brush and wig." A form of apology that she accepted.

They spent time after that studying the identity he'd provided in the envelope. A rich recluse, not often seen, who always wore sunglasses. Easy enough to mimic. More astonishing, Declan even provided fingerprints to slip over her own.

Fancy.

But the prep work to slip into the persona of someone else was for tomorrow. When Carla yawned and went off to bed, leaving Audrey with a drooling Harper on her chest, and Declan, with just a plain sexy chest, she was all too conscious of how she looked and probably smelled.

When she went to rise, Declan was there, grabbing Harper and laying her down in the playpen. It might have been awkward then—what to say, what to do—but he grabbed her by the hand, didn't say a word. Pulled her into the master bedroom and straight into the master bath.

He shut the door, and she protested. "Harper—"

"Is sleeping, and you need a bath or something to relax."

The water ran a moment after he'd declared it, and he sat on the edge of the tub, testing it with his fingers under the jet.

A bath did sound heavenly. Carla would hear if Harper did wake and interrupt if necessary.

Audrey stripped. Shirt, pants, underthings. All of it hit the floor.

His jaw joined them.

It was nice to see she could still have that kind of effect on a man. The other night, in the dark and with blankets, it was easy to pretend she'd not had a child. That her belly was indeed still perfectly flat. The stretch marks not lining her skin.

He didn't seem to see her flaws. He smiled. A big, toothy grin of appreciation.

"Strip," she ordered.

"Yes, ma'am." He tugged off his shirt, leaving his upper body bare. His pants followed, and she saw the proof of his arousal.

She stepped past him into the tub, the warm water swirling around her ankles. The bath only large enough for one.

Pity.

She leaned back and closed her eyes, skin flushed as she felt his gaze devouring her. The heated water soothed her tired muscles. Muscles that tensed the moment he brushed his fingers over her.

She couldn't help a fine tremble as he stroked softly, lightly over her skin. He replaced the callused tips with cloth, the fabric abrading and bringing forth even more shivers of delight.

He spent time rubbing around her nipples, startling her when he bobbed over the edge of the tub to suck at one. The washcloth traveled between her thighs, rubbing against her mound, making her hips roll in the water. He let the cloth drift and touched her. His fingers stroking lightly, teasing her underwater, making her pant with need.

He reached for her and held her atop the water, one arm under her shoulders, pulling her up so that he might suckle her nipple. Drawing sharp cries of pleasure.

His other hand cupped her mound, a finger inserted between her nether lips, something for her pulsing sex to grip. She pumped against his hand, wanting more from him.

There was a rocking of water and a shift in position as he managed to wedge himself into the tub. She gripped the sides, wondering what he did, only to gasp as he lifted her bottom and placed his face between her thighs.

He licked her. Licked her slit and found her clit. He flicked it with his tongue. Teased it. He played her body like a fine instrument, drawing forth the tautest strains of pleasure. Making her gasp to his masterful melody.

He licked her and tasted her, making her pleasure ramp higher and higher. Brought her to the brink, dragged her to him. "Sit on me," he whispered in her ear before nipping it.

She sheathed him, the water making it tight, her body shuddering as she shoved him in and stretched. Oh, how she stretched so delightfully around him.

She clung to his shoulders, bouncing and riding. Exclaiming her pleasure and finally coming all over him. Collapsing against his chest.

Holding him tight.

Never wanting to let go.

What would it be like to live like this every day? To have someone steady in her life? A man she wouldn't have to keep secrets from. A father figure for Harper. A partner in life.

A lover at night...

Could a killer mom have a happily ever after?

CHAPTER TWENTY-FOUR

DECLAN HAD PROBLEMS LETTING GO THE NEXT morning. They'd spent the night entwined, only making love once, her droopy eyes and satisfied expression leading him to put her to bed. He joined her.

He wondered how long he could keep this feeling going. Because he had a fear that once the open house was done, and her mission accomplished, Audrey would leave.

He didn't want that. The emptiness he'd felt when he entered the condo to find her gone wasn't something he wanted to repeat.

But how to make her stay?

He needed to give her a reason. Because he was realistic enough to know that good sex and good times wouldn't be enough to sway her.

What did Audrey need?

For some reason, he flashed back to his academy lessons. Mostly the ones on undercover work.

He could hear the always tweed-wearing professor Monroe saying in his monotone voice, "The keys to a long-lasting, good cover are a home"—easy enough to find if she didn't want to stay with him—"transportation,"—he'd gladly loan her a car, he owned a few—"reason for moving"—a little bit tougher. What excuse would a woman have for coming to the city? And the final tip from the professor on being undercover... "A job. Even if you don't need the cash, you can't just bum around all day."

Which meant, in order for her to stay, Audrey needed a job. She'd said she worked as an interior designer. Which was a nice complement to the realty business when you thought about it. Add in the fact that their office lacked a feminine touch of late...

An idea percolated.

While Declan would have enjoyed sticking around, he did have to prep for the open house and check into a few other things. He had absolutely no problem dropping a kiss on Harper's head before he headed out the door—Audrey got one on the lips.

"See you later." After the open house, he'd make sure he nabbed her and talked to her about staying. By then, he'd have lined up all the arguments for it.

He left the condo, looking like every other business guy heading off for work at nine in the morning. Suits got the perks of making their hours. He missed all the traffic, grabbed a bagel and coffee on the way, and hit the office where he spent a boring few hours.

Around three, Sherry—recovered from her cold—buzzed him. "Some baby stuff just arrived for you."

He frowned. "What baby stuff? I didn't order anything."

Perhaps Audrey had. Which was a good sign. If she

were getting more things, then that probably meant she planned to stay.

He exited his office and headed to the front, noting the back of the delivery guy's tan shirt as the elevator doors closed behind him. He made a beeline for the box sitting on the counter. It had a smiling baby on the front, sitting in a sling.

Harper already had a sling.

The box didn't have any tape holding it shut.

His gut twisted. "Pull the fire alarm." He grabbed the box and held it away from him, as if that would make a difference if the thing exploded. "Evacuate the break room," he hollered as he ran into it. It was already empty.

The microwave opened at the push of a button. He shoved the package inside and slammed the door closed. He dove out of the break room, yanking its door shut behind him.

A glance over at the elevator showed it at floor number three, two, lobby.

Boom.

The break room door buckled but held, the steel frame twisting a bit against the impact. A siren wailed, the fire alarm kicking in.

Another thing kicked in, as well. The realization that someone had attacked him.

Which made it clear that this wasn't necessarily all about Audrey and her ex. The attack at her house was before she met him. A separate thing altogether. Perhaps all along, he was the target. And whoever wanted him dead had just gotten serious about it.

Cool.

Audrey didn't see it in the same light. The moment he

finished telling his story—once he reached the condo and bellowed, "Honey, I'm home," as he walked in —Audrey launched into a tirade.

"You idiot. You almost died!"

"Not even close. There isn't a scratch on me."

Audrey grabbed him by the lapels of his coat and yanked herself close to hiss, "You handled a bomb."

"Secured it."

"I don't care what you call it. It was dumb, and you could have died."

"But didn't. Good thing, or the open house would be off tonight."

Audrey shoved away from him. "Idiot. Your life is more important." Not exactly a declaration of undying love, but he'd take it.

The bomb at the office meant taking more care at the condo. What if his enemy came after him here? It also meant a slight change in plans for the evening.

A plan Audrey would have to accomplish alone. Because as the afternoon hour waned, it was time for Declan to set the stage for the open house.

He just didn't want to leave Audrey.

His gut was tightening again. He made one last attempt to change her mind. "Tell me what to look for, and I'll handle it for you."

She shook her head. "My mission. My responsibility. Besides, what if it's not there? What if your client is innocent? If you're caught, it might cost you big time."

"I don't care about the commission."

Whereas she didn't care what he said. She patted his cheek. "I've got to get ready."

The plan involved Audrey, in her disguise, slipping

unseen from the building and then re-entering again as if she'd just arrived.

He turned to Carla, who sat curled on the couch, a laptop nestled in her lap. "What's the status on the ghosting part of the plan?"

"Cameras are ready to play on a loop for this floor. Elevator one, as well. As soon as Audrey leaves, I'm going to suspend all the logs for the elevator for three minutes. So don't dally." Carla aimed this last bit at Audrey. "Get down to the basement level, but don't go into the garage itself. There will be a car waiting for you by the service entrance. Cameras are trickier there, so you'll have to move fast because I can only suspend them for thirty seconds before someone notices."

Declan didn't appear convinced. "There's still time for me to bring you in as my assistant."

"Because Suarez won't think it's weird at all you've suddenly got one. Don't worry, Zee." She patted his cheek. "This will work."

And if it didn't? Then they'd go to plan B. Which he liked to call winging it.

CHAPTER TWENTY-FIVE

POOR DECLAN HAD HIS FACE IN A KNOT WHEN HE LEFT the condo. He worried. Too much.

Cute, but cramping her style. She could do this. It helped to know that Carla would be guarding the baby, leaving Audrey free to attend the open house with the stolen identity of a rich socialite. They weren't hard to impersonate, most choosing to stay out of the media's eye. They had a certain uniform look to them, as well. One that Audrey achieved with the liberal application of makeup plus an intricate hairstyle. Amazing how easily one could change.

Emerging from the bedroom, she twirled for Carla.

"Not bad. You'll pass." Carla handed her a wallet with the identification they'd fiddled with. "Remember to stick to the timeline. We have no room for error."

"I know. I know." Carla had harped on it numerous times already. "If this works, you'll be on your way home tomorrow."

Carla barked. "As if. You and I both know I'm not

going anywhere until this new problem with your ex is resolved."

"If it's him. Declan seems to think he's the one drawing the problems."

"Maybe he is. What if he's not? I'm gonna stick around until we know for sure. Besides, you could use a hand getting settled in."

"What are you talking about? I'm not living here. Mother already has a new place waiting for me."

Carla cast her a side eye. "You'd be an idiot to go. Tell her you want to stay. She'll make it happen."

"Isn't it crazy, though?"

"Totally. Which is why you should do it. Live a little, Audrey."

She could hear an echoing voice in her head. *Love a little, Audrey.*

Nerves fluttered in her stomach.

Carla pointed a finger at her. "It's time."

"You sure you'll be okay with Harper?"

"You insulting my parenting skills?"

"Of course, not."

"Then shut up and go. I got this. Harper is safe." If someone got past Carla to Harper, then Audrey probably wouldn't have stood a chance. Carla had been with KM a lot longer than Audrey. She came into the agency at the delicate age of nineteen with a baby in tow. Ten years later, the soccer mom slash mercenary could handle herself against just about anything.

"Get those cameras ready." Audrey positioned herself by the door. When Carla gave the signal, she moved, heading quickly down the hall at a brisk pace, hoping that no one would see her as she passed. Not that it would matter much. The chances of whoever was watching also attending the open house were slim. The guest list catered to a select group. Or was it Suarez? Hopefully, by the end of the night, they'd know.

The elevator dinged within seconds of her calling it, and once the doors closed, it plummeted straight to the basement. She was conscious of the clock ticking. This part of the plan—actually the rest of it—relied on everything going smoothly at each stage. She couldn't maintain radio contact with Carla. No earpieces or even jewelry with a signal. They didn't want to take chances with Suarez being so paranoid and the goons checking guests at the door.

As Audrey followed the preset path, she had to hope the cameras were off and no one was watching. She slipped out of the condominium into the rear alley, the town car waiting as promised. It moved the moment she slid into the rear passenger seat.

Blonde hair escaped in curling tendrils from the bulk of it tucked under a driver's cap. A glance in the rearview mirror showed her a face she knew.

"Tanya?" Audrey queried.

"Hey, babe. How's it going?" Tanya maneuvered the large car out of the alley and performed a loop to make it seem as if they arrived from a different direction.

"My house blew up," Audrey offered.

"I heard. That bites."

"Especially since I just repainted the guest bath." All that work, wasted.

"How is the baby?"

"Good. Your boy?"

"He made the competitive hockey team." Tanya

flashed a bright smile in the rearview mirror. "He is a star. Next Gretzky for sure."

KM's Canadian agent took her code name of Hockey Mom too seriously.

"I can't believe Mother sent you and Carla down. I had this handled." Perhaps not as smoothly as she would have liked, but, still, did Mother have no faith in her?

"As if we wouldn't come when we heard asshat might be after you and the baby."

"Mother told you?"

"No secrets, remember?" Not between agents, at least. It was part of making them a family. The only one allowed to hide stuff was Mother.

"We don't know for sure it's Mendez."

"Doesn't matter who it is. We'll keep you safe." Tanya pulled to a stop in front of the condo where the doorman awaited. "I'll be close by in case you need to leave hot."

"Here's to hoping that doesn't happen." Because if she were running for her life, she wouldn't dare grab Harper and drag her into danger, too.

The doorman pulled open the rear passenger door and offered Audrey a hand out. He wasn't the regular fellow she'd observed on previous occasions, even if he wore the uniform. She noted the white hunk of plastic in his ear. His piece would pick up every word spoken, and she wondered if the pin on his lapel was filming guests as they arrived.

She kept her chin high and her gaze disinterested. *I am now a snooty lady of high society.* Entering the lobby, she noted a woman sitting in a chair. Another familiar face. Meredith, another operative, dressed in a business suit, carrying a slim, leather attaché case.

Meredith stood and pulled out a sheet of paper. "Mrs. Grossman. Here are the specs on the property we're about to see."

Sniffing, Audrey—the new Mrs. Grossman—ignored the offering. "Bland numbers and descriptions. You better not have dragged me out to see a dump, Ms. Pattinson."

"As I told you on the phone, it's a very exclusive listing. We're lucky we even managed to get an invite so late."

"Hmmph." Conscious the doorman captured every word, Audrey dared not slip out of her role.

The man escorted them to the private elevator, activating it with the press of his palm. Even within the confines of the box, they didn't dare say anything. Eyes and ears still tracked.

Upon exiting in the vestibule, Audrey took note of the two hulking guards carrying metal detecting wands advancing on them.

She arched a brow. "Is the security in this building so lax that we must resort to extreme vetting?"

Declan chose that moment to emerge from the penthouse looking utterly delicious in his dark suit and sleek hair. "Ladies. So glad you could come. Sorry for the checkpoint. My client values his privacy. I'm sure you understand."

That earned him a disdainful sniff. She passed their muster—her gun having been left behind with Carla—and entered the condo.

It was as if she'd been transported to a sterile landscape. White everywhere she looked as if it had snowed inside, blanketing every surface and leeching every ounce of color. The only contrast was with the people. A dozen or so she noted at first glance—the men wearing suits, the women in a myriad rainbow of fabric from slinky evening dresses to more casual slacks and cashmere sweaters. The one thing everyone had in common was the oozing wealth. It emitted a vibe when gathered in one spot.

Declan pointed to a pile of footwear beside a woven basket filled with booties. "If you wouldn't mind. The owner is quite fond of his carpet."

"I prefer hardwood," was her reply as she slid off her shoes and put on the soft fabric booties. Between them and the carpet underfoot, it would make sneaking around super easy. She'd have to pay attention lest someone surprise her poking her nose where she shouldn't.

"There's wine and snacks in the kitchen area. Which you'll notice contains a plethora of state-of-the-art appliances, including a chef's stove, a walk-in fridge, and dual dishwashers for when you entertain. A perfect place for making cookies." He winked.

Casting a glance at the massive island that could easily sit a dozen people on the stools tucked under the edge, her lip curled. "More white."

"It wouldn't take much to brighten up the place," Declan replied, leading her inside by the elbow. It was hard to pretend nonchalance. His touch electrified. She couldn't react. She wasn't supposed to know him.

"If you'd like to attend to the other guests, I can tour my client," Meredith stated.

"Be sure to poke your head in the office. It's got a fabulous view of the city." A reminder from Declan that he believed Suarez might be hiding the treasure, but Audrey had a different idea. She made a show of checking out the living room, a huge open space with white leather couches, clear glass side tables, and an incredible view of the city lit up and sparkling at night.

There was nowhere to hide anything, short of ripping open cushions, opening walls, or tearing up flooring. She glided into the kitchen and pretended to inspect the cupboards, grimaced at the fridge—*Ugh, just look at all those carbs*—before running her hand over the white marble of the dining table.

Having done her duty for anyone watching in the main rooms, she slid down the hall, popping her head into a guest bath. Then two bedrooms—all white, yet managing to look different. One opting for a woven white theme that gave texture to the wallpapered walls and stitched bedspread. The other bedroom presented a country feel with painted panels and actual cow skin for a rug.

The next room had to be the office. The massive room contained more color than the other spaces, the bookcases on the walls to the left and right as she walked in packed with books. Classics, for the most part, she noted as she perused the titles on the spines. Noticeably absent during the meandering was any staff.

She'd expected to see some of Suarez's people mingling. Declan had expected it, too.

Odd.

She swiped a finger across the white wood desk, the gleam of the grain enhanced by the smooth, clear lacquer.

"Imagine meeting clients here," Meredith gushed. "And did you notice the built-ins?" Audrey's fake realtor crouched and pulled at the closed cupboards lining the bottom. "Dovetail joints. Plenty of storage." While Meredith casually peeked inside the ones on the left, Audrey pretended boredom as she opened a few on her right. "They're not very deep," she noted. Not deep enough for the object.

"According to the specs, the master bedroom has a massive closet. More than enough room to store larger items."

"Because I want to store my prized possessions with my clothes." Audrey tossed her head.

"Why don't we take a peek?" Meredith led the way, and Audrey followed, the long hall between the office and the master bedroom providing separation from the main living area and even the guest quarters. As she entered the bedroom, they noted another couple touring the space, and Audrey had to school her features. Mason of BBI was leading around a corpulent man in a suit.

Her fake realtor didn't have to pretend. "Yummy fellow," Meredith declared. "Hello there, dahling." She drew out the word and held out her hand.

Mason, somewhat startled, gripped it and shook, almost causing Audrey to burst out laughing. Meredith probably expected a kiss on it, not a rapid pump. "Hello. I'm Mason with Bad Boy Inc."

"Meredith with Killer Realty."

"Are you from around here? I don't think we've met before."

"You might not have heard of us. We're very exclusive."

Mason's client snorted. "More like sexist. I've heard of them. It's one of them feminist, bra-burning places that only works with women."

"Because they're smart," Audrey declared. "I want to see this famous closet." She marched away from the man before she smacked him. Attitudes like his were why the Killer brand was needed.

The closet proved grand. Spacious. With an island and room for hundreds of shoes. But...

Audrey counted paces as she exited the room. Then counted more as she hit the hall. It didn't match up. Somewhere between the office and the closet, there were about fifteen feet missing. A hidden room that either Declan neglected to mention, or he didn't know about.

Question was, how to get into it? Because she'd wager she'd found where Suarez hid the object.

Sticking close to Meredith as they headed to the main living area, she whispered, "I need to explore that closet some more." Chances were the entrance was hidden there.

Checking her watch, Meredith muttered, "Give me two minutes."

Two minutes for the diversion part of their plan. Aloud, Audrey declared, "Did the master bedroom closet have a mirror?"

"I think it did."

"Think isn't good enough. At the price they're asking, this place must be perfect." Tossing her head, Audrey stalked back down the hall, conscious of the ticking clock.

The bedroom was empty this time around, and she had to force herself to do a circuit of the room, mentally counting down before she entered the closet. As she exclaimed over the lack of lighting, she moved to the far wall, noting the seams of the organizer. The clear space on the floor in front of it.

Meredith, who'd followed, excused herself. "Can you explore on your own for a moment, Mrs. Grossman? I need to take this call. I'll be right outside." Keeping watch as the seconds ticked down to zero.

The sudden plunge into darkness left Audrey blinking

spots. The power failure not only removed all sources of lights, but power to the cameras, too. She didn't have much time.

The watch she wore, while lovely, also served as a flashlight. She pressed the button on the side and illuminated the pitch-black closet. She immediately began palpating the storage unit, looking for a soft spot, a hook to tug as a lever. She found it inside the top drawer at the back.

Click.

Luckily, the hidden door relied on simple mechanics and not power. It pulled open, and she crept in, listening for a warning. When she didn't hear one, she tugged the hidden door closed behind her just as the power returned, illuminating everything.

She blinked and made sense of what she saw. There was a lot in here to process, starting with the color from the rich tapestry of the woven rug, to the paintings on the wall —one of which she was pretty sure had been stolen recently from a museum in France. Then she saw it by a window, sitting on a pedestal—the urn she'd been sent to find. The hieroglyphics etched on its side told secrets the world wasn't ready to hear.

Remove or destroy. They could discredit images if they had to. But the vase itself...no one could ever examine it.

Before she could lay a hand on it, someone hit her on the back of the head.

CHAPTER TWENTY-SIX

THE POWER FAILURE PLUNGED THE CONDO INTO unexpected darkness. It didn't take a genius to figure out what had happened.

Audrey. She'd probably planned it.

She was that good.

He'd gotten the shock of his life when Audrey arrived, playing the part of Mrs. Grossman, rich trophy wife. Her blonde hair swept into a bun with artful curls. Her eyes hidden by large sunglasses, the lenses more of a smoky gray than concealing. She wore a very well-tailored outfit, the slacks nipped at the waist, loose by the ankles. Her jacket form-fitting with a flair, and embroidered with silver. However, it was her face that startled him most.

He knew it was she. Knew it, yet that recognition came about only because of instinct, a flare of fire from his body, which reacted to her presence. Because he didn't recognize her. The makeup had changed the appearance of her face somehow. Her cheeks seemed hollowed. Her nose a narrow slash. Even the shape of her lips was different.

Incredible. A reminder that she was not only a wonderful mother and lover but also a true professional. A partner.

Which was sexier than expected.

He had to look away from her after he'd led her inside lest someone watching notice the sparks between them. He wanted to melt her fake snooty attitude. Slide his hands inside her blouse and see what she hid.

Could even be a knife. She admitted to carrying a small one. Made of stone so as to avoid detection.

He'd yet to find it on her, but he really wanted a chance to search.

In her guise of client, she wandered around while he entertained those left behind. Faking a bright chatter that was more by rote than interest, he kept a close eye on everyone. Some he already knew, brokers he'd met before. Even some rich faces that enjoyed acquiring properties, collecting them around the world in the Guinness-sized version of Monopoly played with other wealthy patrons.

Screw growing houses into a hotel. Everyone knew retail space was where it was at. You can charge a lot of money for prime locations.

He was sipping a glass of water dyed to look like wine when the power extinguished. He didn't panic, simply listened in the pitch black, his eyes closed.

The lack of lighting didn't last long. Power was quickly restored, and he opened his eyes, not blinded at all, unlike many in the room. By their excited chatter, they'd never been in the sudden dark before. He quickly did a head count. Nobody appeared to be missing except for Audrey and her partner, the realtor.

"Just a glitch, folks," he said, his voice carrying over

them. Voices calmed, and Declan tried to act natural. Meanwhile, he was dying to know if Audrey had found the item.

Doing a circuit of the room, he startled as he came face-to-face with Suarez. The man stood just inside the hall, wearing a dark outfit that emphasized his tanned skin. His brown eyes met Declan's.

When had the man arrived? Why?

They'd discussed—more like Declan had insisted—that Suarez should make himself scarce during the showing. Bad enough the guests were frisked as they came in. The last thing he needed was for Suarez to pull his pompous airs. Declan was here to do a job.

Two of them, actually. The first job might very well succeed, given the very wealthy philanthropist Mason had brought through as his cover had declared he'd be calling the office in the morning with an offer. As to the other reason he was here, he had to garner Audrey enough time to find the stolen vase.

"Mr. Hood." Suarez purred his name.

No way to avoid it. He'd have to stop and chat. Declan pasted a genial smile on his face. "Sir, what are you doing here?"

"It's my home."

It proved a fight not to grit his teeth. "It is getting rave reviews. Rumor has it we should have an offer—"

A hand sliced through the air cut him short. "I'm not interested in rumors. The open house is over."

"Sir? We were supposed to run until ten."

"Shut it down." Suarez shook his head. "I am no longer interested in selling."

The declaration stunned. "Excuse me?"

"Changed my mind. Get everyone out. Now."

Suarez made no attempt to control his tone, and people around them heard. They cast Suarez evil side-eyes, but none would beg to stay. Forget selling this place. Even in the future, these people wouldn't be back.

Rather than argue with Suarez, Declan made an announcement. "Sorry, but the property has just left the market."

Murmurs of discontent went through the room, along with speculation. The less Declan said, the more intrigued they would be. He might have lost the sale on this place, but people would remember him. Wonder what had happened at the open house. Had it sold that quickly?

Once most of the main area had cleared, he went through the place room by room, poking his head into doors. He found Suarez in his office, facing the window overlooking the city. Hands steepled.

"Is it done?"

"Almost, sir. Just making sure everyone left." Because he'd yet to see Audrey and her partner.

"Hurry up. I am a busy man."

Had Declan been able to wear a gun, that might have been the last thing the pompous ass Suarez said. He might not have found anything hardcore about him, but Declan didn't like the guy. He rubbed him wrong.

Leaving, he headed to the last place in the condo left to look. He found Meredith, the realtor, there, sans Audrey.

"Where is she?" he hissed.

Meredith shrugged and mouthed, "*Don't know,*" before saying aloud, "I lost her in the dark."

How could she have lost her? What had Audrey done

now? Declan couldn't ask, not with Suarez suddenly looming in the doorway.

"Is there a problem, Mr. Hood?" Suarez had followed and stood just inside the bedroom.

Yes, there was a problem. Audrey appeared to be missing, but the slight shake of Meredith's head kept those words hidden. "No problem, sir. Just disappointment. Lots of people were interested in the property."

"Yes, there were. It drew a nice crowd, Hood." Suarez had a sly smile. "Saw just the person I wanted."

The claim had an ominous undertone, and Declan wanted to confront the man. Was Suarez implying that he'd caught Audrey? He couldn't exactly ask.

What if Audrey had found her vase and already escaped with it? What if speaking blew whatever chance she had to complete her mission? He couldn't let his emotions interfere, not until he knew for sure.

With Suarez eyeballing them, he led Meredith from the condo, the pair of them silent in the elevator. When they reached the lobby, Declan said, "Listen, I know this property didn't pan out, but I have another your client might like. If you've got a few minutes, I've got the specs at my place, which is coincidentally on another floor."

"Mr. Hood, are you inviting me to your room?"

"If you're worried about a chaperone, don't be. My girlfriend, nanny, and daughter are inside."

"In that case, I'd love to see them."

They maintained the act for anyone watching, taking the second public elevator to the right floor. Him idly mentioning the stats on the supposed property.

He slid the key into the lock and led them into an empty condo.

Expected, yet still jarring. He'd known of the plan. A plan he'd not approved of. Moving Harper out of the condo exposed her. Yet, Audrey had insisted. She felt it was safer if Carla took her somewhere new.

Carla took advantage of the same camera lag that hid Audrey while exiting the building. She vacated the place, getting a ride with Ben, who took them somewhere secure.

Declan had already gotten a text with the all-clear message. One less thing to worry about.

Where was Audrey, though? He fired her a text.

Delivery failed.

Trying again bounced back, too. His lips flattened as he glanced at Meredith and saw her also glaring at her phone.

"I take it she should be replying."

"She's not, but Tanya is." The driver who dropped Audrey off. "Says she's been around the block and checked the three rendezvous points. Audrey's not there."

The words brought a chill. "So we don't know where Audrey is?"

A negative shake. "She might be somewhere safe, and her phone isn't working. Like she could still be inside the condo. I don't know. I lost track of her in the dark."

"Where was the last place you saw her?"

"Master bedroom. She told me to watch the door while she searched the closet. The lights went off, and when they came back on, I went into the closet, but she was gone."

Had she found the vase in the closet? Where? He'd been through it with several people when the open house started. There was nothing along that stupidly long hall to get to the bedroom, not even a door.

It hit him. "Fuck me. That long hallway." He wanted to slap himself for not noticing it before. "There's a room hidden between the office and the closet." Panic rooms were common, and he should have thought of it. Then again, why hadn't Suarez told him about it?

"She could be trapped."

"Or she found the vase and managed to escape with it." He rubbed his chin. "Question is, how do we find out for sure?"

"We try other methods of tracking." Meredith took a seat at the table and placed her folio briefcase atop it. She unzipped it and began pulling out items. Pen, clipped to the front pocket. An eyeglasses case from which she pulled a pair of lenses that perched low on her nose.

The notebook she removed had a hard front and back cover, the middle—with actual notepaper—removed with only a firm yank. She began to tap on it, and the upper part illuminated.

"Hot damn, you've got a slim." One of the newest devices around. Thinner than a tablet, disguisable, too. It was like having the power and ability of a desktop hidden in plain sight.

Nice toy.

Declan preferred to pace as Meredith tapped away.

"Let's say she escaped, where would she have gone if her phone wasn't working?" He paused and glanced at the futuristic laptop.

"One of the three rendezvous points." Meredith slid her finger over a lit square, enlarging a map that showed a few pulsing spots.

"What are those?" he asked, leaning in for a closer look.

"The blue spots pulsing are the places we agreed upon

to meet. The ones Tanya"—she poked at a green spot that was moving—"has been monitoring."

"By driving around in circles? As if that weren't noticeable."

"She stopped and parked at a donut place." Meredith tapped the screen. "She's waiting to see if Audrey pings her."

His gaze tracked over the map and spots. He zeroed in on a purple one. "That's Carla." With the baby.

"Yes. She just texted me the all-clear."

He didn't sigh in relief but felt it. He was worried about Harper. With the little girl safe, he could concentrate on the mother.

"You're one of her friends."

"More than that. We're family." Meredith spared him a quick glance.

"I don't think Audrey knows that." The previous discussion of her issues came to mind.

"She's still pretty new. We're working on her. Takes time to realize not everyone in the world is out to get you." Meredith stopped tapping and frowned. "If she did escape, then she really should have contacted us by now."

"Could be she has her hands full."

"Or she never left. If he had a panic room, then it might be lined to prevent signals from getting in or out."

"So she might still be inside. Fuck." Declan rubbed his beard. "We need to get back in there."

"You're his realtor. Tell him you have an offer."

"Suarez doesn't want an offer. He told me he wasn't selling anymore."

"I don't suppose you want to go up there and grovel for the listing back?"

He shot Meredith a look. "How about we try something less emasculating, such as calling Suarez and claiming someone lost an earring. Ask if I can come look for it."

"He'll have his own people do that."

"Then we'll just have to kick the fucking door in." Once they managed to get past the elevator. Would it still allow him entry upstairs?

"His door will need more than a kick," was her wry reply.

"Good thing I have some explosive clay."

Meredith took a moment before beaming. "That would work."

And would totally blow any cover they had. But if Audrey were in danger, then there was no question. They had to save her.

Knock. Knock.

As if one mind, they looked at the door. Declan snared the gun he'd stashed in the vase by the entrance. He held up his phone and tapped the flashing app for the eyeball in the door.

"It's cool. It's my buddy Mason," Declan announced. Which was actually a bad sign. Why was his friend visiting so openly?

The door shut, and BBI's tech guru got right to the point. "My client wants to buy the condo. Think you can talk Suarez into actually selling it."

"Probably not, given I'm about to blow up his door to get Audrey out."

Mason whistled. "How the hell did she get stuck inside?"

"Either she got trapped in a secret room, or she got caught." Either way, they needed to go looking.

"Give it a few minutes, and you'll have fewer people to deal with. Looks like your client is going on a trip. Ben texted to say a helicopter landed on the roof."

That was a stroke of good news. If indeed Audrey were hidden inside, then they'd have a chance to get her out.

But what if Audrey was in trouble, and this delay cost them? He couldn't forget Suarez's smug smile.

"I did find something interesting," Meredith remarked. She pulled out a toothbrush.

"We already ran fingerprint and hair samples on Suarez." First thing Declan did was collect them so they could try and match Suarez to possible crimes or locations.

"Fingerprints are too easy to change these days, and anyone could see that hair wasn't all his."

"He's wearing a toupee?" A good one, obviously, since Declan never suspected.

"Hair plugs. Looks like he was originally brown-haired, but he had some darker chunks put in."

Declan tucked his hands behind his back. "I'll have someone grab the brush and run it, but it will take a few days. Our lab got roasted." By Audrey. He wondered if Harry would send an invoice to KM for the damages.

"Days?" Meredith snorted. "You boys need to upgrade your toys." She reached for the eyeglass case. Pried it open, snapped the head off the toothbrush, and put it in. She then placed her phone on top of it as if it were an induction mat. The case glowed, pulsing with light, and Mason dropped to his knees to peer at it.

"Is that what I think it is?"

"Portable Molecular Biolab. It runs waves through the samples and breaks down the components in seconds.

What the sample is made of. Plus, it can give us a rudimentary DNA sequence."

"How accurate is it?" Declan asked.

"Accurate enough to give us a baseline to run," Meredith stated, her glasses perched on the tip of her nose as she began studying the information being spat at her on her screen.

"Dude, we totally need to get Harry to buy us one." Mason turned an excited expression on Declan. "I need this in my life."

"Maybe Santa will bring it if you're a good boy," Declan declared. He wandered away from the group and dialed into his home security system back at the loft. The place where Carla had disappeared to with Harper. He zoomed in on the playpen and saw her inside, chest rising and falling, totally unaware that her mother was missing.

"Don't worry, diva. I'll find her," he whispered, even if she couldn't hear him.

"Declan!" Mason's call brought him in a rush.

"What is it? Has something happened?"

Mason handed him the phone. "It's Ben. We have a problem."

He put the cell to his ear. "Talk."

"Suarez is on the move. He's getting into the helicopter."

"And?"

"He's not alone. He's got a woman, and I doubt she's going voluntarily. One of his guards is carrying her."

Audrey. Shit. "Can you stop them from leaving?"

"I can try stalling the blades, but it's windy." Which meant, as good as Ben's sniper abilities were, the odds remained that he'd probably miss.

"Fuck. I'm going to see if I can stop them." He tossed the phone to Mason and bolted out of the condo, Meredith on his heels. He no longer cared about their cover. Suarez was obviously on to them.

I never should have left without Audrey.

The elevator wouldn't get him to the penthouse. They'd have to take the stairs, which were locked before the top floor. He snared a hunk of clay from his pocket. At least he'd thought to bring some. A hunk of the stuff around the knob, a wooden match as an igniter, which meant...short fuse. He ducked down the stairs.

Rumble.

The handle exploded, setting off an alarm. As if he cared about any blaring sirens. He kicked at the remains of the door and then had to repeat the process as he went up one more flight to the roof. Another door barred his way. Another explosion blasted it, and he emerged onto an empty roof deck, the pebbled surface bare. The helicopter already a distant hum.

Declan cursed and whirled as Mason emerged on the roof with him. He barked, "We need to find out where the chopper is going." Because he wanted to be there to meet it when it landed.

They made their way back with haste to the condo. The moment he walked in, he knew there was more bad news. His blood ran cold at the grim expression on Meredith's face. She pointed at her screen.

"I got the DNA results for Suarez."

Declan glanced at the information and didn't immediately grasp what they saw. "What am I looking at?"

A red nail pointed. "We found a match for his DNA."

Shouldn't that be a good thing? Except Meredith's face indicated it wasn't. "Who is it?"

"Suarez is Mendez."

The father of Audrey's child.

A man who'd tried to hurt her.

A killer who'd just kidnapped her.

Oh, shit.

CHAPTER TWENTY-SEVEN

WAKING UP WITH A THROBBING HEADACHE SUCKED.
Especially since she remembered how it happened.

Caught like a rookie. How had she missed the presence
of someone in that hidden room? How could she have
been so stupid?

How much trouble was she in? The fact that Audrey
couldn't move didn't bode well. A tug of her arms showed
them pulled behind her, the wrists taped together. Her legs
were also taped to the legs of the chair she sat on.

The slight stirring drew attention, and a mocking voice
said, "My lovely Edith."

She froze. It couldn't be. The voice was all wrong. But
the name and the way he said it...

Opening her eyes, she saw the tanned countenance of
Suarez. "What are you doing?"

"Anything I like." He smiled. She definitely knew that
smile. "It's been a while, Edith."

"Mendez." She whispered his last name. Forget using
his first. She wouldn't share that kind of intimacy with

him. "How is this possible?" He looked nothing like the man she'd once spied on.

"Surely, a former FBI agent can figure that out. Plastic surgery," Mendez said with a *duh* tone. "A new nose, some cheekbone chiseling, a new haircut…" He smiled. "But the one thing I wouldn't let them touch. My eyes. Which is why I wear these." He swiped at the orbs, pulling away contact lenses, and his blue eyes shone. A washed-out blue that was striking in his tanned face. A handsome man now after surgery, just like he was before.

But how insane did you have to be to change your own face?

"What do you want?" She tugged at her restraints, but he'd secured her well.

"What do you think I want, *Edith*? You took something of mine."

Her heart stilled in her chest. "She's not yours."

At that lie, he laughed. "We both know that's not true. She's my daughter. And I will have her."

"No, you won't."

"How do you intend to stop me?" He crouched in front of her and placed his hands on her thighs, the heavy weight most unwelcome. "You're a little tied up at the moment."

"My friends will protect her."

"Ah, yes, your friends. I'll admit, I am a tad put out they were called in. Just constantly ruining my plans."

"Your plans?" She ogled him.

"You didn't really think you got that mission by accident, did you?" Mendez leaned forward and smiled, his teeth a white gleam against his tan. He'd finally achieved the Spanish appearance he never inherited.

"What are you talking about?"

"The vase. The one you had to either retrieve or destroy," he mocked. "Such an easy-sounding mission, and your specialty according to the person who took the contract."

A cold feeling invaded her stomach. "You're the client."

"I am, and this is the vase you came out of hiding for." He held it up, the fine terra cotta showing the cracks of age. "Nice piece of art. Expensive, too. But expendable in the grand scheme." He smashed it to the floor, and she flinched at the explosion of shards.

"You set a trap for me." She couldn't help her expression of surprise. "But how?" How did he know how to hire her?

"Finding you was a stroke of luck. It's amazing sometimes how small the world is. A friend of mine had someone steal his secrets, and he caught the culprit on camera. Shared it in the hopes someone would recognize the thief. Imagine my surprise when I saw who he'd caught skulking into his office." His smile widened, and her stomach shrank. "It was my lovely Edith. Quite a shock, I will admit. You know, I looked for you after that botched hospital incident."

But she was gone at that point. Not even in the country anymore.

Mendez, who always did like the sound of his own voice, kept talking. "I'd just about given up on finding you. That disappearing act was top-notch. Almost as good as mine." Those white teeth, so perfect and straight, managed to look menacing. "I do have to wonder, though, how did a disgraced former FBI agent get recruited by a high-end mercenary agency? I didn't think you were that good." The genial smile remained, but she recognized the cruel look in his eyes. The same one he wore when he'd admitted that he'd played her for a fool.

"Not going to say anything?" He leaned close, his breath minty fresh. Always. Every hair in its place. Nothing ever messy.

She didn't answer. He'd feed off anything she said. Twist it. Use her own words to hurt her.

"It's probably best you say nothing. After all, how can you defend stealing my child? My daughter." His tone dropped. "Did you really think I'd leave her with you?" He managed to make that sound as if it were the absolute worst thing ever.

Audrey remained still. A statue staring straight ahead.

"Ignore me all you like, *Edith*. You'll soon be begging for my attention. Begging to see my daughter. You can't keep her away from me. I will take back what is mine."

A part of her understood he'd wanted to take Harper away all along, but hearing it so baldly stated, and coldly as if Harper were simply an object not a child, chilled her. A baby needed love, not an owner.

"Harper is not a thing. You can't just take her." The exclamation poured hotly from her.

"I have every right. She's *my* daughter. My child and heir. You will bring her to me."

She spat, "Like fuck. You'll have to kill me first." She wouldn't give him Harper.

Mendez laughed. "Kill? You know, I thought about it. Really, I did. But won't it be more fun for you to live knowing you'll never see the child again? And make no mistake, Harper will come to live with me. Although, I think we're going to change her name. I am rather partial to Sophia."

"Harper's hidden. You won't find her."

"Clever, that thing with the cameras." Mendez leaned against an old desk and crossed his arms. "I might not know exactly where she is, but that will soon change. We've opened negotiations with your lover."

"I have no lover."

"Don't lie," he snarled. "I know what you did. Living with a man. Letting him play at being Daddy. Spreading your thighs for him at night."

Her blood ran cold. "Leave Declan out of this."

"Too late. Your boyfriend should have minded his business instead of getting involved in mine. He should have died with that present I sent."

"You sent the bomb?"

"A dud, obviously. Don't worry, I'll handle his pencil-pushing ass after I get Harper."

Pencil-pushing? Audrey didn't show any emotion as it sank in. Mendez didn't know about Declan. Which meant, he probably didn't know about Bad Boy Inc.

How could she use this to her advantage? She needed to throw Mendez off track.

Sometimes, the best way was direct. "You should leave while you can, before Declan and his buddies kick your butt."

"Do you really think he has the balls to confront me? I think I know your boyfriend better than you. Why do you think I hired him? He is weak. Letting me push him around. No backbone at all." Mendez sneered. "I truly thought maybe he'd finally show some gumption when I made him order booties for the open house. But no, he caved to my ridiculous demands. He'll cave when I make the offer, too."

"What offer?" What bribe did Mendez plan to offer Declan?

"I am going to offer him a trade. You for my daughter."

CHAPTER TWENTY-EIGHT

DECLAN'S PHONE RANG IN THE MIDST OF THE MEETING with Meredith and Mason. It took him a blink to realize he was reading the call display correctly. He lifted a finger to his lips, shushing the other two. They immediately understood. Suarez, aka Mendez, was on the phone.

"Hello?"

"I do believe I found something of yours during the open house."

Forget any guise of pleasantry. Declan barked, "Give her back."

"Such ill manners. What happened to calling me sir?" Sam—short for "Suarez aka Mendez"—mocked.

"I don't need to play games anymore." Finally. No more brown-nosing this prick.

"Indeed, we don't," agreed Sam.

"I know you've got Audrey. Give her back."

"Why would I do that when we have so much to catch up on? Such as the fact that she kept my own daughter from me."

"After what happened, can you blame her?"

"I do blame her. Did she not tell you? She tricked me, and now she pays the price."

"Let her go." Declan lost his cool for a moment, his fear for Audrey overcoming his training.

"I will, once I get my daughter. Really, this is all your fault. The plan was to get my hands on Audrey and have her divulge the location of my daughter. Imagine my delight when she brought the child along."

"So you were the one who tried to kidnap her?"

"Hardly kidnapping. I am merely requesting you give me what is mine."

"You didn't request, you blackmailed," Declan growled.

"Your fault. Things would have happened differently if you'd not foiled my plan by not bringing your nanny and the baby as ordered."

"You used me?" The pieces fell into place as Declan understood Sam's end goal.

"Don't whine. You're still being considered to handle the sale of the condo. Show yourself solid, and that will be just the start of the tidbits I'll throw you. But first, you have to help me. I want my daughter."

"What of Audrey?"

"I've no use for the whore. She's yours in exchange."

The request was stark.

Audrey for Harper. Declan didn't need to hear Audrey's voice to know the answer. He shook his head and said, "No."

"This is not a negotiation. Either you give me what I want, or I'll send you pieces of her until you do. I'll contact you with the trade-off spot in a bit. It goes without saying that I expect you to come alone. No calling the police or you will regret it."

Click. The call disconnected, and Declan cursed as he tossed the phone. For a moment, pure silence existed as they digested the news.

"What are we going to do?" Declan asked.

Neither Meredith or Mason had a reply. He asked it again later at the BBI office where Harry and a few other agents had gathered to discuss the crazy turn of events. In a back office, with reinforced windows and walls, they had Tanya minding the baby, who'd been given a huge security escort.

No way was Declan letting anything happen to her. His dilemma, though, was how to save Audrey so the little girl didn't lose her mother.

On screen was Audrey's handler. The woman kept her privacy by wearing dark shades and a wide-brimmed hat that obscured her features and hair. She pursed scarlet lips. They were already past introductions and discussing the grit of the situation. The woman stated, "We can't allow Mendez to keep Audrey. We'll have to meet his demands."

Harry cleared his throat. "As a father, I think I can safely presume that Audrey would prefer not to have her baby used as a bargaining chip."

"What makes you think we'd let him keep her?" The woman Audrey called Mother tilted her head. "The exchange would be but a ploy."

"You can't use Harper as bait." Declan rose from his chair. "It's too dangerous."

"On the contrary, with Harper in the picture, Mendez won't dare to do anything that might harm his child. Why do you think he kidnapped Audrey rather than attack those with the baby directly?"

"Your plan is nuts. I mean, what do you expect me to do? Walk into his place holding the baby as a shield?" Declan shook his head.

Yet the woman on screen nodded. "That's exactly what I'm suggesting. By all appearances, he has no idea about your connections to BBI and KM. If that's the case, then he won't be expecting an attack."

"An attack means bullets. I don't want Audrey or Harper getting hurt."

"No one will get hurt. Much," Mother added as an afterthought. "Unless your office is incompetent." A challenge that caused some squirming and at least one ball scratch. "Arrange the meeting. Have the operatives shadow you there."

"Ben can get there ahead of time on his bike and scout things out," Harry interjected. "Mason, you can be on-site tech, and Carla"—he angled his head—"can babysit and provide deep online cover. We need to have control of all the eyes in the area."

"Why doesn't he stay here babysitting while I provide on-site?" she huffed. "I am just as good as a man."

"Better because you can actually handle a crying baby, whereas Mason here"—Harry swept a hand—"would probably end up crying beside her."

"Hey, I resent that," muttered Mason. "But it's true. So very true."

"Depending on the location where he's holding Audrey, we'll want an extraction team in place, plus a defensive layer to provide cover if things get a bit noisy. Tanya is a sharpshooter," Mother offered.

"We'll pair her with Ben. Find a pair of good spots to park your asses," Harry ordered.

As the plans took place, Declan felt he had to say something. "What am I doing?"

"Distracting the target while we secure the package."

"I won't be able to distract him for long if I show up empty-handed," was his sarcastic reply. "This is the stupidest plan."

"It is the only chance we have of retrieving Audrey alive." The handler's voice emerged low and serious from the screen. "You don't know Mendez like we do. He is ruthless. If you don't agree to his terms, he will kill her."

Still, any plan that used Harper as bait would mean he'd die if Audrey survived. Because she would kill him. Still, the choices were limited. Keep Harper, and her mother died. Give up Harper, and they had to hope Mendez wouldn't allow her to come to any harm.

However, the more they discussed their options, the more Declan came to see it was the only way. A few modifications made him believe it might just work.

Might.

But he'd take it.

True to his villainous word, Sam called with his instructions. He was sending an Uber to Declan. The easiest thing in the world to hack. Did Sam want Declan to be followed? Did he truly take him for such a rube?

The instructions also came with the admonition to come alone or else. It just needed a soundtrack for a fake ominous tone. Since the ride would arrive shortly, Declan prepared to leave. Someone helped him with the chest harness. Handed him the diaper bag and a bottle.

He waited on the sidewalk outside his work. A car slid

to a stop. A woman sat behind the wheel. Tanya, also known as Hockey Mom. They'd only officially met an hour ago, and he knew about her son's potential on the ice.

It reassured to know he'd go in with one ally who cared about Audrey's safety.

"You call the ride?" she said, rolling down her window and smacking her gum.

"I did," he said, playing the game for anyone watching. He slid into the car, and it rolled off, the pair silent, the stakes too high for them to risk it by saying anything that might be overheard.

As if this were some kind of movie, Mendez chose a warehouse to make the exchange. The parking lot behind the chain-link fence loomed empty. The place closed on weekends.

Tanya dropped Declan off, not saying a word. She didn't have to. He knew the next part of the plan had her parking nearby and covering his backside.

Still, as she rolled off, leaving him alone in that barren parking lot, he felt very much naked. He wore only a chest harness with the baby. The diaper bag in his left hand wouldn't protect him much from bullets, and he doubted the bottle in the other would do him any good either.

He took a few steps towards the building, hoping the plastic listening device in the nipple of the bottle was working. The signal in it was weak on purpose, in the hopes no one would detect it.

The warehouse had two openings—a large roll-up, metal door and a smaller, person-sized one. Guess which one Sam chose to make his entrance?

It made a killer itch to shoot. But he couldn't. That wasn't part of the plan, so he was forced to watch as first the legs, then the bodies of three men appeared. There was Matrix Thug, wearing a black trench coat and dark shades to hide his expression. The front of his jacket was unbuttoned, and he had a hand tucked within. He obviously clutched a gun.

Thug Two, with his mullet, had his weapon slung across his chest. Semi-automatic. Ballsy given the location was still rather public.

In between them? Sam. Wearing a pale gray suit, he stepped out, hands empty. "I am glad to see you saw sense, Mr. Hood."

Actually, his vision was rather red at the moment, but he knew better than to admit it.

Follow the plan.

He held his hands out at his sides and hoped their theories about no one shooting were right. On his chest, Harper gurgled the only recognizable sound being, "Da."

"Yes, it's your father." A man who'd changed his identity, even his actual face, to evade detection. A man with that kind of desperation could be capable of anything. Declan's hand hovered over the baby's belly as if it would provide a shield. His body remained tense, ready to pivot if he needed to protect.

"A shame it was a daughter and not a son the whore whelped," Sam observed as he stepped out from the gloom of the warehouse into daylight. He only barely glanced at Harper as if she were of minimal interest. Fucker. He didn't deserve to be a father.

"Where is she?" Declan asked.

"Who?"

"Don't play fucking stupid."

"Or you'll do what, Mr. Hood? An interesting name, that. I don't suppose you can shoot a bow and arrow."

"I can." He was even better after a few beers. It relaxed him.

"Hand over the child."

The abruptness took him off guard. "Like hell."

"Are you here to trade or not, Mr. Hood? I don't have all day."

"What the heck you gonna do with a baby? Why not leave her with Audrey and figure out some visitation schedule?"

A genuine laugh burst from Sam. "As if Edith would let me walk away. She would rather see me with a bullet in my head."

"It's what all the most famous criminals are wearing these days." Two could ooze cold confidence.

Sam barked another laugh. "Who says I'm a criminal? There've been no charges levied against me."

"Yet. Way I hear it, witnesses have a tendency to disappear."

"Yes, they do." The hand Sam slid inside his coat emerged with a gun. "Will you be one of them, Mr. Hood?"

Sam still hadn't grasped that he'd lost. The moment he didn't do his homework about BBI, he'd sealed his fate. The fact that he dared to hurt Audrey meant he wouldn't be leaving this place alive.

Declan's earpiece gave a small beep before erupting with sound. Mason updated him, "Guards inside neutralized. The package is intact."

Code for "Audrey is okay."

Declan smiled. "I don't suppose you'll do the right thing and turn yourself in."

The gun rose, aiming right at the baby. "Does this answer your question?"

"As a matter of fact, it does." Declan's hand flattened, going right through the baby's body. The hologram rippled before closing over his hand and hiding it.

Yes, hologram. As if he'd actually bring the baby.

Sam snarled and fired a shot. Declan's body armor absorbed it like a punch. It sucked the air from him, and the hologram glitched. Which was fine, it had served its purpose.

Before twisting himself upright, he grabbed the gun strapped to his stomach, hidden before by the fake baby, and aimed.

Pop.

He managed to wing Sam as the man pivoted and lunged. The bullet hit him in the shoulder. With a cry, the villain bolted around the side of the building.

A hum erupted.

"What is that?" Declan yelled. A reply came through his earpiece.

"Fucker has a helicopter next parking lot over."

At the news, Declan took off running. He couldn't let the man escape.

Shots were fired behind him, and Declan barked, "I thought we had his goons contained."

"We did. Someone else is firing on us," Tanya exclaimed. "We're pinned down."

Sam was better prepared than expected. A good thing Declan had not brought the baby. A good thing KM had the technology to fake a baby. He'd never seen anything so clever as that hologram vest, part of a new cloaking technology built into clothing.

Harper remained safe with Carla and a few other agents in the office. It would take an army to get to her.

Someone from the chopper fired on him, the whistle of it zipping past his ear. He sucked in a breath. *Ouch.* A line of fire burned, and his ear dripped hotly.

He ducked behind a parked truck, the side of it promising *Clean Laundry. Clean Service.* He darted a look around the hood, hid quick, avoiding a round of bullets. A body dropped next to him. Chest heaving from exertion.

He blinked at the mirage.

It remained. A disheveled Audrey smiled. "Hey, Zee."

"What are you doing?"

"Giving you cover." She popped up and began firing off shots. Someone had armed Audrey before setting her loose. He couldn't help himself. He leaned over and planted a hard kiss on her lips.

"I'm glad you're not dead." All he had time to say. There was still a man to catch.

With someone to cover him, Declan scuttled out the side and ran for the helicopter in an arc, firing as he ran, pinging bullets off the edge of the helicopter door.

Sam made it in, and the opening on the side slid shut. The metal bird lifted into the air. The blades whipping as they rotated, tugging at Declan's hair. He stopped running and took aim, his feet planted, both hands on the grip. He sighted the blades.

Ping.

The chopper wobbled but kept moving away. He was going to lose the fucker.

Audrey must have realized the same thing. She went

sprinting past him, weapon raised, firing wildly. The chopper kept going, hit but not injured enough to stop.

It kept rising, and Audrey cursed. "Bloody hell. He's escaping."

Which was bad. They couldn't have Sam disappearing again.

"He's not going anywhere." Ben arrived, and Declan had to wonder what movie he was recreating this time as he knelt, cigarette dangling from his lips, expression intent as he aimed the portable missile launcher.

Yes, launcher. Even Audrey gaped, impressed.

The rocket whistled as it sliced through the air. Ben's aim was good. He stood and took a long drag from his cigarette, missile launcher casually leaned on his shoulder.

The helicopter emitted a bright flash at the impact, then exploded, flames and black smoke shooting out.

No survivors.

Audrey slumped against Declan and whispered, "Thank God. It's done."

"D-d-d-d-," the hologram sputtered.

CHAPTER TWENTY-NINE

As the image on Declan's chest stuttered to life, Audrey turned to face him. She eyed the mirage baby then Declan. When he first arrived and stepped out of the car carrying a bottle and Harper, she'd cried out as if the noise would stop the image from unfolding on the screen, which Mendez watched from inside the warehouse.

"No." What was he thinking? How could he bring Harper here?"

Mendez laughed. "Guess he's not the good guy you thought."

She couldn't believe Declan would do that, put Harper in danger. The hologram glitched just in time because she almost put a bullet in him.

"You almost died today," she announced.

"Is this how you say thank you for the rescue?"

No, she wanted to say it to him in a shower, their bodies naked. In bed. With more nakedness. She wanted to hold him close. But fear still held her prisoner. Because he'd almost died.

For me.

"Thank you." Said softly before she walked away.

He marched after her, "Where you going?"

"To find Harper. Where is she?"

"Carla has her. At the office."

Audrey slowed. "She's nowhere close by?"

"Of course, not. You didn't really think I'd let her anywhere near that dude, did you?"

"I wasn't sure."

"Not sure!" He drew himself straight. "I would never do anything to harm her."

The shock and indignation on his face smacked her with guilt. "I couldn't be sure of that. You're not her daddy."

"And?" he snapped. "Do you really think that makes a difference? I would never put a kid in harm's way. Especially not that kid."

"Why?" she asked.

"Can you two lovebirds figure out your shit another time?" Ben barked. "We have cleanup to do."

Declan grimaced. "I got this. Go to my loft. I'll have Harper brought there since it's safe now."

"Maybe I should get a hotel."

He glared at Audrey. "We are not done. So don't you dare run away. I'll be there as quickly as I can."

She didn't argue. The shock of almost dying and thinking Mendez might get his hands on Harper had shaken her. She needed to hold her daughter's weight in her arms. Smell her.

The taxi Declan called her dropped her off on the sidewalk outside the loft. Her feet dragged. Her tired mind was still stunned. She'd been so afraid; afraid not for herself but her child. Now, the relief at knowing the nightmare was over, that she could finally relax, had her almost dead on her feet.

But she kept moving, eagerness to hold Harper kept her going. She made it to the loft door and slid in the key Declan handed her. The lock didn't click, and the keypad didn't demand she enter a code. Had Carla not sealed it when she arrived? Having lost her phone to Mendez, Audrey couldn't text her to be sure.

She pulled the gun Declan had given her. She clutched it as she nudged the door open. The first thing she saw was Carla on the floor, her forehead bleeding. Attacked.

Recently, too. Audrey's heart raced, and then stopped as she caught movement. She saw someone bent over the playpen.

Audrey's mouth turned to a dried husk.

A woman straightened, holding Harper in her arms.

Apparently, she'd misjudged Mendez. He must have had a contingency plan to grab Harper in case his other scheme didn't work out. "Put her down."

"I think not," replied the woman.

"Mendez is dead."

The thin lips pulled taut and disappeared in a face lined with age. "I know."

"Then why are you here? Whatever he asked you to do is pointless now. He's gone. He won't be paying you," Audrey pointed out.

Cold eyes, a faded blue, perused her. Judged her and dismissed her in one fell swoop. "You killed my son."

Oh, shit. Was this Mendez's mother? Audrey had always assumed the woman dead the way he spoke of her.

"Mendez didn't leave me a choice. He tried to take my daughter."

"Don't you mean *his* daughter. My grandchild." Mendez's mother stared down at Harper, no hint of warmth at the display of chubby cheeks and a gap-toothed smile. "It's been a bloody pain trying to get my hands on her."

"What are you talking about?"

"Silly girl. Did you really think he was the one who sent those people after her?" The smile had the predatory hunger of a barracuda. "He was being too nice about it. Fabricated an elaborate plot rather than doing what had to be done."

"You can't just take her."

"Why not? Doesn't seem fair you get to keep your baby when I lost mine."

The contents of Audrey's stomach roiled as fear coalesced and churned it. Was this woman talking of kidnapping Harper or worse? "You're family. Her only grandmother. It would be nice if you were a part of her life." Audrey would say and promise anything to move this woman with the icy gaze away from her child.

"Visit?" The amusement at odds with the expression. "Are you trying to bribe me with something so paltry after what you did?"

What about what Mendez did? The words burned on the tip of her tongue. Yet she instinctively knew yelling them wouldn't sway this woman. The crazy obviously didn't fall far from the tree.

"What do you want? You can't expect me to give you custody of Harper."

"Custody?" The woman laughed. "What need have I

for a snot-nosed child born of a snake? I have grandchildren. Ones with much better bloodlines. What I don't have is my son because you took him, and now, I'll take your child as retribution."

The woman pulled a gun before Audrey's horrified gaze. Her mouth rounded. She dashed towards them, knowing she wouldn't make it in time.

A perfect hole erupted.

Red on the edges, black inside.

It took a moment for the blood to seep and the body to fall.

Another second still for Harper to let out a lusty wail as her killer grandma dropped to the floor.

In seconds, Audrey held her daughter, sobbing. She felt more than saw Declan as he moved in behind her, his arms clasping her while he murmured, "Hush now baby, don't say a word."

Through a throat clogged with tears, Audrey mumbled, "Momma's gonna buy you a mockingbird."

"And if that mockingbird won't sing." He brushed his lips in her hair. "Then Daddy will fucking shoot it and buy you a diamond ring."

"That's a horrible verse," she said through her sniffles.

"Guess I need practice."

"Or maybe you shouldn't sing."

"Hey," he chided, leading them away from the body. "Is that any way to encourage me?"

She saw what he did. Lightened the situation to stop her from shaking. It didn't entirely work.

"What da fuck happened?" groaned Carla.

"Language," admonished Declan, the very inanity of it

as they stood over a dead body bringing hysterical laughter.

It didn't last long. Audrey focused on her daughter, safe and asleep in her arms. She paid little mind to what happened around her, from the cleanup crew that disposed of the body to the assurances that this would be the end of it.

Would it?

Eventually, everyone left. Even Carla with her head bandaged and a bruised ego.

The door shut. Declan armed his security system then took Harper from Audrey, placing the baby in the playpen before returning to take her into his arms.

He held her. Not saying anything. Just holding her close.

It was heaven.

"You saved me," Audrey eventually said.

"You owe me cookies."

"You risked your life for cookies?"

"Hot from the oven," he corrected.

"Why?" The word whispered from her.

"I'll always save you," was his gruff reply. "Haven't you figured it out yet? I love you, Audrey Edith whatever the fuck your last name is now."

She managed a tremulous smile. "According to my new driver's license, it's Coxson."

He recoiled and winced. "Ouch. Good thing I showed up to make an honest woman of you. I'd hate for Harper to have to go through life with that as her last name."

"What are you saying?"

"I'm saying, I think it's time I settled down. With you. In case that wasn't clear. Marry me."

"We barely know each other." What had it been? Days since they met? Felt so much longer.

"We'll have a lifetime to do that."

"You can't propose now."

"I guess the loft isn't too romantic, huh. Got it. I'll find a better location. Guess I should get a ring, too."

The way he kept ignoring her had her muttering, "What is wrong with you? We're not getting married."

"Fine. You want to hold off, then we'll hold off. Live with me."

She blinked. "I'm supposed to be going to Nebraska."

"Say no. Ask to be reassigned. Here. With me."

"You want to work together?" She couldn't help the seeping doubt.

"Think of it. Me, the realtor hotshot. You, my lovely interior designer. We could flip places."

"What about Harper?"

"We'll hire a nanny." At her moue, he laughed. "A real one this time, with a flexible schedule."

"Do you have any idea what you're talking about doing? Having a kid isn't all fun and games."

"I know it's not. Harry explained it to me. It's shitty diapers and waking up in the middle of the night to walk her. It's never having a clean shirt. It's screaming when my television gets taken over by cartoons on football Sunday. It's feeling like king of the world when she smiles at me."

She worried her lower lip. "Is this proposal and all just about being Harper's daddy then?"

"Oh, hell no." He grinned. "Does someone need me to show her exactly how much I desire her?"

"Maybe." The reply was coy. His response was anything but.

They put his shower to good use. The bench in it just the right height for her to drape her legs around his neck. His bed didn't creak when they finally made it to the sheets. She clung to him, reveling in his strength, his warmth, and his love.

His arms provided a warm haven and a promise. She awoke feeling refreshed, and something even more astonishing. She felt as if she'd finally come home.

"What are you thinking?" he asked.

She tilted her head to find him watching her. "If I do stay, you have to realize it won't be easy."

"I get that. You like to hog the bed." He wiggled under her splayed body. "You'll want to put tampons in the cupboard. Yogurt in the fridge."

She slapped his arm. "I meant it's hard being a parent."

"I don't doubt it is. But I'm a quick study." He hopped out of bed and tugged on some track pants a moment before Harper let out a yodel.

"Coming, diva."

Was there anything sexier than a half-dressed man getting up to grab a waking baby?

She leaned back and just absorbed it.

The little traitor grinned as her favorite guy lifted her high. "How's my sweet diva this morning?" He held her overhead until Harper chortled.

Proud of himself, Declan declared, "See, Ree. I'll make a killer daddy."

To his credit, he didn't drop the baby when a gob of drool landed on his mouth.

And Audrey didn't go to Nebraska.

EPILOGUE

"I can't believe Ree is making me move to suburbia," Declan groaned.

"It's a financially sound investment. You'll gain more space," Calvin noted as he flipped a burger, one of many on his man-sized grill.

"It would be nice if Harper had her own room. I get that, but do you know what else she said to me?" Declan lowered his voice. "Ree says we should shop for a minivan. A minivan! What's next? Matching golf shirts?"

"It's not that bad," Calvin commiserated. "Have you seen all the features you can get in them?"

Declan gasped. "Brother, say it isn't so."

Calvin offered a rueful grin. "We pick ours up next week."

Look at the domesticated killer who was also happier than Declan ever recalled seeing him. He had reason. "When's Lily due?" Declan asked with a glance at Lily. She had a hand pressed to the middle of her back as she watched her daughter on the swing. Her belly extended so far, it was a wonder she didn't fall over.

"Doc says by the end of the month."

"Are you ready?"

A snort erupted from Calvin. "I don't think any man is ever ready, but guess I'll cope. I figure if morons around the world can manage a half-assed attempt at parenting every day, then someone with my skills and intelligence can do a decent job."

At that, Declan laughed. "The most complex mission of your life."

"Damned straight. I won't fail."

Neither could Declan. The stakes were too high.

Harper toddled to him. Her stick legs getting her to places upright, and he'd been there for the very first steps. The feeling when she wobbled to him that first time was indescribable.

And sappy. He chugged his beer before asking, "Those burgers about ready? Because I am starved."

What he wasn't, though, was unhappy. Life was good. More than good.

There was a time that the idea of settling down and even moving to the—gasp—'burbs might have made him fall on the floor laughing—or shoot the person suggesting it. But that was before.

Before he'd found love. Before he'd discovered the joys of being a family man.

Now...

Now, he'd kill to keep it.

———

MEANWHILE, one state over, a soccer mom with a kid of her own and a couple extra to fill in the seats of her minivan, received a text just as she slammed the trunk shut over the sweaty equipment.

You're needed.

Unknown number. No name. No other message, but it was enough.

Carla swung into the noisy van and said to her son in the passenger seat beside her, "Mom's work just called. I gotta go out of town for a bit."

"Do you have to? Aunt Judy is so strict," grumbled her tween son.

Little did he know, Aunt Judy wasn't a real aunt.

"I'll be back before you know it."

Half a million dollars richer in her offshore account.

But little did *she* know how this job would change her life.

STAY TUNED FOR THIS BAD BOY SPIN-OFF. KILLER MOMS, WITH BOOK ONE, *SOCCER MOM*, COMING SOON.

More books at EveLanglais.com